NICOLA CORNICK

"This entertaining story is sure to please."
—*The Romance Reader* on *The Earl's Prize*

"Cornick's characters pull you into their world
and hold you there."
—*Rakehell.com*

"A charming tale!"
—*Romantic Times* on *The Penniless Bride*

**Coming soon from HQN Books and the
two rising stars of historical romance!**

**Julia Justiss's
THE COURTESAN
December 2005**

**Nicola Cornick's
DECEIVED
July 2006**

MARY BALOGH
JULIA JUSTISS
NICOLA CORNICK

CHRISTMAS KEEPSAKES

HQN™

ISBN 0-373-77094-4

CHRISTMAS KEEPSAKES

Copyright © 2005 by Harlequin Books S.A.

The publisher acknowledges the copyright holders of the individual works as follows:

A HANDFUL OF GOLD
Copyright © 1998 by Mary Balogh

THE THREE GIFTS
Copyright © 2005 by Janet Justiss

THE SEASON FOR SUITORS
Copyright © 2005 by Nicola Cornick

This edition published by arrangement with Harlequin Books S.A.

® and TM are trademarks of the publisher. Trademarks indicated with ® are registered in the United States Patent and Trademark Office, the Canadian Trade Marks Office and in other countries.

www.HQNBooks.com

Printed in U.S.A.

CONTENTS

A HANDFUL OF GOLD   9
Mary Balogh

THE THREE GIFTS   155
Julia Justiss

THE SEASON FOR SUITORS   285
Nicola Cornick

Dear Reader,

I was delighted when I learned that Harlequin was to republish my novella "A Handful of Gold" in this new anthology. I have written a large number of books and novellas centered about Christmas, but this story has always been one of my personal favorites.

Christmas is the most wonderful season of the year about which to weave a love story, since it is a time of peace and giving and love and joy. It is a time of hope and healing and new beginnings. It is a time for the human heart to reflect upon all that is most truly meaningful in life—and what could ever be more meaningful than love? Out of love for her family, Verity Ewing, the heroine of "A Handful of Gold," gives herself for Christmas to Julian Dare, Viscount Folingsby, a man who knows only how to take. But the magic of the season and of a new birth and of love itself transform Julian and return her gift a thousandfold to Verity.

I do hope you will enjoy rereading this novella—or reading it for the first time. I know I am going to enjoy reading Julia Justiss's and Nicola Cornick's stories. It is a pleasure to be sharing this anthology with them. Have a warm and wonderful and love-filled Christmas.

Mary Balogh

A HANDFUL OF GOLD

Mary Balogh

To Robert, Jacqueline, Christopher and Siân—
my family, who are the meaning of Christmas to me.

Chapter One

THE GENTLEMAN sprawled before the dying fire in the sitting room of his London lodgings was looking somewhat the worse for a night's wear. His gray knee breeches and white stockings were of the finest silk, but the latter were wrinkled and he had long before kicked off his shoes. His long-tailed evening coat, which had molded his frame like a second skin when he had donned it earlier in the evening, had now been discarded and tossed carelessly onto another chair.

His finely embroidered waistcoat was unbuttoned. His neckcloth, on the arrangement of which his valet had spent longer than half an hour of loving artistry, had been pulled open and hung unsymmetrically against his left shoulder. His dark hair, expertly cut to look fashionably disheveled, now looked unfashionably untidy from having had his fingers pass through it one too many times. His eyes were half-closed—and somewhat bloodshot. An empty glass dangled from one hand over the arm of the chair.

Julian Dare, Viscount Folingsby, was indisputably foxed.

He was also scowling. Drinking to excess was not among his usual vices. Gaming was. So was womanizing. And so was reckless living. But not drinking. He had always been careful to exclude from habit anything that might prove to also be addictive. He had every intention of one day "settling down," as his father phrased it, of being done with his "wild oats," another of the Earl of Grantham's clichés. It would be just too inconvenient to have to deal with an addiction when the time came. Gambling was not an addiction with him. Neither were women. Though he was exceedingly fond of both.

He yawned and wondered what time it was. Daylight had not yet dawned, a small comfort when this was December and daylight did not deign to show itself until well on into the morning. Certainly it was well past midnight. *Well* past. He had left his sister's soirée before midnight, but since then he had been to White's club and to one or two—was it one or two?—card parties at which the play had been deep and the drinking deeper.

He should get himself up from his chair and go to bed, but he did not have the energy. He should ring for his valet, then, and have the man drag him off to bed. But he did not have even the energy to get up and ring the bell. Doubtless he would not sleep anyway. He knew from experience that when he was three sheets to the wind, an approximately vertical position was preferable to a horizontal one.

Why the devil had he drunk so deep?

But drunkenness had not brought oblivion. He remembered very well why. That heiress. Miss Plunkett. No, *Lady* Sarah Plunkett. What a name! And unfortunately the chit had the face and disposition to match it. She was going to be at Conway for Christmas with her mama and papa. Emma, his youngest sister, had mentioned the fact in the letter that had reached him this morning—no, yesterday morning. He had put two and two together without further ado and had come up with the inevitable total of four. But he had not needed to use any arithmetical or deductive skills.

His father's letter, which he had read next, had been far more explicit. Not only were the Plunkett chit and the Plunkett parents to join their family gathering for Christmas, but also Julian would oblige his father by paying court to the girl and fixing his interest with her. He was nine-and-twenty years old, after all, and had shown no sign of choosing anyone for himself. His father had been extremely patient with him. But it was high time he finished with his wild oats and settled down. As the only son among five sisters, three of them still unmarried and therefore still unsettled, it was his duty....

Viscount Folingsby passed the fingers of his free hand through his hair again, unconsciously restoring it almost to simple dishevelment, and eyed the brandy decanter a short distance away. An impossible distance away.

He was not going to do it—marry the girl, that was. It was as simple as that. No one could make him, not even his stern but annoyingly affectionate father. Not even his fond mama and doting sisters. He grimaced. Why had he been blessed with a singularly close and loving family? And why had his mother produced nothing but daughters after the initial triumph of his birth as heir to an earldom and vast properties and fortune—almost every last half penny of which was entailed and would pass to a rather distant cousin if he failed to produce at least one heir of his own?

His lordship eyed the brandy decanter again with some determination, but he could not somehow force resolution downward far enough to set his legs in motion.

There had been another letter in the morning's post. From Bertie. Bertrand Hollander had been his close friend and coconspirator all through school and university. They were still close even though Bertie spent most of his time now overseeing his estates in the north of England. But Bertie had a hunting box in Norfolkshire and a mistress in Yorkshire and intended to introduce the two to each other over Christmas. He was avoiding his own family with the excuse that he was going to go shooting with friends over the holiday. He intended instead to spend a week with his Debbie away from prying eyes and the need for propriety. He wanted Julian to join him there with his own mistress.

Julian did not currently have a resident mistress. He had dismissed the last one several months before on the grounds that evenings spent in her company had become even more predictable and every bit as tedious as evenings spent at the insipid weekly balls at Almack's. Since then he had had a mutually satisfactory arrangement with a widow of his acquaintance. But she was a respectable woman of good ton, hardly the sort he might invite to spend a cozy week of sin in Norfolkshire with Bertie and his Debbie.

Damn! He was more foxed than he knew, Julian

thought suddenly. He had gone somewhere tonight even before attending Elinor's soirée. He had gone to the opera. Not that he was particularly fond of music—not opera at least. He had gone to see the subject of the newest male gossip at White's. There was a new dancer of considerable charms, so it was said. But in the few weeks since she had made her first onstage appearance, she had not also made her first appearance in any of the beds of those who had attempted to entice her there. She was either waiting for the highest bidder or she was waiting for someone she fancied or she was a virtuous woman.

Julian, his father's summons and Bertie's invitation fresh in his mind, had gone to the opera to see what the fuss was all about.

The fuss was all about long, shapely legs, a slender, lithe body, and long titian hair. Not red, nothing so vulgar. Titian. And emerald eyes. Not that he had been able to see their color from the box he had occupied during the performance. But he had seen it through his quizzing glass as he had stood in the doorway of the greenroom afterward.

Miss Blanche Heyward had been surrounded by a court of appropriately languishing admirers. His lordship had looked her over unhurriedly through his glass and inclined his head to her when her eyes had met his across the room. And then he had joined the even larger crowd of gentlemen gathered about Hannah Dove, the singer who sang like her name, or so one of her court had assured her. For which piece of gross flattery he had been rewarded with a gracious smile and a hand to kiss.

Julian had left the greenroom after a few minutes and taken himself off to his married sister's drawing room.

It might be interesting to try his own hand at assaulting the citadel of dubious virtue that was Blanche Heyward. It might be even more interesting to carry her off to Bertie's for Christmas and a weeklong hot affair. If he went to Conway, all he would have was the usual crowded, noisy, enjoyable Christmas, and the Plunkett chit. If he went to Norfolkshire...

Well, the mind boggled.

What he *could* do, he decided, was make her decision his, too. He would ask her. If she said yes, then he would go to Norfolkshire. For a final fling. As a swan song to freedom and wild oats and all the rest of it. In the spring, when the season brought the fashionable world to town, the Plunkett girl among them, he would do his duty. He would have her big with child by *next* Christmas. The very thought had him holding his aching head with the hand that had been holding his glass a minute before. What the devil had he done with it? Dropped it? Had there been any brandy left in it? Couldn't have been or he would have drunk it instead of sitting here conspiring how he might reach the decanter, on legs that refused to obey his brain.

If she said no—Blanche, that was, not the heiress—then he would go down to Conway and embrace his fate. That way he would probably have a child *in the nursery* by next Christmas.

Julian lowered his hand from his head to his throat with the intention of loosening his neckcloth. But someone had already done it for him.

Dammit, but she was gorgeous. Not the heiress. Who the devil was gorgeous, then? Someone he had met at Elinor's?

There was a quiet scratching at the sitting room door, and it opened to reveal the cautious, respectful face of his lordship's valet.

"About time," Julian told him. "Someone took all the bones out of my legs when I was not looking. Deuced inconvenient."

"Yes, my lord," his man said, coming purposefully toward him. "You will be wishing someone took them from your head before many more hours have passed. Come along then, sir. Put your arm about my neck."

"Deuced impertinence," his lordship muttered. "Remind me to dismiss you when I am sober."

"Yes, my lord," the valet said cheerfully.

SEVERAL HOURS before Viscount Folingsby found himself sprawled before the fire in his sitting room with boneless legs and aching head, Miss Verity Ewing let herself into a darkened house on an unfashionable street in London, using her latchkey and a considerable amount of stealth. She had no wish to waken anyone. She would tiptoe upstairs without lighting a candle, she decided, careful to avoid the eighth stair, which creaked. She would undress in the darkness and hope not to disturb Chastity. Her sister was, unfortunately, a light sleeper.

But luck was against her. Before she could so much as set foot on the bottom stair, the door to the downstairs living room opened and a shaft of candlelight beamed out into the hall.

"Verity?"

"Yes, Mama." Verity sighed inwardly even as she put a cheerful smile on her face. "You ought not to have waited up."

"I could not sleep," her mother told her as Verity followed her into the sitting room. She set down the candle and pulled her shawl more closely about her shoulders. There was no fire burning in the hearth. "You know I worry until you come home."

"Lady Coleman was invited to a late supper after

the opera," Verity explained, "and wanted me to accompany her."

"It was very inconsiderate of her, I am sure," Mrs. Ewing said rather plaintively. "It is thoughtless to keep a gentleman's daughter out late almost every night of the week and send her home in a hackney cab instead of in her ladyship's own carriage."

"It is kind of her even to hire the hackney," Verity said. "But it is chilly and you are cold." She did not need to ask why there was no fire. A fire after ten o'clock at night was an impossible extravagance in their household. "Let us go up to bed. How was Chastity this evening?"

"She did not cough above three or four times all evening," Mrs. Ewing said. "And not once did she have a prolonged bout. The new medicine seems really to be working."

"I hoped it would." Verity smiled and picked up the candle. "Come, Mama."

But she could not entirely avoid the usual questions about the opera, what Lady Coleman had worn, who else had made up their party, who had invited them for supper, what they had eaten, what topics of conversation had been pursued. Verity answered as briefly as she could, though she did, for her mother's sake, give a detailed description of the costly and fashionable gown her employer had worn.

"All I can say," Mrs. Ewing said in a hushed voice as they stood outside the door of her bedchamber, "is that Lady Coleman is a strange sort of lady, Verity. Most ladies hire companions to live in and run and fetch for them during the day when time hangs heavy on their hands. They do not allow them to live at home, and they do not require their services mostly during the evenings when they go out into society."

"How fortunate I am to have discovered such a lady, then," Verity said, "and to have won her approval. I could not bear to have to live in and see you and Chastity only on half days off. Lady Coleman is a widow, Mama, and needs company for respectability when she goes out. I could scarcely ask for more pleasant employment. It pays reasonably well, too, and will get better. Only this evening Lady Coleman declared that she is pleased with me and is considering raising my salary quite substantially."

But her mother did not look as pleased as Verity had hoped. She shook her head as she took the candle. "Ah, my love," she said, "I never thought to see the day when a daughter of mine would have to seek employment. The Reverend Ewing, your papa, left us little, it is true, but we might have scraped by quite comfortably if it had not been for Chastity's illness. And if General Sir Hector Ewing were not unfortunately in Vienna for the peace talks, he would have helped us, I am certain. You and Chastity are his own brother's children after all."

"Pray do not vex yourself, Mama." Verity kissed her mother's cheek. "We are together, the three of us, and Chastity is recovering her health after seeing a reputable physician and being prescribed the right medicine. Really, those are the only things that matter. Good night."

A minute later she had reached her own room and had entered it and closed the door. She stood for a moment against it, her eyes closed, her hands gripping the knob behind her back. But there was no sound apart from quiet, even breathing from her sister's bed. Verity undressed quickly and quietly, shivering in the frigid cold. After she had climbed into bed, she lay on her side, her knees drawn up, and pulled the covers up over her ears. Her teeth were chattering, though not just with the cold.

It was a dangerous game she played.

Except that it was no game.

How soon would it be, she wondered, before Mama discovered that there was no Lady Coleman, that there was no genteel and easy employment? Fortunately they had moved to London from the country so recently and under such straitened circumstances that they had few friends and none at all who moved in fashionable circles. They had moved because Chastity's chill, contracted last winter not long after their father's death, had stubbornly refused to go away. It had become painfully clear to them that they might well lose her if they did not consult a physician more knowledgeable than the local doctor. They had feared she had consumption, but the London physician had said no, that she merely had a weak chest and might hope to recover her full health with the correct medicines and diet.

But his fees and the medicines had been exorbitantly expensive and the need for his services was not yet at an end. The rent of even so unfashionable a house as theirs was high. And the bills for coal, candles, food and other sundries seemed always to be piling in.

Verity had searched and searched for genteel employment, assuring her mother that it would be only temporary, until her uncle returned to England and was apprised of their plight. Verity placed little faith in the wealthy uncle who had had nothing to do with them during her father's life. Her grandfather had held aloof from his youngest son after the latter had refused an advantageous match and had married instead Verity's mother, the daughter of a gentleman of no particular fortune or consequence.

In Verity's opinion, the care of her mother and sister fell squarely on her own shoulders and always would. And so when she had been unable to find employment as a governess or companion or even as a shop assistant or seamstress or housemaid, she had taken up the unlikely offer of an audition as an opera dancer. She was quite fit, after all, and she had always adored dancing, both in a ballroom and in the privacy of a shrubbery or empty room at the rectory. To her intense surprise she had been offered the job.

Performing on a public stage in any capacity—as an actress, singer or dancer—was not genteel employment for a lady. Indeed, Verity had been well aware even before accepting the employment that, in the popular mind, dancers and actresses were synonymous with whores.

But what choice had she?

And so had begun her double life, her secret life. By day, except when she was at rehearsals, she was Verity Ewing, impoverished daughter of a gently born clergyman, niece of the influential General Sir Hector Ewing. By night she was Blanche Heyward, opera dancer, someone who was ogled by half the fashionable gentlemen in town, many of whom attended the opera for no other purpose.

But it was a dangerous game. At any time she might be recognized by someone she knew, though no one from her neighborhood in the country was in the habit of staying in London and sampling its entertainments. More important, perhaps, she was making **it** impossible to mingle with polite society in the future if the general should ever decide to help them. But she did not anticipate that particular problem.

There were more immediate problems to deal with.

But what she earned as a dancer was just not enough.

Verity huddled deeper beneath the bedcovers and set her hands between her thighs for greater warmth.

"Verity?" a sleepy voice asked.

Verity pushed back the covers from her face again. "Yes, love," she said softly, "I am home."

"I must have fallen asleep," Chastity said. "I always worry so until you are home. I *wish* you did not have to go out alone at night."

"But if I did not," Verity said, "I would not be able to tell you about all the splendid parties and theater performances I attend. I shall describe the opera to you in the morning or, more to the point, the people who were in the audience. Go back to sleep now." She kept her voice warm and cheerful.

"Verity," Chastity said, "you must not think that I

am not grateful, that I do not know the sacrifice you are making for my sake. One day I will make it all up to you. I *promise*."

Verity blinked back tears from her eyes. "Oh yes, you will, love," she said. "In the springtime you are going to dance among the primroses and daffodils, unseasonable roses in your cheeks. Then you will have repaid me double—no, ten times over—for the little I am able to do now. Go to sleep, you goose."

"Good night." Chastity yawned hugely and only a minute or two later was breathing deeply and evenly again.

There was one way in which a dancer might augment her income. Indeed she was almost expected to do so. Verity hid her head beneath the covers once more and tried not to develop the thought. But it had been nagging at her for a week or more. And she had said those words to Mama earlier, almost as if she were preparing the way. *Lady Coleman declared that she is pleased with me and is considering raising my salary quite substantially.*

She had acquired quite a regular court of admirers in the greenroom following each performance. Two of the gentlemen had already made blatant offers to her. One had mentioned a sum that she had found quite dizzying. She had told herself repeatedly that she was not even tempted. Nor was she. But it was not a matter of temptation. It was a matter for cold decision.

The only possible reason she would do such a thing was her mother's and Chastity's security. A great deal more money was going to have to be found if Chass was to continue to have the treatment she needed. It was a matter of her virtue in exchange for Chastity's life, then.

Phrased that way, there was really no decision to make.

And then she thought of the advent of temptation that had presented itself to her just that evening in the form of the gentleman who had stood in the doorway of the greenroom, looking at her insolently through his quizzing glass for a minute or so before joining the crowd of gentlemen gathered about Hannah Dove. His actions had suggested that he was not after all interested in her, Verity—or rather in Blanche—and yet she had been left with the strange notion that he had watched her all the time he was in the greenroom.

He was Viscount Folingsby, a notorious rake, another dancer had told her later. Verity would likely have guessed it anyway. Apart from being almost incredibly handsome—tall, well formed, very dark, with eyes that were both penetrating and slumberous—there was an air of self-assurance and arrogance about him that proclaimed him to be a man accustomed to having his own way. There was also something almost unbearably sensual about him. A rake, yes. Without a doubt.

Yet she had been horribly tempted for that minute. If he had approached her, if he had made her an offer…

Thank heaven he had not done either.

But soon, *very* soon, she was going to have to consider and accept someone's offer. There! Finally she was calling a spade a spade. She was going to have to become someone's mistress. No, that was calling a spade a utensil. She was going to have to become someone's *whore*.

For a dizzying minute the room spun about her, closed eyes notwithstanding.

For Chastity, she told herself determinedly. For Chastity's life.

Chapter Two

JULIAN VISITED the greenroom at the opera house two evenings after his previous appearance there. There were a few men talking with Blanche Heyward. Hannah Dove was invisible amidst her court of admirers. His lordship joined them and chatted amiably for a while. It was not part of his plan to appear overeager. Several minutes passed before he strolled over to make his bow to the titian-haired dancer.

"Miss Heyward," he said languidly, holding her eyes with his own, "your servant. May I commend you on your performance this evening?"

"Thank you, my lord." Her voice was low, melodic. Seductive, and deliberately schooled to sound that way, he guessed. Her eyes looked candidly—and shrewdly?—back into his. He did not for a moment believe she was a virtuous woman. Or that what little virtue she had was not for hire.

"I have just been commending Miss Heyward on her talent and grace, Folingsby," Netherford said. "Damme, but if she were in a ballroom, she would put every other lady to shame. No gentleman would wish to dance with anyone but her, eh? Eh?" He dug one elbow into his lordship's ribs.

There were appreciative titters from the other gentlemen gathered about her.

"Dear me," his lordship murmured. "I wonder if Miss Heyward would wish to court such—ah, fame."

"Or such notoriety," she said with a fleeting smile.

"Damme," Netherford continued, "but one would love to watch you waltz, Miss Heyward. Trouble is, every other man present would want to stand and watch, too, and there would be no one to dance with all the other chits." There was a general gust of laughter at his words.

Julian raised his quizzing glass to his eye and caught a suggestion of scorn in the dancer's smile.

"Thank you, sir," she said. "You are flatteringly kind. But I am weary, gentlemen. It has been a long evening."

And thus bluntly she dismissed her court. They went meekly, after making their bows and bidding her good-night—three of them out the door, one to join the crowd still clustered about Hannah Dove. Julian remained.

Blanche Heyward looked up at him inquiringly. "My lord?" she said, a suggestion of a challenge in her voice.

"Sometimes I find," he said, dropping his glass and clasping his hands at his back, "that weariness can be treated as effectively with a quiet and leisurely meal as with sleep. Would you care to join me for supper?"

She opened her mouth to refuse—he read the intent in her expression—hesitated, and closed her mouth again.

"For supper, my lord?" She raised her eyebrows.

"I have reserved a private parlor in a tavern not far from here," he told her. "I would as soon have company as eat alone." And yet, he told her with his nonchalant expression and the language of his body, he would almost as soon eat alone. It mattered little to him whether she accepted or not.

She broke eye contact with him and looked down at her hands. She was clearly working up a refusal again. Equally clearly she was tempted. Or—and he rather suspected that this was the true interpretation of her behavior—she was as practiced as he in sending the message she wished to send. A reluctance and a certain indifference, in this case. But a fixed intention, nevertheless, of accepting in the end.

He made it easier for her, or rather he took the game back into his own hands.

"Miss Heyward." He leaned slightly toward her and lowered his voice. "I am inviting you to supper, not to bed."

Her eyes snapped back to his and he read in them the startled knowledge that she had been bested. She half smiled.

"Thank you, my lord," she said. "I *am* rather hungry. Will you wait while I fetch my cloak?"

He gave a slight inclination of his head, and she stood up. He was surprised by her height now that he was standing close to her. He was a tall man and dwarfed most women. She was scarcely more than half a head shorter than he.

Well, he thought with satisfaction, the first move had been made and he had emerged the winner. She had agreed only to supper, it was true, but if he could not turn that minor triumph into a week of pleasure in Norfolkshire, then he deserved the fate awaiting him at Conway in the form of the ferret-faced Lady Sarah Plunkett.

He did not expect to lose the game.

And he did not believe, moreover, that she intended he should.

IT WAS a square, spacious room with timbered ceiling and large fireplace, in which a cheerful fire crackled. In the center of the room was one table set for two, with fine china and crystal laid out on a crisply starched white cloth. Two long candles burned in pewter holders.

Viscount Folingsby must have been confident, Verity concluded, that she would say yes. He took her cloak in silence. Without looking at him, she crossed the room to the fire and held out her hands to the blaze. She felt more nervous than she had ever felt before, she believed, even counting her audition and her first onstage performance. Or perhaps it was a different kind of nervousness.

"It is a cold night," he said.

"Yes." Not that there had been much chance to notice the chill. A sumptuous private carriage had brought them the short distance from the theater. They had not spoken during the journey.

She did not believe it was an invitation just to supper. But she still did not know what her answer would be to the inevitable question. Perhaps it was understood in the demimonde that when one accepted such an invitation as this, one was committing oneself to giving thanks in the obvious way.

Could it possibly be that before this night was over she would have taken the irrevocable step?

What would it *feel* like? she wondered suddenly. And how would she feel in the morning?

"Green suits you," Lord Folingsby said, and Verity despised the way she jerked with alarm to find that he was close behind her. "Not all women have the wisdom and taste to choose clothes that suit their coloring."

She was wearing her dark green silk, which she had always liked though it was woefully outmoded and almost shabby. But its simple high-waisted, straight-sleeved design gave it a sort of timeless elegance that did not date itself as quickly as more fussy, more modish styles.

"Thank you," she said.

"I fancy," he said, "that some artist must once have mixed his paints with care and used a fine brush in order to produce the particular color of your eyes. It is unusual, if not unique."

She smiled into the dancing flames. Men were always lavish in their compliments on her eyes, though no one had ever said it quite like this before.

"I have some Irish blood in me, my lord," she said.

"Ah. The Emerald Isle," he said softly. "Land of red-haired, fiery-tempered beauties. Do you have a fiery temper, Miss Heyward?"

"I also have a great deal of English blood," she told him.

"Ah, we mundane and phlegmatic English." He sighed. "You disappoint me. Come to the table."

"You like hot-tempered women, then, my lord?" she asked him as he seated her and took his place opposite.

"That depends entirely on the woman," he said. "If I believe there is pleasure to be derived from the taming of her, yes, indeed." He picked up the bottle of wine that stood on the table, uncorked it and proceeded to fill her glass and then his own.

While he was so occupied, Verity looked fully at him for the first time since they had left the theater. He was almost frighteningly handsome, though why there should be anything fearsome about good looks she would have found difficult to explain. Perhaps it was his confidence, his arrogance more than his looks that had her wishing she could go back to the greenroom and change her answer. They seemed very much alone together, though two waiters were bringing food and setting it silently on the table. Or perhaps it was his sensual appeal and the certain knowledge that he wanted her.

He held his glass aloft and extended his hand halfway across the table. "To new acquaintances," he said, looking very directly into her eyes in the flickering light of the candles. "May they prosper."

She smiled, touched the rim of her glass to his and

drank. Her hand was steady, she was relieved to find, but she felt almost as if a decision had been made, a pact sealed.

"Shall we eat?" he suggested after the waiters had withdrawn and closed the door behind them. He indicated the plates of cold meats and steaming vegetables, the basket of fresh breads, the bowl of fruit.

She was hungry, she realized suddenly, but she was not at all sure she would be able to eat. She helped herself to a modest portion.

"Tell me, Miss Heyward," the viscount said, watching her butter a bread roll, "are you always this talkative?"

She paused and looked unwillingly up at him again. She was adept at making social conversation, as were most ladies of her class. But she had no idea what topics were suited to an occasion of this nature. She had never before dined tête-à-tête with a man, or been alone with one under any circumstances for longer than half an hour at a time or beyond a place where she could be easily observed by a chaperon.

"What do you wish me to talk about, my lord?" she asked him.

He regarded her for a few moments, a look of amusement on his face. "Bonnets?" he said. "Jewels? The latest shopping expedition?"

He did not, then, have a high regard for women's intelligence. Or perhaps it was just her type of woman. *Her type.*

"But what do *you* wish to talk about, my lord?" she asked him, taking a bite out of her roll.

He looked even more amused. "You," he said without hesitation. "Tell me about yourself, Miss Heyward. Begin with your accent. I cannot quite place its origin. Where are you from?"

She had not done at all well with the accent she had assumed during her working hours, except perhaps to disguise the fact that she had been gently born and raised.

"I pick up accents very easily," she lied. "And I have lived in many different places. I suppose there is a trace of all those places in my speech."

"And someone," he said, "to complicate the issue, has given you elocution lessons."

"Of course." She smiled. "Even as a dancer one must learn not to murder the English language with every word one speaks, my lord. If one expects to advance in one's career, that is."

He gazed silently at her for a few moments, his fork suspended halfway to his mouth. Verity felt herself flushing. What career was he imagining she wished to advance?

"Quite so," he said softly, his voice like velvet. He

carried his fork the rest of the way to his mouth. "But what are some of these places? Tell me where you have lived. Tell me about your family. Come, we cannot munch on our food in silence, you know. There is nothing better designed to shake a person's composure."

Her life seemed to have become nothing but lies. In each of her worlds she had to withhold the truth about the other. And withholding the truth sometimes became more than a passive thing. It involved the invention of lie upon lie. She had some knowledge of two places—the village in Somersetshire where she had lived for two-and-twenty years, and London, where she had lived for two months. But she spoke of Ireland, drawing on the stories she could remember her maternal grandmother telling her when she was a child, and more riskily, of the city of York, where a neighborhood friend had lived with his uncle for a while, and about a few other places of which she had read.

She hoped fervently that the viscount had no intimate knowledge of any of the places she chose to describe. She invented a mythical family—a father who was a blacksmith, a warmhearted mother who had died five years before, three brothers and three sisters, all considerably younger than herself.

"You came to London to seek your fortune?" he asked. "You have not danced anywhere else?"

She hesitated. But she did not want him to think her inexperienced, easy to manipulate. "Oh, of course," she said. "For several years, my lord." She smiled into his eyes as she reached for a pear from the dish of fruit. "But all roads lead eventually to London, you know."

She was startled by the look of naked desire that flared in his eyes for a moment as he followed the movement of her hand. But it was soon veiled behind his lazy eyelids and slightly mocking smile.

"Of course," he said softly. "And those of us who spend most of our time here are only too delighted to benefit from the experience in the various arts such persons as yourself have acquired elsewhere."

Verity kept her eyes on the pear she was peeling. It was unusually juicy, she was dismayed to find. Her hands were soon wet with juice. And her heart was thumping. Suddenly, and quite inexplicably, she felt as if she had waded into deep waters, indeed. The air fairly bristled between them. She licked her lips and could think of no reply to make.

His voice sounded amused when he spoke again. "Having peeled it, Miss Heyward," he said, "you are now obliged to eat it, you know. It would be a crime to waste good food."

She lifted one half of the pear to her mouth and bit into it. Juice cascaded to her plate below, and some of it trickled down her chin. She reached for her napkin in some embarrassment, knowing that he was watching her. But before she could pick it up, he had reached across the table and one long finger had scooped up the droplet of juice that was about to drip onto her gown. She raised her eyes, startled, to watch him carry the finger to his mouth and touch it to his tongue. His eyes remained on her all the while.

Verity felt a sharp stabbing of sensation down through her abdomen and between her thighs. She felt a rush of color to her cheeks. She felt as if she had been running for a mile uphill.

"Sweet," he murmured.

She jumped to her feet, pushing at her chair with the backs of her knees. Then she wished she had not done so. Her legs felt decidedly unsteady. She crossed to the fireplace again and reached out her hands as if to warm them, though she felt as if the fire might better be able to take warmth from her.

She drew a few steadying breaths in the silence that followed. And then she could see from the corner of one eye that he had come to stand at the other side of the hearth. He rested one arm along the high mantel. He was watching her. The time had come, she thought. She had precipitated it herself. Within moments the question would be asked and must be answered. She still did not know what that answer would be, or perhaps she did. Perhaps she was just fooling herself to believe that there was still a choice. She had made her decision back in the greenroom— no, even before that. This was a tavern, part of an inn. No doubt he had bespoken a bedchamber here, as well as a private dining room. Within minutes, then…

How would it feel? She did not even know exactly what she was to expect. The basic facts, of course…

"Miss Heyward," he asked her, making her jump again, "what are your plans for Christmas?"

She turned her head to look at him. Christmas? It was a week and a half away. She would spend it with her family, of course. It would be their first Christmas away from home, their first without the friends and neighbors they had known all their lives. But at least they still had one another and were still together. They had decided that they would indulge in the extravagance of a goose and make something special of the day with inexpensive gifts that they would make for one another. Christmas had always been Verity's favorite time of the year. Somehow it restored hope and reminded her of the truly important things in life—family and love and selfless giving.

Selfless giving.

"Do you have any plans?" he asked.

She could hardly claim to be going home to that large family at the smithy in Somersetshire. She shook her head.

"I will be spending a quiet week in Norfolkshire with a friend and his, ah, lady," he said. "Will you come with me?"

A quiet week. A friend and his lady. She understood, of course, exactly what he meant, exactly to what she was being invited. If she agreed now, Verity thought, the die would be cast. She would have stepped irrevocably into that world from which it would be impossible to return. Once a fallen woman, she would never be able to retrieve either her virtue or her honor.

If she agreed?

She would be away from home at Christmas of all times. Away from Mama and Chastity. For a whole week. Could anything be worth such a sacrifice, not to mention the sacrifice of her very self?

It was as if he read her mind. "Five hundred pounds, Miss Heyward," he said softly. "For one week."

Five hundred pounds? Her mouth went dry. It was a colossal sum. Did he know what five hundred pounds meant to someone like her? But of course he knew. It meant irresistible temptation.

In exchange for one week of service. Seven nights. Seven, when even the thought of one was insupportable. But once the first had been endured, the other six would hardly matter.

Chastity needed to see the physician again. She needed more medicine. If she were to die merely because they could not afford the proper treatment for her illness, how would she feel, Verity asked herself, when it had been within her power to see to it that they *could* afford the treatment? What had she just been telling herself about Christmas?

Selfless giving.

She smiled into the fire. "That would be very pleasant, my lord," she said, and then listened in some astonishment to the other words that came unplanned from her mouth, "provided you pay me in advance."

She turned her head to look at him when he did not immediately reply. His elbow was still on the mantel, his closed fist resting against his mouth. Above it his eyes showed amusement.

"We will, of course, agree to a compromise," he told her. "Half before we leave and half after we return?"

She nodded. Two hundred and fifty pounds before she even left London. Once she had accepted the payment, she would have backed herself into a corner. She could not then refuse to carry out her part of the agreement. She tried to swallow, but the dryness of her mouth made it well nigh impossible to do.

"Splendid," he said briskly. "Come, it is late. I will escort you home."

She was to escape for tonight, then? Part of her felt a knee-weakening relief. Part of her was strangely disappointed. The worst of it might have been over within the hour if, as she had expected, he had reserved a room and had invited her there. She felt a deep dread of the first time. She imagined, perhaps naively, that after that, once it was an accomplished fact, once she was a fallen woman, once she knew how it felt, it would be easier to repeat. But now it seemed that she would have to wait until they left for Norfolkshire before the deed was done.

He had fetched her cloak and was setting it about her shoulders. She came to attention suddenly, realizing what he had just said.

"Thank you, no, my lord," she said. "I shall see myself home. Perhaps you would be so kind as to call a hackney cab?"

He turned her and his hands brushed her own aside and did up her cloak buttons for her. He looked up into her eyes, the task completed. "Playing the elusive game until the end, Miss Heyward?" he asked. "Or is there someone at home you would rather did not see me?"

His implication was obvious. But he was, of course, right though not in quite the way he meant. She smiled back at him.

"I have promised you a week, my lord," she said. "That week does not begin with tonight, as I understand it?"

"Quite right," he said. "You shall have your hackney, then, and keep your secrets. I do believe Christmas is going to be more…interesting than usual."

"I trust you may be right, my lord," she said with all the coolness she could muster, preceding him to the door.

Chapter Three

JULIAN WAS FEELING weary, cold and irritable by the time Bertrand Hollander's hunting box hove into view at dusk on a particularly gray and cheerless afternoon, two days before Christmas. He would feel far more cheerful, he told himself, once he was indoors, basking before a blazing fire, imbibing some of Bertie's brandy and contemplating the delights of the night ahead. But at the moment he could not quite convince himself that this Christmas was going to be one of unalloyed pleasure.

He had ridden all the way from London despite the fact that his comfortable, well-sprung traveling carriage held only one passenger. During the morning, he had thought it a clever idea—she would be intrigued to watch him ride just within sight beyond the carriage windows; he would comfort himself with the anticipation of joining her within during the afternoon. But during the noon stop for dinner and a change of horses, Miss Blanche Heyward had upset him quite considerably. No, that was refining too much on a trifle. She had *annoyed* him quite considerably.

And all over a mere bauble, a paltry handful of gold.

He had been planning to give it to her for Christmas. A gift was perhaps unnecessary since she was being paid handsomely enough for her services. But Christmas had always been a time of gift giving with him, and he knew he was going to miss Conway and all its usual warm celebrations. And so he had bought her a gift, spending far more time in the choosing of it than he usually did for his mistresses and instinctively avoiding the gaudy flash of precious stones.

On impulse he had decided to give it to her in the rather charming setting of the inn parlor in which they dined on their journey, rather than wait for Christmas Day. But she had merely looked at the box in his outstretched hand and had made no move to grab it.

"What is it?" she had asked with the quiet dignity he was beginning to recognize as characteristic of her.

"Why do you not look and see?" he had suggested. "It is an early Christmas gift."

"There is no need of it." She had looked into his eyes. "You are paying me well, my lord, for what I will give in return."

Her words had sent an uncomfortable rush of tightness to his groin, though he was not at all sure she had intended them so. He had also felt the first stirring of annoyance. Was she going to keep him with his hand outstretched, feeling foolish, until his dinner grew cold? But she had reached out a hand slowly, taken the box and opened it. He had watched her almost anxiously. Had he made a mistake in not choosing diamonds or rubies, or emeralds, perhaps?

She had looked down for a long time, saying nothing, making no move to touch the contents of the box.

"It is the Star of Bethlehem," she had said finally.

It was a star, yes, a gold star on a gold chain. He had not thought of it as the Christmas star. But the description seemed apt enough.

"Yes," he had agreed. He had despised himself for his next words, but they had been out before he could stop them. "Do you like it?"

"It belongs in the heavens," she had said after a lengthy pause during which she had gazed at the pendant and appeared as if she had forgotten about both him and her surroundings. "As a symbol of hope. As a sign to all who are in search of the meaning of their lives. As a goal in the pursuit of wisdom."

Good Lord! He had been rendered speechless.

She had looked up then and regarded him very directly with those magnificent emerald eyes. "Money ought not to be able to buy it, my lord," she had said. "It is not appropriate as a gift from such as you to such as I."

He had gazed back, one eyebrow raised, containing his fury. *Such as he?* What the devil was she implying?

"Do I understand, Miss Heyward," he had asked, injecting as much boredom into his voice as he could summon, "that you do not like the gift? Dear me, I ought to have had my man pick up a diamond bracelet instead. I shall inform him that you agree with my opinion that he has execrable taste."

She had looked into his eyes for several moments longer, no discernible anger there at his insult.

"I am sorry," she had surprised him by saying then. "I have hurt you. It is very beautiful, my lord, and shows that you have impeccable taste. Thank you." She had closed the box and placed it in her reticule.

They had continued with their meal in silence, and suddenly, he had discovered, he was eating straw, not food.

He had mounted his horse when they resumed their journey and left her to her righteous solitude in his carriage. And for the rest of the journey he had nursed his irritation with her. What the devil did she mean *it is not appropriate as a gift from such as you?* How dared she! And why was it inappropriate, even assuming that the gold star was intended to be the Star of Bethlehem? The star was a symbol of hope, she had said, a sign to those who pursued wisdom and the meaning of their own lives.

What utter balderdash!

Those three wise men of the Christmas story—*if* they had existed, and *if* they had been wise, and *if* there had really been three of them—had they gone lurching off across the desert on their camels, clutching their offerings, in hopeful pursuit of wisdom and meaning? More likely they had been escaping overly affectionate relatives who were attempting to marry them off to the biblical era equivalent of the Plunkett chit. Or hoping to find something that would gratify their jaded senses.

They must all have been despicably rich, after all, to be able to head off on a mad journey without fear of running out of money. It was purely by chance that they had discovered something worth more than gold, or those other two commodities they had had with them. What the deuce were frankincense and myrrh anyway?

Well, he was no wise man even though he had set out on his journey with his pathetic handful of gold.

And even though he was hoping to find gratification of his senses at the end of the journey. That was all he *did* want—a few congenial days with Bertie, and a few energetic nights in bed with Blanche. To hell with hope and wisdom and meaning. He knew where his life was headed after this week. He was going to marry Lady Sarah Plunkett and have babies with her until his nursery was furnished with an heir and a spare, to use the old cliché. And he was going to live respectably ever after.

It was going to snow, he thought, glancing up at the heavy clouds. They were going to have a white Christmas. The prospect brought with it none of the elation he would normally feel. At Conway there would be children of all ages from two to eighty gazing at the sky and making their plans for toboggan rides and snowball fights and snowman-building contests and skating parties. He felt an unwelcome wave of nostalgia.

But they had arrived at Bertie's hunting box, which looked more like a small manor than the modest lodge Julian had been expecting. There were the welcome signs of candlelight from within and of smoke curling up from the chimneys. He swung down from his horse, wincing at the stiffness in his limbs, and waved aside the footman who would have opened the carriage door and set down the steps. His lordship did it himself and reached up a hand to help down his mistress.

And that was another thing, he thought as she placed a gloved hand in his and stepped out of the carriage. She was not looking at all like the bird of paradise he had pictured himself bringing into the country. She was dressed demurely in a gray wool dress with a long gray cloak, black gloves and black half boots. Her hair—all those glorious titian tresses—had been swept back ruthlessly from her face and was almost invisible beneath a plain and serviceable bonnet. There was not a trace of cosmetics on her face, which admittedly was quite lovely enough without. But she looked more like a lady than a whore.

"Thank you, my lord," she said, glancing up at the house.

"I trust," he said, "you were warm enough under the lap robes?"

"Indeed." She smiled at him.

One thing at least was clear to him as he turned with her toward Bertie, who was standing in the open doorway, rubbing his hands together, a welcoming grin on his face. He was still anticipating the night ahead with a great deal of pleasure, perhaps more so than ever. There was something unusually intriguing about Miss Blanche Heyward, opera dancer and authority on the Star of Bethlehem.

VERITY FELT embarrassment more than any other emotion for the first hour or so of her stay at Bertrand Hollander's hunting box, and what a misnomer *that* was, she thought, looking about at the well-sized, cozy, expensively furnished house that a gentleman used only during the shooting season. And, of course, for clandestine holidays with his mistress.

It was that idea that caused the embarrassment. Mr. Hollander appeared to be a pleasant gentleman. He had a good-looking, amiable face and was dressed with neat elegance. He greeted them with a hearty welcome and assured them that they must make themselves at home for the coming week and not even think of standing on ceremony.

He greeted her, Verity, with gallantry, taking her hand and raising it to his lips before tucking it beneath his arm and leading her into the house while begging her to call upon him at any time if he might be of service in increasing her comfort.

And yet there was something in his manner—a certain familiarity—that showed he was a gentleman talking, not with a lady, but with a woman of another class entirely. There was the frank way, for example, that he looked her over from head to toe before grinning at Viscount Folingsby. It was not quite an insolent look. Indeed, there was a good deal of appreciation in it. But he would not have looked at a lady so, not at least while she was observing him doing it. Nor would he have called a lady by her first name. But Mr. Hollander used hers.

"Come into the parlor where there is a fire, Blanche," he said. "We will soon have you warmed up. Come and meet Debbie."

Debbie was the other woman, Mr. Hollander's mistress. She was blond and pretty and plump and placid. She spoke with a decided Yorkshire accent. She did not rise from the chair in which she lounged beside the fire, but smiled genially and lazily at the new arrivals.

"Sit down there, Blanche," she said, pointing to the chair at the other side of the fire. "Bertie will send for tea, won't you, love? Ee, you look frozen, Jule. You'd better pull a chair closer to the fire unless you want to sit with Blanche on your lap."

She was addressing Viscount Folingsby, Verity realized in some shock as she took the offered chair and removed her gloves and bonnet, since no servant had offered to take them in the hall. She directed a very straight look at her new protector, but he was bowing over Debbie's outstretched hand and taking it to his lips.

"Charmed," he said. "I do hope you are not planning to order tea for me, too, Bertie?"

His friend barked with laughter and crossed the

room to a sideboard on which there was an array of decanters and glasses. The viscount pulled up a chair for himself, Verity was relieved to find, but Mr. Hollander, when he returned with glasses of liquor for his friend and himself, raised his eyebrows at Debbie. She sighed, hoisted herself out of the chair, and then settled herself on his lap after he had sat down.

Verity refused to feel outrage. She refused to show disapproval by even the smallest gesture. These were two gentlemen with their mistresses. She was one of the latter, by her own choice. There was already more than two hundred pounds safely stowed away in a drawer at home. The rest of the advance payment had been spent on another visit to the physician for Chastity and more medicine. A small sum was in her purse inside her reticule. It was too late to go back even if she wanted to. The money was not intact to be returned.

And so she resigned herself to what must be. But she had made one decision during the days since she had accepted Viscount Folingsby's proposition. She was not going to act a part besides what she had already committed herself to. She spoke with some sort of accent to disguise the refinement of her lady's voice. She had invented a family at a smithy in Somersetshire. But beyond those things she was not going to go. She was not going to try to be deliberately vulgar or stupid or anything else she imagined a mistress would be.

She had brought with her the clothes she usually wore at home. She had dressed her hair as she usually wore it there. She had kept her end of the bargain by coming here. She would keep it by staying over Christmas and allowing Viscount Folingsby to do *that* to her. Her mind still shied away from the details and from the alarming fact that she was ignorant of many of them. She had hardly been in a position to ask her mother, as she would have done had she been getting married and was facing a wedding night.

She had told Mama and Chastity that Lady Coleman was going into the country for Christmas and required her presence. She had told them that she was being paid a very generous bonus for going, though she had not mentioned the incredible sum of five hundred pounds. They had both been upset at the prospect of her absence over Christmas, and she had shed a few tears with them, but they had consoled themselves with the belief that as a member of a house party she would have a wonderful time.

"Are you warmer now?" Viscount Folingsby asked suddenly, bringing Verity's mind back to Mr. Hollander's sitting room, into which a servant was just carrying a tea tray. He leaned forward and took one of her hands in both of his. His were warm; hers was not.

"Perhaps I should have cuddled you on my lap after all."

"I believe the fire and the tea between them will do the trick nicely for now, my lord," she said before turning her attention to Mr. Hollander, who was smiling genially at them. "I have never before been into this part of the world, sir. Do tell me about it. What beauties of nature characterize it? And what history and buildings of note are there here?"

She would no longer be mute, wondering what topics of conversation were appropriate for an opera dancer and a gentleman's mistress.

"Ee, Bertie, love," Debbie said, "there is a right pretty garden out back. Tell Blanche about it. Tell her about the tree swing."

It was not tree swings exactly that Verity had had in mind, but she settled back in her chair with a smile as the servant handed her her tea. Viscount Folingsby relinquished her hand.

"For now," he murmured. "But later, Blanche, I beg leave to do service in place of the fire and the tea."

It took her a moment to realize he was referring to her earlier words. When she did so, she wished she were sitting a little farther back from the fire. Her face felt as if it were being scorched.

It did not seem, she thought suddenly, as if Christmas was close. Tomorrow would be Christmas Eve. For a few moments there was the ache of tears in her throat.

THERE MUST have been a goodly number of bedchambers in the house, Julian guessed later that night as he ascended the staircase with Blanche on his arm. But Bertie, of course, had assigned them only one. It was a large room overlooking the small wooded park at the back of the house. It was warmed by a log fire in a large hearth and lit by a single branch of candles. Heavy velvet curtains had been drawn back from the large canopied bed and the covers had been turned down.

He was glad he had not had her before, he decided as he closed the door behind them and extinguished the single candle that had lit their way upstairs. Pleasurable anticipation had been building in him for over a week. It had reached a crescendo of desire this evening. She had been looking almost demure in the green silk dress she had worn the evening they first supped together, her hair dressed severely but not unattractively.

And she had been acting the part of a lady, keeping the conversation going during dinner and in the sitting room afterward with observations about their journey, about the Christmas decorations and carol singers in London, and about—of all things—the peace talks that were proceeding in Vienna now that Napoleon Bonaparte had been defeated and was imprisoned on the island of Elba. She had asked Bertie what plans had been made for their own celebration of Christmas. Bertie had looked surprised and then blank. He obviously had no plans at all beyond enjoying himself with his pretty, buxom Debbie.

Paradoxically Julian had found Blanche's demure appearance and ladylike behavior arousing. He considered both erotic. She had too many charms to hide effectively.

"Come here," he said now.

She had gone to stand in front of the fire. She was holding out her hands to the blaze. But she turned her head, smiled at him and came to stand in front of him. She was clever, he thought. She must know that an overeagerness on her part would somehow dampen his own. Though there was just a chance she was not quite as eager as he. This was a job to her, after all. He would soon change that. He set his hands on either side of her waist and drew her against him, fitting her body against his own from the waist down. He could feel the slimness of her long legs, the flatness of her abdomen. His breath quickened. She looked back into his eyes, a half smile on her lips.

"At last," he said.

"Yes." Her smile did not waver. Neither did her eyes.

He bent his head and kissed her. She kept her lips closed. He teased them with his own and touched his tongue lightly to the seam, moving it slowly across in order to part her lips and gain entrance. Her head jerked back.

"What are you doing?" She sounded breathless.

He stared blankly at her. But before he could frame an answer to such a nonsensical question, her look of shock disappeared, she smiled again, and her hands came up to rest on his shoulders.

"Pardon me," she said. "You moved just a little too fast for me. I am ready now." She brought her mouth back to his, her lips softly parted this time, and trembling against his own.

What the devil?

His mind turned cold with suspicion. He closed his arms about her and thrust his tongue deep into her mouth without any attempt at subtlety. She made no move to pull away, but she went rigid in every limb for a few moments before relaxing almost to limpness. He moved his hands forward quite deliberately and cupped her breasts with them, his thumbs seeking and pressing against her nipples. Again there was the momentary tensing followed by relaxation.

He was looking down at her a moment later, his

eyes half-closed, his hands again on either side of her waist.

"Well, Miss Heyward," he asked softly, "how have you enjoyed your first kiss?"

"My first…" She gazed blankly at him.

"I suppose it would be strange indeed," he said, "if I were to discover in a few minutes' time on that bed that you are not also a virgin?"

She had nothing to say this time.

"Well?" he asked her. "Shall I put the matter to the test?" He watched her swallow.

"Even the most hardened of whores," she said at last, "was a virgin once, my lord. For each there is a first time. I will not flinch or weep or deny you your will, if that is what you fear. You are paying me well. I will do all that is required of me."

"Will you, indeed?" he said, releasing her and crossing the room to the hearth to push a log farther into the blaze with his foot. He watched the resulting shower of sparks. "I am not paying for the pleasure of observing martyrdom."

"I was not acting the martyr," she protested. "You took me by surprise. I did not know… I am perfectly willing to do whatever you wish me to do. I am sorry that I will be awkward at first. But I will learn tonight, and tomorrow night I will know better what it is you expect of me. I hope I…perhaps under the circumstances you will decide that you have already paid me handsomely enough. I believe you have. I will try to earn it."

Did she realize, he wondered in some amazement, that she was throwing a pail of cold water over his desire with every sentence she uttered? Anger was replacing it—no, fury. Not so much against her. She had told him no lies about her experience, had she? His fury was all against himself and his own cleverness. He would keep her for Bertie's, would he? He would savor his anticipation, would he, until it was too late to change his mind, to go to Conway as he ought to have done? He would have one last fling, would he, before he did his duty by his family and name? Well, he had been justly served.

In the middle of the desert, far from home, had the wise men ever called themselves all kinds of fool?

"I do not deal in virgins, Miss Heyward," he said curtly.

"Ah," she said, "you do not like to face what it is you are purchasing, then, my lord?"

He raised his eyebrows in surprise and regarded her over his shoulder in silence for a few moments. This woman had sharp weapons and did not scruple to wield them. "Is your need for the money a personal one?" he asked her, turning from the fire. "Or is it your family that is in need?" He did not want to know, he realized after the questions were out. He had no wish to know Blanche Heyward as a person. All he had wanted was one last sensual fling with a beautiful and experienced and willing partner.

"I do not have to answer that," she said. "I will pay back all I can when we have returned to London. But I am still willing to earn my salary."

"As I remember," he said, "our agreement was for a week of your company in exchange for a certain sum, Blanche. There was no mention of your warming my bed during that week, was there? We will spend the week here. It is too late now for either of us to make other arrangements for Christmas. Besides, those were snow clouds this afternoon if ever I have seen any. We will salvage what we can of the holiday, then. It might be the dreariest Christmas either of us has ever spent, but who knows? Maybe not. Maybe I will decide to give you lessons in kissing so that your next, ah, employer will make his discovery rather later in the process than I did. Undress and go to bed. There is a dressing room for your modesty."

"Where will you sleep?" she asked him.

He looked down at the floor, which was fortunately carpeted. "Here," he said. "Perhaps you will understand that I have no wish for Bertie to know that we are not spending the night in sensual bliss to-gether."

"You have the bed," she said. "I will sleep on the floor."

He felt an unexpected stirring of amusement. "But I have already told you, Blanche," he said, "that I have no wish to gaze on martyrdom. Go to bed be-fore I change my mind."

By the time she came back from the dressing room a few minutes later, dressed in a virginal white flannel nightgown, her head held high, her cheeks flushed and her titian hair all down her back, he had made up some sort of bed for himself on the floor close to the fire with blankets he had found in a drawer and a pillow he had taken from the bed. He did not look at her beyond one cursory glance. He waited for her to climb into the bed and pull the covers up over her ears, and then extinguished the candles.

"Good night," he said, finding his way back to his bed by the light of the fire.

"Good night," she said.

What a marvelously just punishment for his sins, he thought as he lay down and his body registered the hardness of the floor. But why the devil was he doing this? She had been willing and he was paying her handsomely. Heaven knows, he had wanted her badly enough, and still did.

It was not any real reluctance to violate innocence, he decided, or any unwillingness to deal with awkwardness or the inevitable blood. It was exactly what he had said it was. He had no desire to watch martyrdom or to inflict it.

I will not flinch or weep or deny you your will.

If there were less erotic words in the English language, he could not imagine what they might be. Sheer martyrdom! If only she had wanted it, wanted *him* just a little bit, even if she had been nervous…

Miss Blanche Heyward, he was discovering to his cost, was not the average, typical opera dancer. In fact she was turning out to be a royal pain.

A fine Christmas this was going to be. He thought glumly of Conway and of what he would be missing there tomorrow and the day after. Even the Plunkett chit was looking mildly appealing at this particular moment.

"What would you have done for Christmas," a soft voice asked him as if she had read his thoughts, "if you had not come here with me?"

He breathed deeply and evenly and audibly.

Perhaps tomorrow he would teach her to see a night spent in bed with him as fitting a different category of experience from Christians being prodded into the arena with slavering lions. But unlike his usual confident self, he did not hold out a great deal of hope of succeeding.

Surprisingly he slept.

Chapter Four

VERITY DID NOT sleep well during the night. But as she lay staring at the window and the suggestion of daylight beyond the curtains, she was surprised that she had slept at all.

There were sounds of deep, even breathing coming from the direction of the fireplace. She listened carefully. There were no sounds from beyond the door. Did that mean no one was up yet? Of course, Mr. Hollander and Debbie had probably been busy all night and perhaps intended to be busy for part of the morning, too.

It should have been all over by this morning, she thought. She should be a fallen woman beyond all dispute by now. And he had been wrong. It would not have felt like martyrdom. Even in the privacy of her own mind she was a little embarrassed to remember how exciting his hard man's body had felt against her own and how shockingly pleasurable his open mouth had felt against her lips. All her insides had performed some sort of vigorous dance when he had put his tongue into her mouth. What an alarmingly intimate thing to do. It should have been disgusting but had not been.

Well, she thought with determined honesty, she had actually wanted to experience the whole of it. And deny it as she would, she had to confess to herself that there had been some disappointment in his refusal to continue once he had realized the truth about her.

And so here they were in this ridiculous predicament with all of Christmas ahead of them. How could she possibly earn five hundred pounds when one night was already past and he had slept on the floor?

All of Christmas was ahead of them. What a depressing thought!

And then something in the quality of the light beyond the window drew her attention. She threw back the bedcovers, ignored her shivering reaction to the frigid air beyond their shelter and padded across the room on bare feet. She drew aside the curtain.

Oh!

"Oh!" she exclaimed aloud. She turned her head

and looked eagerly at the sleeping man. "Oh, do come and look."

His head reared up from his pillow. He looked deliciously tousled and unshaven. He was also scowling.

"What?" he barked. "What the devil *time* is it?"

"Look," she said, turning back to the window. "Oh, look."

He was beside her then, clad only in his shirt and last night's knee breeches and stockings. "For this you have dragged me from my bed?" he asked her. "I told you last night that it would snow today."

"But look!" she begged him. "It is sheer magic."

When she turned her head, she found him looking at her instead of at the snow beyond the window, blanketing the ground and decking out the bare branches of the trees.

"Do you always glow like this in the morning?" he asked her. "How disgusting!"

She laughed. "Only when Christmas is coming and there is a fresh fall of snow," she said. "Can you imagine two more wonderful events happening simultaneously?"

"Finding a soft warm bed when I am more than half asleep and stiff in every limb," he said.

"Then have my bed," she said, laughing again. "I am getting up."

"A fine impression Bertie is going to have of my

power to keep you amused and confined to your room," he said.

"Mr. Hollander," she told him, "will doubtless keep to his room until noon and will be none the wiser. Go to bed and go to sleep."

He did both. By the time she emerged from the dressing room, clad in the warmest of her wool dresses, her hair brushed and decently confined, he was lying in the place on the bed where she had lain all night, fast asleep. She stood gazing down at him for a few moments, imagining that if she had not been so gauche last night...

She shook her head and straightened her shoulders. Mr. Hollander had made no preparations for Christmas. Doubtless he thought that spending a few days in bed with the placid Debbie would constitute enough merrymaking. Well, they would see about that. She was not being allowed to earn her salary in the expected way. The least she could do, then, was make herself useful in other ways.

Two COACHMEN, one footman, one groom, a cook, Mr. Hollander's valet, and four others who might in a more orderly establishment have been dubbed a butler, a housekeeper and two maids were in the middle of their breakfast belowstairs. A few of them scrambled awkwardly to their feet when Verity appeared in their midst. A few did not. Clearly it was not established in any of their minds whether they should treat her as a lady or not. The cook looked as if she might be the leader of the latter faction.

Verity smiled. "Please do not get up," she said. "Do carry on with your breakfast. Doubtless you all have a busy day ahead."

If they did, their expressions told Verity, this was the first they had heard of it.

"Preparing for Christmas," she added.

They might have been devout Hindus for all the interest they showed in preparing for Christmas.

"Mr. Hollander don't want no fuss," the woman who might have been the housekeeper said.

"He said we might do as we please provided he has his victuals when he is ready for them and provided the fires are kept burning." The possible-butler was the speaker this time.

"Oh, splendid," Verity said cheerfully. "May I have some breakfast with you, by the way? No, please do not get up." No one had made any particular move to do so. "I shall just help myself, shall I?" She did so. "If you have been given permission to please yourselves, then, you may be pleased to celebrate Christmas. In the traditional way, with Christmas foods and wassail, with carol singing and gift giving and decorating the house with holly and pine boughs and whatever else we can devise with only a day's warning. Everyone can have a wonderful time."

"When I cook a goose," the cook announced, "nobody needs a knife to cut it. Even the edge of a fork is too sharp. It melts apart."

"Ooh, I do love a goose," one of the maids said wistfully. "My ma used to cook one as a treat for Christmas whenever we could catch one. But it weren't never cooked tender enough to cut with a fork, Mrs. Lyons," she added hastily.

"And when I make mince pies," the cook continued as if she had not been interrupted, "no one can stop eating after just one of them. *No one.*"

"Mmm." Verity sighed. "You make my mouth water, Mrs. Lyons. How I would love to taste just one of those pies."

"Well, I can't make them," Mrs. Lyons said, a note of finality in her voice. "Because I don't have the stuff."

"Could the supplies be bought in the village?" Verity suggested. "I noticed a village as I passed through it yesterday. There appeared to be a few shops there."

"There is nobody to go for them," Mrs. Lyons said. "Not in all this snow."

Verity smiled at the groom and the two coachmen, all of whom were trying unsuccessfully to blend into the furniture. "Nobody?" she said. "Not for the sake of goose tomorrow and mince pies and probably a dozen other Christmas specialties, too? Not for Mrs. Lyons's sake when it sounds to me as if she is the most skilled cook in all of Norfolkshire?"

"Well, I am quite skilled," the cook said modestly.

"There are pine trees and holly bushes in the park, are there not?" Verity asked of no one in particular. "Is there mistletoe anywhere?" She turned her eyes on the younger of the two maids. "What is Christmas without a few sprigs of mistletoe appearing in the most unlikely places and just over the heads of the most elusive people?"

The maid turned pink and the valet looked interested.

"There used to be some on the old oaks," the butler said. "But I don't know about this year, mind."

"The archway leading from the kitchen to the back stairs looks a likely place to me for one sprig," Verity said, looking critically at the spot as she bit into a piece of toast.

Both maids giggled and the valet cleared his throat.

After that the hard work seemed to be behind her, Verity found. The idea had caught hold. Mr. Hollander had given his staff carte blanche even if he had not done so consciously. And the staff had awakened to the realization that it was Christmas and that they might celebrate it in as grand a manner as they chose. All lethargy magically disappeared, and Verity was able to eat her eggs and toast and drink down two cups of coffee while warming herself at the kitchen fire and listening to the servants make their animated plans. There were even two volunteers to go into the village.

"You cannot all be everywhere at once, though," Verity said, speaking up again at last, "much as I can see you would like to be. You may leave the gathering of the greenery and just come to help drag it all indoors. Mr. Hollander, Lord Folingsby, Miss, er, Debbie, and I will do the gathering."

Silence and blank stares met this announcement until someone sniggered—the groom.

"I don't think so, miss," he said. "You won't drag them gents out of doors to spoil the shine on their boots nor 'er to spoil 'er complexion. You can forget that one right enough."

The valet cleared his throat again, with considerably more dignity than before. "You will speak with greater respect of Mr. Hollander, Bloggs," he told the groom, who looked quite uncowed by the reprimand.

Verity smiled. "You may safely leave Mr. Hollander and the others to me," she said. "We are *all* going to enjoy Christmas. It would be unfair to exclude them, would it not?"

Her words caused a burst of merriment about the table, and Verity tried to imagine Julian pricking his aristocratic fingers in the cause of gathering holly. He would probably sleep until noon. But she had done him an injustice. He appeared in the archway that was not yet adorned with mistletoe only a moment later, as if her thoughts had summoned him. He was dressed immaculately despite the fact that he had not brought his valet with him.

"Ah," Julian said languidly, fingering the handle of his quizzing glass, "here you are, Blanche. I began to think you had sprouted wings and flown since there are no footprints in the snow leading from the door."

"We have been planning the Christmas festivities," she told him with a bright smile. "Everything is organized. Later you and I will be going out into the park with Mr. Hollander and Debbie to gather greenery with which to decorate the house."

Suddenly that part of the plan seemed quite preposterous. His lordship raised his quizzing glass all the way to his eye and moved it about the table, the better to observe all the conspirators seated there. It came to rest finally on her.

"Indeed?" he said faintly. "What a delightful treat for us."

JULIAN WAS SITTING awkwardly on the branch of an ancient oak tree, not quite sure how he had got up there and even less sure how he was to get down again without breaking a leg or two or even his neck. Blanche was standing below, her face upturned, her arms spread as if to catch him should he fall. Just a short distance beyond his grasp was a promising clump of mistletoe. Several yards away from the oak, Bertie was standing almost knee-deep in snow, one glove on, the other discarded on the ground beside him, complaining about a holly prick on one finger with all the loud woe of a man who had just been run through with a sword. Debbie was kissing it better.

A little closer to the house, in a spot sheltered by trees and therefore not as deeply covered with snow, lay a pathetically small pile of pine boughs and holly branches. Pathetic, at least, considering the fact that they had been outdoors and hard at work for longer than an hour, subjected to frigid temperatures, buffeting winds and swirling flakes of thick snow. The heavy clouds had still not finished emptying their load.

"Oh, do be careful," Blanche implored as Julian leaned out gingerly to reach the mistletoe. "Don't fall."

He paused and looked down at her. Her cheeks were charmingly rosy. So was her nose. "Did I imagine it, Blanche," he asked, using his best bored voice, "or did the drill sergeant who marched us out here and ordered me up here really wear your face?"

She laughed. No, she did not—she giggled. "If you kill yourself," she said, "I shall have them write on your epitaph—He Died In The Execution Of A Noble Deed."

By dint of shifting his position on the branch until he hung even more precariously over space and scraping his boot beyond redemption to get something of a toehold against the gnarled trunk, he finally succeeded in his mission. He had dislodged a handful of mistletoe. There was no easy way down to the ground. Indeed, there was no possible way down. He did what he had always done as a boy in a similar situation. He jumped.

He landed on all fours and got a faceful of soft snow for his pains.

"Oh, dear," Blanche said. "Did you hurt yourself?" He looked up at her and she giggled again. "You look like a snowman, a snowman whose dignity has been bruised. Do you have the mistletoe?"

He got to his feet and brushed himself off with one hand as best he could. His valet, when he got back to London, was going to take one look at his boots and resign.

"Voilà!" He held up his snow-bedraggled prize. "Oh, no, you don't," he said when she reached for it.

He swept it up out of her reach. "Certain acts have certain consequences, you know. I risked my life for this at your instigation. I deserve my reward, you deserve your punishment."

She grinned at him as he backed her against the tree and held her there with the weight of his body. He was still holding the mistletoe aloft.

"Yes, my lord," she said meekly.

His mind was not really on the night before, but if it had been, he might have reflected with some satisfaction that she had learned well her first lesson in kissing. Her lips were softly parted when he touched them with his own, and when he teased them wider and licked them and the soft flesh behind them with his tongue, she made quiet sounds of enjoyment. The contrast between chilled flesh and hot mouths was heady stuff, he decided as he slid his tongue deep. She sucked gently on it. Through all the layers of their clothing he could feel the tautly muscled slenderness of her dancer's body. Total femininity.

Someone was whistling. Bertie. And someone was telling him to be quiet and not be silly, love, and come away to look at *this* holly.

"Well," Julian said, lifting his head and feeling a little dazed and more than a little aroused. He had not anticipated just such a kiss. "The mistletoe *was* your idea, Blanche."

"Yes." Her nose was shining like a beacon. She looked healthy and girlish and slightly disheveled and utterly beautiful. "And so it was."

He was cold and wet, from the snow that had slipped down inside his collar and was melting in trickles down his back, and utterly happy. Or for the moment anyway, he thought more cautiously when he remembered the situation.

Someone was clearing his throat from behind Julian's back—Bertie's groom, Julian saw when he looked. The man was looking for Bertie, who stuck his head out from behind the holly bushes at the mention of his name.

"What is it, Bloggs?" he asked.

Bloggs told his tale of a carriage half turned over into the ditch just beyond the front gates with no hope of its being hauled out again until the snow stopped falling and the air warmed up enough to melt some of it. And the snow was so deep everywhere, he added gloomily, that there was no going anywhere on foot either any longer, even as far as the village. He should know. He and Harkiss had had the devil's own time of it wading home from there all of two hours since, and the snowfall had not abated for a single second since that time.

"A carriage?" Bertie frowned. "Any occupants,

Bloggs?" A foolish question if ever Julian had heard one.

"A gentleman and his wife, sir," Bloggs reported. "And two nippers. Inside the house now, sir."

"Oh, good Lord," Bertie said, grimacing in Julian's direction. "It looks as if we have unexpected guests for Christmas."

"The devil!" Julian muttered.

"Oh, the poor things!" Blanche exclaimed, pushing away from the tree and striding houseward through the snow. "What has been done for their comfort, Mr. Bloggs? Two children, did you say? Are they very young? Was anyone hurt? Have you…"

Her voice faded into the distance. Strange, Julian thought before following her with Bertie and Debbie. Most women who had had elocution lessons spoke well except when they were not concentrating. Then they tended to lapse into regionalism and worse. Why did the opposite seem to happen with Blanche? Bloggs was trotting after her like a well-trained henchman, just as if she were some grand duchess ruling over her undisputed domain.

Funnily enough, she had just *sounded* rather like a duchess.

Chapter Five

THE REVEREND HENRY MOFFATT had been given unexpected leave from the parish at which he was a curate in order to spend Christmas at the home of his wife's family thirty miles distant. Rashly—by his own admission—he had made the decision to begin the journey that morning despite the fact that the snow had already begun to fall and he had the safety of two young children to concern himself with—not to mention that of his wife, who was in imminent expectation of another interesting event.

He was contrite over his own foolishness. He was distressed over the near disaster to which he had brought his family when his carriage had almost overturned into the ditch. He was apologetic about foisting himself and his family upon strangers on Christmas Eve of all days. Perhaps there was an inn close by?

"In the village three miles away," Verity told him. "But you would not get there in this weather, sir. You must, of course, stay here. Mr. Hollander will insist upon it, you may be sure."

"Mr. Hollander is your husband, ma'am?" the Reverend Moffatt asked.

"No." She smiled. "I am a guest here, too, sir. Mrs. Moffatt, do come into the sitting room so that you may warm yourself by the fire and take the weight off your feet. Mr. Bloggs, would you be so kind as to go down to the kitchen and request that a tea tray be sent up? Oh, and something for the children, as well. And something to eat." She smiled at the two little boys, who were gazing about with open curiosity. The younger one, a mere infant of three or four years, was unwinding a long scarf from his neck. She reached out a hand to each of them. "Are you hungry? But that is a foolish question, I know. In my experience little boys are always hungry. Come into the sitting room with your mama and we will see what Cook sends up."

It was at that moment that Mr. Hollander came inside the house with Debbie and Viscount Folingsby close behind him. The Reverend Moffatt introduced himself again and made his explanations and his apologies once more.

"Bertrand Hollander," that young gentleman said,

extending his right hand to his unexpected guest. "And, er, my wife, Mrs. Hollander. And Viscount Folingsby."

Verity was leading Mrs. Moffatt and the children in the direction of the sitting room, but she stopped so that the curate could introduce them to his host.

"You have met my wife, the viscountess?" Julian asked, his eyes locking with Verity's.

"Yes, indeed." The Reverend Moffatt made her a bow. "Her ladyship has been most kind."

One more lie to add to all the others, Verity thought. Her new husband, having divested himself of his outdoor garments, followed her into the sitting room, where she directed the very pregnant Mrs. Moffatt and the little boys to chairs close to the fire. The viscount stood beside Verity, one hand against the back of her waist. But during the bustle of the next few minutes, she felt her left hand being taken in a firm grasp and bent up behind her back. While Julian smiled genially about him as the tea tray arrived and cups and plates were passed around and everyone made small talk, he slid something onto Verity's ring finger.

It was the signet ring he normally wore on the little finger of his right hand, she saw when she withdrew the hand from her back and looked down at it. The ring was a little loose on her, but with some care she would be able to see that it did not fall off. It was a very tolerable substitute for a wedding ring. A glance across the room at Debbie assured her that that young woman's left hand was similarly adorned.

One could only conclude that Viscount Folingsby and Mr. Hollander were born conspirators and had had a great deal of practice at being devious.

"I will hear no more protests, sir, if you please," Mr. Hollander was saying with all his customary good humor and one raised hand. "Mrs. Hollander and I will be delighted to have your company over Christmas. Much as we have been enjoying that of our two friends, we have been regretting, have we not, my love, that we did not invite more guests for the holiday. Especially those with children. Christmas does not seem quite Christmas without them."

"How kind of you to say so, sir," Mrs. Moffatt said, one hand resting over the mound of her pregnancy.

"Ee," Debbie said, "it is going to be right good fun to hear the patter of little feet about the house and the chatter of little voices. You sit down, too, Rev, and make yourself at home. Set your cup and saucer down on that table there. It must have been a right nasty fright to land in the ditch like that."

"We tipped up like *this*," the older of the little boys

said, listing over sharply to one side, his arms out-spread. "I thought we were going to turn over and over in a tumble-toss. It was ever so exciting."

"I was not scared," the younger boy said, gazing up at Verity before depositing his thumb in his mouth and then snatching it determinedly out again. "I am not scared of anything."

"That will do, Rupert," their father said. "And David. You will speak when spoken to, if you please."

But Rupert was pulling at his father's sleeve. "May we go out to play?" he whispered.

"Children!" Mrs. Moffatt laughed. "One would think they would be glad enough to be safe indoors after that narrow escape, would you not? And on such a cold, stormy day. But they love the outdoors."

"Then I have just the answer for them," Julian said, raising his eyebrows and fingering the handle of his quizzing glass. "There is a pile of Christmas greenery out behind the house in dire need of hands and arms to carry it inside. We will never be able to celebrate Christmas with it if it remains out there, will we?" He leveled his glass at each of the boys in turn, a frown on his face. "I wonder if those hands and arms are strong enough, though. What do you think, Bertie?"

Two pairs of eyes turned anxiously Mr. Hollander's way. *Please yes, please yes*, those eyes begged while both children sat with buttoned lips in obedience to their father's command.

"What do I think, Jule?" Mr. Hollander pursed his lips. "I think—but wait a minute. Is that a muscle I spy bulging out your coat sleeve, lad?"

The elder boy looked down with desperate hope at his arm.

"It is a muscle," Mr. Hollander decided.

"And have you ever seen more capable fingers than this other lad's, Bertie?" Julian asked, magnifying them with the aid of his glass. "I believe these brothers have been sent us for a purpose. You will need to put your scarves and hats and gloves back on, of course, and secure your mama's permission. But once that has been accomplished, you may follow me."

Verity watched in wonder as two rather bored and jaded rakes were transformed into kindly, indulgent uncles before her eyes. The two boys were jumping up and down before their mother's chair in an agony of suspense lest she withhold her permission.

"You are too kind, my lord," she said with a weary smile. "They will wear you out."

"Not at all, ma'am," he assured her. "It is a sizable pile."

"Oh," Verity said, beaming down at the children, "and after you have it all inside and dried off, you may help decorate the house with it. There are mistletoe and holly and pine boughs. And Mrs. Simpkins has found ribbons and bows and bells in the attic. Deb—Mrs. Hollander and I will sort through them and decide what can be used. Before Christmas comes tomorrow, this house is going to be bursting at the seams with good cheer. I daresay we will have one of the best Christmases anyone ever had."

Her eyes met Viscount Folingsby's as she spoke. He regarded her with one raised eyebrow and a slightly mocking smile. But she was no longer fooled by such an expression. She had seen him without his mask of bored cynicism. Not just here with the two little boys. She had seen him climb a tree like a schoolboy, not just because she had asked him to do so, but because the tree was there and therefore to be climbed. She had seen him with a twinkle in his eye and a laugh on his lips.

And she had—oh dear, yes—she had felt his kiss. It was not one she could censure even if it had occurred to her to do so. He had earned it, not with five hundred pounds, but with the acquisition of mistletoe. The mistletoe had sanctified the kiss, deep and carnal as it had been.

"It seems," the Reverend Moffatt said as the other two gentlemen left the room with the exuberant children, "that we are to be guests here at least until tomorrow. It warms my heart to have been stranded at a place where we have already been made to feel welcome. Sometimes it seems almost as if a divine hand is at play in guiding our movements, taking us where we had no intention of going to meet people we had no thought of meeting. How wonderful that you are all preparing with such enthusiasm to celebrate the birth of our Lord."

"I am going to make a kissing bough," Debbie announced, looking almost animated. "We had kissing boughs to half fill the kitchen ceiling when I was a girl. Nobody escaped a few good bussings in our house. I had almost forgotten. Christmas was always a right grand time."

"Yes, Mrs. Hollander," Mrs. Moffatt said with a smile. "It is always a grand time, even when we are forced to spend it away from part of our families as I assume we are all doing this year. Your husband is being very kind to our boys. And yours, too, my lady." She turned her smile on Verity. "They have been in the carriage all day and have a great deal of excess energy."

"There will be no going into the village tonight or tomorrow morning if what you said is true, Lady Folingsby," the Reverend Moffatt said. "You will be unable to attend church as I daresay you intended to do. I shall repay a small part of my debt to you, then. I shall conduct the Christmas service here. We will all take communion here together. With Mr. Hollander's permission, of course."

"What a splendid idea, Henry," his wife said.

"Ee," Debbie said, awed into near- silence.

Verity clasped her hands to her bosom and closed her eyes. She had a sudden image of the church at home on the evening before Christmas, the bells pealing out the news of the Christ child's birth, the candles all ablaze, the carved Nativity scene carefully arranged before the altar, her father in his best vestments smiling down at the congregation. Christmas had always been his favorite time of the liturgical year.

"Oh, sir," she said, opening her eyes again, "it is we who will be in your debt. Deeply in your debt." She blinked away tears. "I would like it of all things. I am sure Mr. Hollander and Vi—and my husband will agree."

"It is going to be a grand Christmas, Blanche," Debbie said. "I did not expect it, lass. Not in this way, any road."

"Sometimes we come to grace by unexpected paths," the Reverend Moffatt commented.

"DO YOU EVER have the impression that events have galloped along somewhat out of your control, Jule?" Bertie asked his friend just before dinner was served and they stood together in the sitting room waiting for everyone else to join them. They were surrounded by the sights and smells of Christmas. There was greenery everywhere, artfully draped and colorfully decorated with red bows and streamers and silver bells. There was a huge and elaborate kissing bough suspended over the alcove to one side of the fireplace. There was a strong smell of pine, more powerful for the moment than the tantalizing aromas wafting up from the kitchen.

"And do you ever have the impression," Julian asked without answering the question, which was doubtless rhetorical anyway, "that you ought not to simply label a woman as a certain type and expect her to behave accordingly?" Blanche, changing for dinner a few minutes before in the dressing room while he made do with the bedchamber, had informed him with bright enthusiasm that the Reverend Moffatt was planning to conduct a Christmas service in this very room sometime after dinner. And that the servants had asked to attend. And that they were going to have to see to it on the morrow that

the little boys had a wonderful Christmas. If there
was still plenty of snow, they could…

He had not listened to all the details. But Miss
Blanche Heyward, opera dancer, would have made a
superlative drill sergeant if she had just been a man,
he had thought. Consider as a point in fact the way
she had organized them all—*all* of them—over the
decorations. They had rushed about and climbed and
teetered and adjusted angles at her every bidding. She
had been flushed and bright-eyed and beautiful.

On the whole, he concluded as an afterthought,
he was glad she was not a man.

"And have you ever had a cook for all of three or
four years, Jule," Bertie continued, "and suddenly
discovered that she could *cook?* Not that I have
tasted any of the things that go with those smells yet,
but if smell is anything to judge by…well, I *ask* you."

The staff, it seemed, had been as busy belowstairs
as all of them had been above. But their busyness had
had the same instigator—Miss Blanche Heyward.
Julian even wondered if somehow she had conjured
up the clergyman and his family out of the blizzard.
What a ghastly turn of events that had been.

"Do you suppose," he asked, "anyone noticed the
sudden appearance of rings on our women's fingers,
Bertie?"

But the door opened at that moment to admit

their mistresses, who had come down together. Debbie clucked her tongue.

"Now did I do all that work on the kissing bough just to see it hang over there and you men stand here?" she asked. "Go and get yourself under it, Bertie, love, and be bussed."

"Again?" he said, grinning and waggling his eyebrows and instantly obeying.

They had all sampled the pleasures of the kissing bough after it had been hung. Even the Reverend Moffatt had kissed his wife with hearty good humor and had pecked Debbie and Blanche respectfully on the cheek.

"Well, Blanche." Julian looked her up and down. She was dressed in the dark green silk again. Her hair was neatly confined at the back of her head. She should have looked drably dreary but did not. "Are you enjoying yourself?"

Some of the sparkle that had been in her eyes faded as she looked back at him. "Only when I forget my purpose in being here," she said. "I have already taken a great deal of money from you and have done nothing yet to earn it."

"Perhaps I should be the judge of that," he said.

"Perhaps tonight I can make some amends," she said. "I have had a day in which to grow more accustomed to you. I may still be awkward—I daresay

I will be because I am very ignorant of what happens, you know—but I will not be afraid and I will not act the *martyr.* Indeed, I believe I might even enjoy it. And it will be a relief to know that at last I have done something to earn my salary."

If Bertie and Debbie, now laughing like a pair of children and making merry beneath the kissing bough, had been the only other occupants of the house apart from the servants, Julian thought he might have excused Blanche and himself from dinner and taken her up to bed without further ado. Despite the reference to earning salaries, he found her words arousing. He found *her* arousing. But there were other guests. Besides, he was not sure he would have done it anyway.

If this stay in Norfolkshire had proceeded according to plan, he would have enjoyed a largely sleepless night with Blanche last night. They would have stayed in bed until noon or later this morning. They would have returned to bed for much of the afternoon. By now he would have been wondering how long into the coming night his energies would sustain him. But there would have been all day tomorrow to look forward to—in bed.

The prospect had seemed appealing to him all last week and up until just last night. Longer than that. He had felt disgruntled and cheated all through the night and when he had woken this morning. Or when she had awoken him, rather, with her excited discovery that it had snowed during the night.

But surprisingly he had enjoyed the day just as it had turned out. And the kiss against the oak tree had seemed in some strange way as satisfying as a bedding might have been. There had been laughter as well as desire involved in that kiss. He had never before thought of laughter as a desirable component of a sexual experience.

"You are disappointed in me," Blanche said now. "I am so sorry."

"Not at all," he told her, clasping his hands at his back. "How could I possibly be disappointed? Let me see. A night spent on the floor, an early wake-up call in the frigid dawn to watch snow falling, an expedition out into the storm in order to climb trees, murder my boots and risk my neck. The arrival of a clergyman as a houseguest, an hour spent finding occupation for two energetic infants, another hour of climbing on furniture and pinning up boughs only to move them again when it was discovered that they were half an inch out of place, a church service in the sitting room to look forward to. My dear Miss Heyward, what more could I have asked of Christmas?"

She was laughing. "I have the strangest feeling," she said, "that you *have* enjoyed today."

He raised his quizzing glass to his eye and regarded her through it. "And you believe that you might enjoy tonight," he said. "We will see, Blanche, when tonight comes. But first of all, Bertie's guests. I believe I hear the patter of little feet and the chatter of little voices approaching, as Debbie so poetically phrased it. I suppose we are to be subjected to their company as well as that of their mama and papa since there is no nursery and no nurse."

"For all your expression and tone of voice," Blanche said, "I do believe, my lord, you have an affection for those little boys. You do not deceive me."

"Dear me," Julian said faintly as the sitting room door opened again.

THERE WAS a spinet in one corner of the sitting room. Verity had eyed it a few times during the day with some longing, but its lid was locked, she had discovered. While the Reverend Moffatt was setting up the room after dinner for the Christmas service, his wife asked about the instrument. Mr. Hollander looked at it in some surprise, as if he were noticing it for the first time. He had no idea where the key was. It hardly mattered anyway unless someone was able to play it.

There was a short silence.

"I can play," Verity said.

"Splendid!" The Reverend Moffatt beamed at her.

"Then we may have music with the service, Lady Folingsby. I would lead the singing if I had to, but I have a lamentably poor ear for pitch, do I not, Edie? We would be likely to end a hymn several tones lower than we started it." He laughed heartily.

Mr. Hollander went in search of the key. Or rather, he went in search of a servant who might know where it was.

"Where did you learn to play, Blanche?" Debbie asked.

"At the rectory." Verity smiled and then wished she could bite out her tongue. "The rector's wife taught me," she added hastily. That was the truth, at least.

Mr. Hollander came back in triumph, a key held aloft. The spinet was sadly out of tune, Verity discovered, but not impossibly so. There was no music, but she did not need any. All her favorite hymns, as well as some other favorite pieces, had been committed to memory when she was still a girl.

A table had been converted into an altar with the aid of a crisp white cloth one of the maids had ironed carefully, candles in silver holders, and a fancy cup and plate the housekeeper had found somewhere in the nether regions of the house and the other maid had polished to serve as a paten and chalice. The butler had dusted off a bottle of Mr. Hollander's best wine. The cook had found time and space in her oven to bake a round loaf of unleavened bread. The Reverend Moffatt had clad himself in vestments he had brought with him and suddenly looked very young and dignified and holy.

The sitting room, Verity thought, gazing about her, had become a holy place, a church. Everyone, even the children, sat hushed as they would in a church, waiting for the service to begin. Verity did not wait. She began to play quietly some of her favorite Christmas hymns.

It was Christmas, she thought, swallowing and blinking her eyes. She had not thought it would come for her this year except in the form of an ugly self-sacrifice. But for all the lies and deceptions— with every glance down at her hands she saw the false wedding ring—Christmas had come. Christmas, she reminded herself, and the reminder had never been more apt, was for sinners, and they were all sinners: Mr. Hollander, Debbie, Viscount Folingsby and she. But Christmas had found them out, despite themselves, in the form of the clergyman and his family, stranded by a snowstorm. And Christmas was offering all its boundless love and forgiveness to them in the form of the bread and the wine, which were still at this moment just those two commodities.

A child had been born on this night more than eighteen hundred years ago, and he was about to be born again as he had been each year since then and would be each year in the future. Constant birth. Constant hope. Constant love.

"My dear friends." The clergyman's voice was quiet, serene, imposing, unlike the voice of the Reverend Moffatt who had conversed with them over tea and dinner. He smiled about at each one of them in turn, bathing them—or so it seemed—in the warmth and peace and wonder of the season.

And so the service began.

It ended more than an hour later with the joyful singing of one last hymn. They all sang lustily, Verity noticed, herself included. Even one of the coachmen, who was noticeably tone-deaf, and the housekeeper, who sang with pronounced vibrato. Mr. Hollander had a strong tenor voice. Debbie sang with a Yorkshire accent. David Moffatt sang his heart out to a tune of his own devising. They would not have made a reputable choir. But it did not matter. They made a joyful noise. They were celebrating Christmas.

And then Mrs. Moffatt spoke up, a mere few seconds after her husband had said the final words of the service and wished them all the compliments of the season.

"I do apologize, Mr. and Mrs. Hollander," she said, "for all the inconvenience I am about to cause you. Henry, my dear, I do believe we are going to have a Christmas child."

Chapter Six

HENRY MOFFATT was pacing as he had been doing almost constantly for the past several hours.

"One would expect to become accustomed to it," he said, pausing for only a moment to stare, pale faced and anxious eyed, at Julian and Bertie, who were sitting at either side of the hearth, hardly any less pale themselves, "after two previous confinements. But one does not. One thinks of a new child—one's own—making the perilous passage into this world. And one thinks of one's mate, flesh of one's own flesh, heart of one's heart, enduring the pain, facing all the danger alone. One feels helpless and humble and dreadfully responsible. And guilty that one does not have more trust in the plans of the Almighty. It seems trivial to recall that we have hoped for a daughter this time."

He resumed his journey to nowhere, back and forth from one corner of the room to the other. "Will it never end?"

Julian had never before shared a house with a woman in labor. When he thought about it, about what was going on abovestairs—and how could he *not* think about it?—he felt a buzzing in his ears and a coldness in his nostrils and imagined in some horror the ignominy of fainting when he was not even the prospective father. He remembered how glibly just a few days before he had planned to have a child of his own in the nursery by next Christmas or very soon after.

It must hurt like hell, he thought, and that was probably the understatement of the decade.

There was no doctor in the village. There was a midwife, but she lived, according to the housekeeper, a mile or so on the other side of the village. It would have been impossible to reach her, not to mention persuading her to make the return journey, in time to deliver the child who was definitely on its way.

Fortunately, Mrs. Moffatt had announced with a calm smile—surely it had been merely a brave facade—she had already given birth to two children, as well as attending the births of a few others. She could manage very well alone, provided the housekeeper would prepare a few items for her. It was getting late. She invited everyone else to retire to bed and promised not to disturb them with any loud noises.

Julian had immediately formed mental images of someone screaming in agony.

Debbie had looked at Bertie with eyes almost as big as her face.

"If you are quite sure, ma'am," Bertie had said, as white as his shirt points.

"Come, Henry," Mrs. Moffatt had said, "we will put the children to bed first. Perhaps I can see you in here for a few minutes afterward, Mrs. Simpkins."

Mrs. Simpkins had been looking a delicate shade of green.

That was when Blanche had spoken up.

"You certainly will *not* manage alone," she had assured the guest. "It will be quite enough for you to endure the pain of labor. You will leave the rest to us, Mrs. Moffatt. Sir," she said, addressing the clergyman, "perhaps you can put the children to bed yourself tonight? Boys, give your mama a kiss. Doubtless there will be more than one wonderful surprise awaiting you in the morning. The sooner you fall asleep, the sooner you will find out what. Mrs. Lyons, will you see that a large pot of water is heated and kept ready? Mrs. Simpkins, will you gather together as many clean cloths as you can find? Debbie—"

"Ee, Blanche," Debbie had protested, "no, love."

"I am going to need you," Blanche had said with a smile. "Merely to wield a cool, damp cloth to wipe Mrs. Moffatt's face when she gets very hot, as she will. You can do that, can you not? I will be there to do everything else."

Everything else. Like delivering the baby. Julian had stared, fascinated, at his opera dancer.

"Have you done this before, Blanche?" he had asked.

"Of course," she had said briskly. "At the rectory— ah. I used to accompany the rector's wife on occasion. I know exactly what to do. No one need fear."

They had all been gazing at her, Julian remembered now. They had all hung on her every word, her every command. They had leaned on her strength and her confidence in a collective body.

Who the hell *was* she? What had a blacksmith's daughter been doing hanging around a rectory so much? Apart from learning to play the spinet without music, that was. And apart from delivering babies.

Everyone had run to do her bidding. Soon only the three men—the three useless ones—had been left in the sitting room to fight terror and nausea and fits of the vapors.

The door opened. Three pale, terrified faces turned toward it.

Debbie was flushed and untidy and swathed in an apron made for a giant. One hank of blond hair hung to her shoulder and looked damp with perspiration. She was beaming and looking very pretty, indeed.

"It is all over, sir," she announced, addressing herself to the Reverend Moffatt. "You have a new…baby. I am not to say what. Your wife is ready and waiting for you."

The new father stood very still for a few moments and then strode from the room without a word.

"Bertie." Debbie turned tear-filled eyes toward him. "You should have been there, love. It came out all of a rush into Blanche's hands, the dearest little slippery thing, all cross and crying and—and human. Ee, Bertie, love." She cast herself into his arms and bawled noisily.

Bertie made soothing noises and raised his eyebrows at Julian. "I was never more relieved in my life," he said. "But I am quite thankful I was not there, Deb. We had better get you to bed. You are not needed any longer?"

"Blanche told me I could go to bed," Debbie said. "She will finish off all that needs doing. No midwife could have done better. She talked quietly the whole time to calm my jitters and Mrs. Simpkins's. Mrs. Moffatt didn't have the jitters. She just kept saying she was sorry to keep us up, the daft woman. I have never felt so—so honored, Bertie, love. Me, Debbie Markle, just a simple, honest whore to be allowed to see *that*."

"Come on, Deb." Bertie tucked her into the crook of his arm and bore her off to bed.

Julian followed them up a few minutes later. He had no idea what time it was. Some unholy hour of the morning, he supposed. He did not carry a candle up with him and no one had lit the branch in his room. Someone from belowstairs had been kept working late, though. There was a freshly made-up fire burning in the hearth. He went to stand at the window and looked out.

The snow had stopped falling, he saw, and the sky had cleared off. He looked upward and saw in that single glance that he had been wrong. It was not an *unholy* hour of the morning at all.

He was still standing there several minutes later when the door of the bedchamber opened. He turned his head to look over his shoulder.

She looked as Debbie had looked but worse. She was bedraggled, weary and beautiful.

"You should not have waited up," she said.

"Come." He beckoned to her.

She came and slumped tiredly against him when he wrapped an arm about her. She sighed deeply.

"Look." He pointed.

She did not say anything for a long while. Neither did he. Words were unnecessary. The Christmas star beamed down at them, symbol of hope, a sign for all who sought wisdom and the meaning of their lives. He was not sure what either of them had learned about Christmas this year, but there was something. It was beyond words at the moment and even beyond coherent thought. But something had been learned. Something had been gained.

"It is Christmas," she said softly at last. Her words held a wealth of meaning beyond themselves.

"Yes," he said, turning his face and kissing the untidy titian hair on top of her head. "Yes, it is Christmas. Did they have their daughter?"

"Oh yes," she said. "I have never seen two people so happy, my lord. On Christmas morning. Could there be a more precious gift?"

"I doubt it," he said, closing his eyes briefly.

"I held her," she said softly. "What a gift that was."

"Blanche," he asked after a short while, "where was this rectory you speak of? Close to the smithy?"

"Yes," she said.

"And you went to school there," he said, "and were given lessons in playing the spinet and delivering babies."

"Y-yes." She had the grace to sound hesitant.

"Blanche," he said, "I have the strange suspicion that you may be the biggest liar of my acquaintance."

She had nothing to say to that.

"Go and get ready for bed," he told her. "I am not sure whether it would be more accurate to say it is late or early."

She lifted her head then and looked at him. "Yes, my lord," she said—the martyr being brave.

He was in bed when she came from the dressing room, wearing the virginal nightgown again with her hair down her back. She was still looking brave, he saw in the dying light of the fire. She approached the bed without hesitation.

"Get in," he told her, holding back the bedcovers and stretching out his other arm beneath her pillow.

"Yes, my lord."

He turned her as she lay down, and drew her snugly against him in order to warm her. He tucked the bedcovers neatly behind her. He found her mouth with his own and kissed her with lingering thoroughness.

"Go to sleep now," he told her when he was done.

That brought her eyes snapping open. "But—" she began.

"But nothing," he said. "You are at the point of total exhaustion, Blanche, and would be quite unable either to enjoy or to be enjoyed. Go to sleep."

"But—" she began again, a protest he silenced with another kiss.

"I have no desire to hear about five hundred pounds and the necessity of earning it," he said. "You promised to be mine for a week, obedient to my will. This is my command for tonight, then. Go to sleep."

He waited for her protest. All he heard instead was a quiet, almost soundless sigh, deepened breathing and total relaxation. She was asleep.

And the funny thing was, he thought, feeling her slim, shapely woman's body pressed to his from toes to forehead, he did not feel either frustrated or deprived. Quite the contrary. He felt warm and relaxed and sleepy, more like a man who had just had good sex than one who had had none at all.

He followed her into sleep.

VERITY AWOKE a little later than usual in the morning. She snuggled sleepily into the warmth of the bed and then came fully awake when she realized that she was alone. She opened her eyes. He was gone. He was not in the room, either, she saw when she looked about.

It was Christmas morning.

He had slept with her last night. Just that. He had *slept* with her. He had had her in bed with him, he had held her close, and he had told her to go to sleep. It had not taken her long to obey. But had there been tenderness in his arms and his kiss? Had she imagined it? Certainly there had been no anger.

He was a likable man, she thought suddenly, throwing back the covers and making for the dressing room. It was a surprising realization. She had thought him impossibly attractive from the start, of course. But she had not expected to find him a pleasant person. Certainly not a *kind* one.

She washed in the tepid water that stood on the washstand and dressed in the white wool dress she had made herself back in the autumn to wear after she left off her mourning. It was very simply styled, with a high neckline, straight long sleeves, and an unadorned skirt flaring from beneath her bosom. She liked its simplicity. She brushed her hair and dressed it in its usual knot at the back of her head. She took one last look at herself in the looking glass and hesitated.

Should she? She looked at the plain neckline of her dress.

She opened the drawer in which she had placed most of her belongings and stared at the box before drawing it out and opening it. It really was beautiful. It must have cost a fortune. Not that its charm lay in its monetary value. It was well crafted, tasteful. The chain was fine and delicate. It was easily the most lovely possession she had ever owned. She touched a finger to the star, withdrew, and then, after hesitating a moment longer, lifted the chain from its silken nesting place. She undid the catch, lowered her head and lifted her arms.

"Allow me," a voice said from behind her, and hands covered her own and took the chain from her.

She kept her head bent until he had secured the chain.

"Thank you," she said, and looked up into the glass.

His hands were on her shoulders. He was dressed with his usual immaculate elegance, she could see.

"It is beautiful," she told him. It really was the perfect ornament for the dress.

"Yes." He turned her to face him. "Is that sadness I see in your eyes, Blanche? It is where it belongs, you know. You have earned the right to wear the Christmas star on your bosom."

She smiled and touched a hand to it. "It is a lovely gift," she said. "I have something for you, too."

She had spoken entirely on impulse. When she left London, she had given no thought to a Christmas gift. She had expected him to be merely an employer, who would pay her for the unlimited use of her body. She had not expected him to become...yes, in some strange way he had become her friend. Someone she cared about. Someone who had shown her care.

She turned to the drawer and reached to the back of it. She could not believe she was about to give away such a treasure and to *him* of all people. And yet she knew that she wanted to do it, that it was the right thing to do. Not that it was either an elaborate or a costly gift. But it had been Papa's.

"Here," she said, holding it out to him on her palm. It was not even wrapped. "It is precious to me. It was my father's. He gave it to me when I left home. I want you to have it." All it was was a handkerchief, folded into a square. It was of the finest linen, it was true. But still only a handkerchief.

He transferred it to his own palm and then looked into her eyes. "I believe," he said, "your gift might be more valuable than mine, Blanche. Mine only cost money. You have given away part of yourself. Thank you. I will treasure it."

"Happy Christmas, my lord," she said.

"And to you." He leaned toward her and set his lips against hers in what was a gentle and achingly sweet kiss. "Happy Christmas, Blanche."

And she felt happy, she thought, even though her thoughts had gone to her mother and Chastity, celebrating the day without her. But they had each other, and she had…

"I wonder how the baby is this morning," she said eagerly. "I can scarcely wait to see her again. Did she sleep? I wonder. Did Mrs. Moffatt sleep? And have the little boys met their new sister yet? I wonder if their papa will have time to spend with them today. It is Christmas Day, such an important day for children. Perhaps—"

"Perhaps, Blanche," Viscount Folingsby said, looking and sounding his bored, cynical self again suddenly, "you will conceive ideas again, as you did yesterday, for everyone's delectation. I do not doubt that the boys and the rest of us will be worn to a thread by the time you have finished with us."

"But did you not enjoy yesterday?" she asked him. Surely he had. "It is *Christmas*, my lord, and Mr. Hollander had made no plans to celebrate it. What choice did I have? Poor man, I daresay he has always had a mother or some other relatives to plan the holiday for him."

"Precisely." He sighed. "It was our idea to escape such plans this year, Blanche. To spend a quiet week instead with the women of our choice. Not gathering greenery in the teeth of a blizzard, but making love in a warm bed. Not loading down the house with Christmas cheer and making merry noise with Christmas carols and entertaining energetic little boys and delivering babies, but—well, making love in a warm bed."

"You did *not* enjoy yesterday," she said, dismayed.

"And you *are* disappointed. I *have* failed you. And I have ruined the holiday for Mr. Hollander, too. And—" He had set two fingers firmly against her lips.

"The baby slept through the night," he said, "and has only just begun to fuss. Mrs. Moffatt had a few hours of sleep and declares herself to be refreshed and in the best of health this morning. The Reverend Moffatt is in transports of delight and proclaims himself to be the most fortunate man alive—as well as the cleverest, I do believe—to have begotten a daughter.

"The little boys have been given their gifts and have met their sister, with whom they seem far less impressed than their papa. They are roaring around the sitting room, obeying the paternal command to confine their energies to it until they hear otherwise. Cook is banging around the kitchen with great zeal and has every other servant moving at a brisk trot. Bertie and Debbie have not yet put in an appearance. I daresay they are making love in a warm bed. And you are looking more beautiful than any woman has any right to look. Virginal white becomes you."

"I am sorry it is not the Christmas you intended," she said.

"Are you?" He smiled lazily. "I am not sure I am,

Blanche. Sorry, I mean. It is an interesting Christmas, to say the very least. And it is not over yet. *Do* you have plans for us?"

She felt herself flush. "Well," she said, "I did think that since there are children here and their mother is indisposed and their father will wish to spend much of the day with her…and I thought that since there are still heaps of snow out there even though no more is falling…and I thought that since the rest of us have nothing particular to do all day except…" Her cheeks grew hotter.

"Make love in a warm bed?" he suggested.

"Yes," she said. "Except that. I thought that perhaps we could…that is, unless you wish to do the other. I am quite willing. It is what I came here to do, after all."

He was grinning at her. "Outdoor sports," he said. "I wonder how Bertie and Debbie will greet the happy prospect?"

"Well," she said, "they cannot spend *all* day in bed, can they? It would not be at all polite to the Reverend and Mrs. Moffatt."

He merely chuckled. "Let the day begin," he said, offering her his arm. "I would not miss it for the world, you know, or even for all the warm beds in the world, for that matter."

Chapter Seven

JULIAN did not change his mind all through the day though he had hardly exaggerated when he had predicted that Blanche would have run them all ragged before they were done with Christmas.

As soon as breakfast was over, they took the children outside to play in the snow. *They* being he and Blanche until Bertie and Debbie came out to join them. They romped in the snow for what seemed only minutes but must have been hours until Bloggs appeared to inform them that their Christmas dinner was ready. His expression suggested also that Cook would have their heads if they did not come immediately to partake of it.

But long before that they had engaged in a vigorous snowball fight, which turned out to be grossly unfair in Julian's estimation—and he complained loudly about it—as he and Bertie were pitted against both boys as well as both the ladies, two against four. And if Debbie had ever been a member of a rifle regiment, there would surely not be a Frenchman left in France without a hole through his heart. She had a deadly accurate aim and was wildly cheered by her side, and herself, whenever she demonstrated it.

They built snowmen. Or at least Julian and Bertie did while the boys danced around "helping" and Debbie ran off to beg ashes and carrots and one ancient straw hat from the kitchen. Blanche, reclining on a snowbank, declared that as judge she had the hardest job of all. She awarded the prize of one leftover carrot to Bertie and David.

They made snow angels until Rupert declared with loud disgust that it was a girl's game. Blanche and Debbie continued with the sport notwithstanding while the men constructed a long slippery slide on a bit of a slope and risked their necks zooming along it. Somehow Julian ended up with David on his shoulders, clinging to his hair after his hat had proved to be an untrustworthy anchor. The child whooped with mingled fright and glee.

Debbie sought out the tree swing, brushed the snow off it and cleared a path beneath it before summoning everyone else. They all sampled its delights, singly and in pairs, all of them as noisy and exuberant as children. The adults continued even after the children had rushed away at the appearance of their father to bury him up to his neck in snow.

"The snow is starting to melt," Blanche said wistfully as they were going indoors for dinner. "How sad."

"It is in the nature of snow," Julian said, wrapping one arm about her waist. "Just as it is in the nature of time to pass. That is why we have memories."

"The children have had a marvelous morning, have they not?" she said, beaming happily at him.

"Now to which children are you referring?" he asked, kissing her cold red nose. "To the very little ones? Or to the rest of us? For myself I would as soon have been sitting with my feet up before a roaring fire."

She merely laughed.

Christmas dinner proved to be a culinary delight beyond compare. They all ate until they were close to bursting and then Bertie sent for the cook and made a rather pompous speech of congratulation.

But that was not enough for Blanche, of course. If Mr. Hollander would be so good, she suggested, perhaps all the staff could be invited to the sitting room for a drink of the excellent wassail. She for one would like to thank them all for the hard work they had put into giving everyone such a wonderful Christmas.

"I can only echo your sentiments, Lady Folingsby," the Reverend Moffatt remarked. "Though by my observations, the servants are not the only ones who have been hard at work. My wife and I will not soon forget the warm welcome we have received here and the efforts you have all put into entertaining our children. Not to mention last night for which we will never be able to repay you, my lady, and you, Mrs. Hollander. We will not try, of course, as we know that you acted out of the goodness of your hearts. We humbly accept the gift from two true ladies."

Debbie sniffled and blew her nose in the handkerchief Bertie handed her. "That is one of the nicest things anyone ever said to me," she said. "But it was Blanche who did all the work."

The servants spent the best part of an hour in the sitting room, eating cakes and mince pies and drinking wassail and accepting Christmas bonuses from their employer, as well as from both Julian and the Reverend Moffatt. Julian was never afterward sure who suggested singing Christmas carols again, though he did not doubt it was Blanche. They did so anyway to her accompaniment on the spinet and sang themselves into a thoroughly genial and sentimental mood.

And then after the servants had gone back below-stairs, Mrs. Moffatt made a surprise appearance in the sitting room with the baby.

Julian had always been fond of children. He had had to be, for there had always been enough of them at family gatherings to make life miserable for any-one who was not. But he had never been much for infants or newborns. They were a woman's preserve, he had always thought, needing only to be fed and rocked and sung to and changed.

But he felt a certain proprietary interest in the lit-tle Moffatt girl, he discovered. Her birth had some-how brought Christmas alive for him more than ever before. And Blanche had delivered her. And now Blanche was holding her and gazing down at her with such a look of tenderness in her face that he felt dazzled. She looked so right thus, dressed with simple elegance, glowing with health and vital-ity and warmth, holding a newborn infant in her arms.

If it were her child, his…

He jerked his mind free of such an alarming day-dream and found himself gazing deep into her eyes. She smiled at him.

Ah, Blanche. It was hard to believe that just a week ago he had looked on her only as a desirable candidate for his bed. He had seen her beauty—the long, shapely legs, the taut slender body, the glorious hair and lovely face—and not given even one moment's consideration to the fact that there must be a person behind the facade.

And what a person was there. Even more beautiful, perhaps, than the body in which she resided.

He was in love with her, he thought in some astonishment. He had never been in love before. He had been in lust more times than he could recall and had sometimes called it love, especially when he had been younger. But he had never before felt this ache of longing for a *person*. It was not just that he wished to bed her, though he did, of course. It was more than that. Much more. He wanted to be a part of her, a part of her life, not just a very temporary occupant of her body.

He smiled back at her a little uncertainly.

"I daresay," Mrs. Moffatt said, having noticed perhaps the exchange of smiles, "you and her ladyship have not been married long, my lord." Not long enough for the union to have been fruitful, her words implied.

"Not long, ma'am," he agreed.

He was glad, he thought some hours later, after tea, after the vigorous indoor games Blanche and the Reverend Moffatt had organized for the amusement of the children and everyone else that he had not gone to Conway for Christmas. He had been thinking about it on and off all day and had been missing his family. Had his Christmas gone according to plan, he realized now, he would be regretting his decision. The sort of activity he had planned would not have been any way to celebrate such an occasion. But as events had turned out, he had discovered everything one was surely meant to discover at Christmas—love, hospitality, merriment, kindness, sharing, decency… The list could go on and on.

Sometimes it seemed almost as if one were led blind by some guiding hand toward something for which one had not known one searched. By a star perhaps. To the stable at Bethlehem perhaps. Perhaps he had more in common with the wise men than he had realized until this moment.

The children, yawning and protesting, were finally led away by their father to bed after hugging their adopted "uncles" and "aunts" as if they had known them all their lives.

"I do not believe we will be far behind them, Deb," Bertie said, yawning hugely after they had left. "Have you enjoyed Christmas?"

"Ee, love," Debbie said, "it has been the grandest Christmas since I left home. Maybe grander than then. The Rev is the kindest of gents and the boys are darlings. And the baby! I will never forget last night. I never will. It has been a Christmas to end Christmases."

"I believe," Bertie said, pulling her down onto his lap, perhaps feeling free to do so since the clergyman had expressed his intention of joining his wife and the baby after he had put the boys to bed, "we have you to thank for much of the joy of the past two days, Blanche."

"Oh," she said, "how foolish. It is Christmas. Christmas has a way of happening without any assistance from anyone."

"Nonsense," Julian said. "It needed a whole host of angels to get the shepherds moving off their hillside. It has taken one angel to set us off on a similar pilgrimage."

"Do you mean me?" she asked, blushing. "A strange angel indeed. One with very tarnished wings."

He got to his feet and held out a hand for hers. "It has been a long day," he said, "and you had only a few hours of sleep last night. It is bedtime."

Her eyes met his as she took his hand. There was not even a hint of martyrdom in their expression.

"Good night, Mr. Hollander," she said as the two couples took their leave of one another. "Good night, Debbie. Thank you for helping make Christmas such a joy."

HE WAS STANDING at the window when she came out of the dressing room. He was wearing a nightshirt. The room was warm from the fire that had been built high.

"Is the star still there?" she asked him, going to stand at his side and looking up.

"Gone," he said. "Or merely hidden by clouds. It is warming up out there. The snow will disappear rapidly tomorrow."

"Ah." She sighed. "Christmas is over."

"Not quite." He set an arm about her, and she rested her head on his shoulder. It felt perfectly right to do so. She felt strangely comfortable with him as if, perhaps, she had come to believe the myth that they belonged together. She had even found herself imagining downstairs during the afternoon that that newborn baby was hers, theirs.

"Blanche," he said softly.

And then they were in each other's arms, pressed together, kissing each other with such passion that it seemed indeed that they were one, that they were not meant to be two separate beings, that they would find wholeness and happiness and peace only together like this.

"Blanche." He was kissing her temples, her jaw, her throat, her mouth again. "Ah, my dear one."

It was not enough to touch him with her mouth, her tongue, her arms, her hands. She touched him with her breasts, her hips, her abdomen, her thighs. She wanted…ah, she wanted and wanted. He was warm and hard muscled. He smelled musky and male. And he felt safe, solid, dependable. He felt like a missing part of herself for which she craved. She wanted him. She wanted wholeness.

She did not know how her nightgown had become unbuttoned down the front. She did not care. She needed him closer. She needed his hands and then his mouth on her breasts. She needed…ah, yes.

"Ah, yes," she said from somewhere deep in her throat, and she twined her fingers in his hair and tipped her head back as he suckled first one nipple and then the other, sucking gently, laving the tips with his tongue, sending raw aches down between her thighs and up through her throat into her nostrils. "Ah, yes. Please." Her knees no longer quite belonged to her.

"Come, my love," he whispered against her mouth, lifting her into his arms. "Come to bed."

He slid her nightgown down over her feet after setting her down and pulled his nightshirt off over his head. She gazed at him in the flickering light of the fire, her eyes half-closed. He was beautiful, beautiful.

"Come." She lifted her arms to him. "Come."

His hands and his mouth moved over her, worshiping her, arousing her. She touched him, explored him, rejoiced in the feel of him, the heat of him. But she could not touch him *there*, though she became increasingly aware of that part of him, thick and long and hard. He touched her where she had never thought to be touched with a hand, with fingers. She felt an ache so intense it was pain and pleasure all strangely mixed together. And she heard wetness and was curiously unembarrassed.

She could not wait—for she knew not what.

"Please," she begged him, her voice sounding not quite her own. "Please."

"Yes," he said, coming to her open arms, coming down into them, coming down between her thighs, pressing them apart with his own, coming heavy and warm and eager to her nakedness. "Yes, my love. Yes."

She would not believe at first that it could be possible. He pressed against her and she was almost surprised, although she knew her own body, when he found an opening there and pushed into it, stretching her wide, not stopping, coming and coming.

"Don't tense," he murmured against her ear. "Just relax. Ah, my dear one, my love. I don't want to hurt you."

But it did not hurt. Not really. It only surprised her and filled her with wonder and gave her a moment's panic when she thought he could come no farther but he pressed on. There was what she expected to be pain, and then he pressed past it until he was deep, deep inside. She lifted her legs from the bed and twined them about his. He moaned.

And then, just when she thought ecstasy had been arrived at and finally relaxed, he moved. He moved to leave her.

"No," she murmured in protest.

He lifted his head, looked down into her face and kissed her. "Yes," he said. "Like this, you see." And from the brink of her he pressed deep again. And withdrew and pressed deep.

Final ecstasy came several minutes or hours later—time no longer had any meaning—after they had loved together with sweet, strong rhythm, with a sharing of bodies and pleasure, with a mingling of selves. It came with a building of almost unbearable need, with an involuntary tightening of every inner muscle, and with a final relinquishing of self, a final trust in the power of union. It came as shivering relaxation and quiet peace. It came with shared words.

"My sweet life," he whispered. "My dear angel."

"My love," she heard herself murmuring. "My love, my love."

She fell asleep moments later, after he had drawn out of her and rolled onto his side, taking her with him and keeping her against him. Just after he drew the bedcovers warmly about her.

JULIAN DID NOT fall asleep for a long while, even though he lay in a pleasant lethargy. He was sexually sated. He was also deeply happy.

He had never set much store by happiness. It was strange, perhaps, when for all his adult years he had directed almost all his energies into activities that would bring him pleasure or gratification in varying degrees. But he had never really believed in *happiness*. He had never either expected or craved it for himself.

Happiness, he thought, was a feeling of rightness, of having arrived at a place one had always sought, however halfheartedly, but never quite believed existed. With a person of whose existence one had always dreamed, even if not always consciously, but had never thought to find. Happiness was a moment in time when one was at peace with life and the universe, when one felt one had found the meaning of one's existence. And it was more than a moment. It was a direction for the rest of life, an assurance that the future, though not, of course, a happily ever after, would nevertheless be well worth living.

He had never really believed in romantic love.

But he was in love with Blanche Heyward.

There was more to it than that, though. He would

perhaps, even now, have laughed at himself if that had been all. But it was not. He *loved* her. She had become in the course of a few days—though he felt he had known her from the eternity before birth— as essential to his life as the air he breathed.

Fanciful thoughts. He would be writing a poem to her left eyebrow if he did not watch himself. He mocked himself as he smoothed the hair back from her sleeping face and settled her head more comfortably in the hollow between his neck and shoulder. He had been teased by her for a few days, that was all, and had finally had very good sex indeed with her. In a few weeks' time, when they were back in London and he had set her up properly as his mistress, he would already be tiring of her. He had quickly tired of every mistress he had ever kept.

He kissed her brow and then her lips. She made little protesting sounds but did not wake.

No, it was not so. He wished it were. She was a blacksmith's daughter and an opera dancer. He was a viscount, heir to an earldom. No other relationship was possible between them but that of protector and mistress. He could not…

But as he stared into the darkness, lit only by the dying embers of the fire, he knew that there was one thing he would never be able to do. He could never marry anyone else. Ever. Even though he owed it to his father to secure the succession for the next generation. Even though he owed it to his mother and his sisters to secure their future. Even though he owed it to his birth, his upbringing, his position.

If he could not marry Blanche—and he did not see how he ever could—then he would not marry anyone.

Perhaps he would see things differently tomorrow, next week, next year. He did not know. All he did know now was that he loved, that he was happy, that—he had been led to one of those earth-shattering experiences one sometimes read about that changed the whole direction of his life.

He would wake her up later, he decided, and make slow, lazy love to her again. And if they stayed awake afterward, he would take the risk of telling her how he felt. It was no very great risk, he thought. She felt about him as he felt about her. That was a part of the miracle. Unworthy as he was of her, she felt as he did. *My love*, she had called him over and over again as he had spilled his seed into her. And her body had told him the same thing even if she had not spoken the words aloud, and their minds and their very souls had intertwined as their bodies had merged.

Later he would love her again. In the meantime he slept.

NOT FOR ONE moment did Verity feel disoriented when she awoke. Neither did she entertain any illusions.

She had given in to naïveté and passion and the sentimentality that had surrounded Christmas. She had given in to a practiced seducer. Not that she would have resisted even if she had realized the truth at the time. She would not have done so. She would have given her body just as unprotestingly. She would have done so as part of the bargain she had made with him in London. But she would have guarded her heart. She would not so foolishly have imagined that it was a love encounter.

He had been a man claiming his mistress.

She had been a woman at work, earning her pay.

And now, beyond all argument, she was a fallen woman. A whore. She had done it for Chastity. Strange irony, that. But that fact notwithstanding, she was and always would be a whore.

She could not bear to face him in the morning. She could not bear to see the knowing look in his eyes, the triumph. She could not bear to play a part. She could not bear to become his regular mistress, to be used at his convenience until he tired of her and discarded her. She could not even bear to finish out this week, after which she would be free to withdraw from any future commitment.

Perhaps at the end of the week she would not have the strength to do so.

She could not bear to face him in the morning and see from his whole attitude how little their encounter had meant to him.

She had no choice but to live out the week. Even if there were a way of leaving now, she still had two hundred and fifty pounds to earn. And he had already paid her that same amount. Had she earned that advance? With what had happened here a few hours ago? With her willingness to allow it to happen on the two previous nights? *Two hundred and fifty pounds?* If she were a governess, she would be fortunate to earn that amount in four years.

There *was* a way of leaving. There was a village three miles away. A stagecoach stopped there early each morning. She had heard the servants mention it. But there was snow on the ground. And would the stage run on the day after Christmas? The snow had been melting since yesterday afternoon. It had been a cloudy night, perhaps a mild night. Why would the stage *not* run?

She would surely wake him if she tried to get out of bed, if she tried to dress and creep away.

But now that the mad, impossible idea had entered her mind, she could not leave it alone. She *could* not face him in the morning. If she felt nothing for him, she would do so with all the cheerful good sense she could muster. She had taken this employment quite deliberately, after all, knowing what was involved. She had been prepared to do what she had done with him earlier as many times as he chose. It was not from that she shrank.

In her naïveté she had not realized that her feelings might become involved. It had not occurred to her that spending a few days in close proximity with a man would reveal him to her as a person, or that she would find this particular man likable, charming, lovable. She had never for one moment expected to fall in love. She had done even worse than that. She had *loved* and still did and always would.

After removing herself from his arms while he grumbled sleepily, she edged her way across and then out of the bed. The room was cold, she realized, shivering, and she was naked and stiff. She silently gathered up her nightgown from the floor and tiptoed to the dressing room, the door of which was fortunately ajar. She slipped inside and shut the door slowly. Fortunately the hinges were well oiled and made no sound.

She lit a single candle, washed quickly in the ice-cold water, dressed in her warmest clothes, packed her belongings, and wondered if her luck would hold while she tried to leave the house undetected.

She had not packed everything. She had left his signet ring on the washstand. And one other thing. She wasted several precious moments gazing at it, spread across the top of the chest of drawers, where she had put it the night before. Should she take it? She wanted desperately to do so. It would be the one memento. But she would not need a memento. And it had been too extravagant a gift, especially under the circumstances.

She set one fingertip lightly to the gold star on its chain and then left it where it was. She did not go back into the bedchamber. There was a door leading directly from the dressing room to the corridor beyond.

It had always seemed rather silly, she thought as she made her way cautiously downstairs and let herself out of the front door, to talk about a heart aching. How could a heart *ache*? But this morning it no longer seemed silly. She hurried along the driveway to the road, past the still-stuck carriage, relieved to see that the snow had melted sufficiently that she should be able to walk to the village without any great difficulty.

Her heart ached for a little gold star and chain that would fit into the palm of her hand. And for the Christmas star that had brought such joy and such hope this year and had lured her into a great fool-

Chapter Eight

IT TOOK Julian three months to find her. Though even then he had the merest glimpse of her only to lose her again without a trace, it seemed. Just as he had lost her on Christmas night.

He had woken up by daylight and been half amused, half exasperated to find her gone from bed and from their room. He had washed and shaved and dressed in leisurely fashion, hoping she would return before he was ready, and had then gone in search of her. Even when he had not found her in any of the day rooms or in the kitchen he had not been alarmed, or even when he had peered out of doors and not seen her walking there. He had assumed she must be in the only possible place left, Mrs. Moffatt's room, admiring the baby.

The morning had been well advanced before he

had discovered the truth. She was gone and so were all her possessions except the star and chain. He had picked up the necklace, squeezed it tight in his palm and tipped back his head in silent agony.

She had left him.

Why?

He had returned to London the same day, having concocted a whole arsenal of new lies for the edification of Bertie, Debbie and the Moffatts. And so had begun his search for her. She had left her job at the opera without a word to anyone there. She had not gone to any other theater—he had checked them all. And none of her former co-workers knew of her whereabouts. They had not seen or heard of her since before Christmas.

Eventually he bribed the manager of the opera house to give him her address, but it was a false one. There was no one by the name of Blanche Heyward living there, the landlady informed him, and no one of her description, either, except that Miss Ewing, who used to live there, had been tall. But Miss Ewing had been no opera dancer and nor had any other lady who had ever rented her house. The very idea! She had glared at him with indignation. He became almost desperate enough to travel down to Somersetshire in search of the smithy that had been her home. But how many smithies must there be in Somersetshire?

Blanche clearly did not want to be found.

He tried to put her from his mind. Christmas had been an unusually pleasurable interlude, largely thanks to Blanche, and sleeping with her had been the icing on an already scrumptious cake. But really there was no more to it than that. One could not carry Christmas about all year long, after all. One had to get back to the mundane business of everyday life.

But he did at the end of January make a three-day visit to Conway, where he was greeted with such affection by his parents and such a scold from his youngest sister that he almost lost his courage. He found it again when sitting alone with his father in the library one afternoon. He would not marry Lady Sarah Plunkett, he had announced quite firmly. And before his father could draw breath to ask him—as he was obviously about to do—whom he *would* marry then, he had added that there was only one woman in the world he would consider marrying, but she would not marry him and anyway she was ineligible.

"Ineligible?" his father had asked, eyebrows raised.

"Daughter of a blacksmith," his son had told him.

"Of a *blacksmith*." His father had pursed his lips. "And *she* will not marry *you*, Julian? She has more sense than you."

"I love her," Julian had said.

"Hmm" was all the comment his father had made.

Perhaps that was all the comment he had thought necessary since the marriage seemed in no danger of becoming a reality.

Back in London Julian had searched hopelessly, aimlessly, until the afternoon in March when he spotted her on a crowded Oxford Street. She was on the opposite side of the street, coming out of a milliner's shop. He came to an abrupt halt, unable to believe the evidence of his own eyes. But then her eyes locked on his and he knew he was not mistaken. He started forward as she turned abruptly and hurried away along the pavement.

At the same moment a gentleman's curricle and a tradesman's wagon decided to dispute the right-of-way along the street, whose width had been narrowed by the presence of a large carriage picking up two passengers loaded with parcels. They confronted each other head-on and refused to budge an inch for each other.

The tradesman swore foully and the gentleman only a little more elegantly; the horses protested in the way horses did best. A whole host of bystanders took sides or merely gathered to enjoy the spectacle, and Julian got caught up in the tangle for a few seconds too long. He was across the street in less than a minute, but during that minute Blanche Heyward had disappeared totally. He hurried along the street in the direction she had taken, peering into every shop and along every alley. But there was no sign of her. Or of the young girl who had been with her.

One thing was clear to him. If she had ever regretted running away from Bertie's hunting box, she regretted it no longer. She had no wish to be found. She had no wish even to claim the second half of her week's salary.

She had played the martyr after all, then, on that night and with such courage that he had not even known that she played a part. Fool that he was, he had thought her feelings matched his own. He had thought she enjoyed losing her virginity to a rake who had paid for her favors. What a fool!

He gave up looking for her. Let her live out her life in peace. He just hoped that the two hundred and fifty pounds had proved sufficient to cover whatever need at the smithy had impelled her to accept his proposition, and that there had been some left over for her.

But his resolve slipped when he attended a rout at his eldest sister's in April. Her drawing room and the two salons that had been opened up for the occasion were gratifyingly full, she told him, her arm drawn through his as she led him through. New families were arriving in town every day for the season. But he drew her to a sudden halt.

"Who is that?" he asked, indicating with a nod of the head a thin, pretty young girl who was standing with an older lady and with General Sir Hector Ewing and his wife.

"The general?" she asked. "You do not know him, Julian? He—"

"The young girl with him," he said.

She looked archly at him and smiled. "She *is* pretty, is she not?" she said. "She is the general's niece, Miss Chastity Ewing."

Ewing. *Ewing!* The name of the tall lady who had lived at the false address given to the opera house manager by Blanche Heyward. And Miss Chastity Ewing was the young lady who had been with Blanche on Oxford Street.

"I have an acquaintance with the general, Elinor," he said, "but not a close one. Present me to Miss Ewing, if you please."

"Smitten after one glance," his sister said with a laugh. "This is *very* interesting, Julian. Come along, then."

"WHO?" Verity asked faintly. She had waited up for Chastity even though it was late and even though they no longer shared a room. She was sitting on her sister's bed.

"Viscount Folingsby," Chastity said. "At least I

think I have the name correct. He is Lady Blanch-ford's brother. He is *very* handsome and *very* charming, Verity."

There was a slight buzzing in her head. It had been almost inevitable, of course. She knew that he was in London—she had *seen* him—and that therefore, he would attend ton events, especially now that the season was beginning. Since her uncle had returned from Vienna the week after Christmas, brought them all to live with him, and was now undertaking to introduce Chastity to society, then Chass would surely attend some of the same balls and parties as he. Verity had just hoped that pretty and healthy as Chastity was, she would be just too youthful to attract the notice of Viscount Folingsby.

"Is he?" she said in answer to her sister's words.

But Chastity was smiling at her with bright mischief and came to sit on the bed beside her, still clad in her evening gown. "Of course he is," she said. "You know him, Verity."

Her heart performed a somersault. "Oh?" she said. "Do I?"

Chastity laughed merrily and clapped her hands. "Of course you do," she said, "and I can tell from your guilty expression that you remember him very well. He *told* us. About Christmas."

Verity could feel the blood draining out of her head, leaving it cold and clammy and dizzy.

Chastity took one of her sister's cold, nerveless hands in her own. "Dear Verity," she said. "I daresay you have convinced yourself that he did not really notice you. But I knew it would happen sooner or later. I *told* you, did I not? How could any gentleman look at your beauty and not be struck by it and by *you*. No matter who you were."

"Does Mama know?" Verity was whispering.

"Of course," Chastity said, laughing gleefully. "She was there with me and our uncle."

"*Uncle* knows?" They would all be turned out on the street tomorrow, she thought. Was there any way of persuading him to dismiss her alone? She had already displeased him by refusing to participate in any of the social entertainments of the season. She had pleaded advanced age. Could Mama and Chastity be saved?

"The viscount knew that Lady Coleman went to Scotland the day after Christmas," Chastity said. "He assumed you had gone with her. Imagine his surprise and gratification to learn that you had not, that you were here in London."

"*What?*" There *was* no Lady Coleman, and he did not know her as Verity Ewing.

"Oh, Verity, you silly goose." Chastity raised her sister's hand to her cheek and held it there. "Did you think he would not notice you because you were merely a lady's companion? Did you think he would not wish to renew the acquaintance? He told Mama how you quietly set about making everyone's Christmas comfortable and joyful, not just Lady Coleman's. He told us about the clergyman's family being stranded and about you delivering the baby. Oh, Verity, why did you not tell us about that? And he confessed to Mama that he had kissed you beneath the kissing bough. He has the most roguish smile."

"Oh," Verity said.

"And you thought he would forget you?" Chastity said. "He has not forgotten. He asked Mama if he might call upon you. And he asked Uncle for a private word. They went walking off together. Verity, he is *wonderful*. Almost wonderful enough for you, I do believe. Viscountess Folingsby. Yes." She laughed again. "It will suit. I declare it will. And *now* I know why you have refused to go into society. You have been afraid of meeting him. You have been afraid he would not remember you. You goose!"

Verity could only cling to her sister's hand and stare wide-eyed. He knew who she was! Somehow Mama or Chastity must have mentioned Lady Coleman to him and he had played along with the game. And he wanted to see her. Why? To pay her the rest of her salary? But she had not earned it. To demand part of the other half back, then? The irony of that was that her sacrifice had been unnecessary. Her uncle had taken over their care and the payment of Chastity's medical bills within two days of her return to London.

Perhaps he wanted her to earn what he had already paid her. Perhaps he wanted her to be his mistress here, in town. But he knew she was General Sir Hector Ewing's niece.

She did not *want* to see him. The very thought of doing so was enough to throw her into a panic, as the reality had that afternoon on Oxford Street.

And yet in almost four months the pain had not diminished even one iota. It only seemed to grow worse. She had even found herself bitterly disappointed, as well as knee-weakeningly relieved, when she had discovered that their one encounter had not borne fruit.

"Verity." Her sister's eyes were softly glowing. "You *have* remembered him. You are in love with him. Do not think you can deceive me. How splendid this is. How very romantic. It is like a fairy tale."

Verity snatched her hand away and jumped to her feet. "Foolish girl," she said. "It is high time you were asleep. You have recovered your health even if you are still just a little too thin, but you must not tax your strength. Go to bed now. Turn around and let me undo your buttons."

But Chastity was not so easily distracted. She got to her feet, too, and flung her arms about her sister. Her eyes shone with tears. "I am healthy because of the sacrifice you made for me," she said. "I will never *ever* forget what I owe you, Verity. But you are going to be rewarded. You never would have met him if you had not taken employment with Lady Coleman and if you had not given up your Christmas with us to go away with her. So you see it is a just reward. And I am so happy I could *weep*."

"Go to bed and to sleep," Verity said firmly. "You are drawing far too many conclusions from Viscount Folingsby's courtesy this evening. Besides, I do not like him above half."

Chastity was laughing softly as she left the room.

Verity stood against the door of her own room after she had closed it behind her, her eyes tight shut.

He had found her. But did she want to be found? Perhaps, after all, she needed to be. There was a yawning emptiness in her life, a sense of something unresolved, unfinished. Perhaps it should be finished. She did not know quite why he wished to see her—certainly not for any of the reasons Chastity imagined—but perhaps she should find out. Perhaps if she saw him again, if she found out exactly what it was he wanted of her, she would finally be able to close the book on that episode from the past and move on into the future.

Perhaps she would be able to stop loving him.

HE HAD SPOKEN with her uncle the evening before. He had met him again during the morning in order to discuss and settle details. And now, this afternoon, he had spoken with her mother. Mrs. Ewing had gone to send her daughter down to the visitors' salon in which he waited, feeling more nervous than he had ever felt in his life before.

The door opened and closed quietly. She stood against it, her hands behind her, probably still gripping the knob. She was dressed in pale green muslin, a dress of simple design. Her hair was dressed plainly, too. She had lost some weight and some color. But even if she tried twice as hard she would never be able to disguise the fact that she was an extraordinarily beautiful woman. He made her his most elegant bow.

"Miss Ewing?" he said.

She stared at him for several moments before releasing her hold on the knob and curtsying. "My lord."

"Miss *Verity* Ewing," he said. "You were misnamed." She had nothing to say to that.

"Verity," he said.

"I have two hundred pounds left," she told him

then, her voice soft, her chin up, her shoulders back. "I have not needed it after all. I will return it to you. I hope you will agree to forget the fifty pounds. I did partly earn it, after all."

The younger girl had been ill. Verity Ewing had taken employment in order to pay the physician's bills and to buy medicines. She had worked as a companion to Lady Coleman. She had done it for her sister.

"I believe your virginity was worth fifty pounds," he said. "Where is the rest?"

"Here."

She carried a small reticule over her arm, he saw. She opened it and took a roll of banknotes from it. She held them out to him and then brought them to him when he did not move. He took the money with one hand and the reticule with the other and set them down on the chair beside him.

"You are satisfied now?" he asked her. "It is all finished now?"

She nodded, looking down at the money. "I should have returned it to you before," she said. "I did not know quite how. I am sorry."

"Verity," he said softly. "My love."

She closed her eyes and kept them closed. "No," she said. "It is finished. I will not be your mistress. I will always be a...a fallen woman, but I will not be your mistress. Please leave now. And thank you for not exposing me to my mother and sister. Or to my uncle."

"My love." He was not at all sure of himself. Verity Ewing, alias Blanche Heyward, was, as he knew from experience, a woman of strong will and firm character. "Must I go? Or may I stay—forever? Will you marry me?"

She opened her eyes then and raised them to his chin. She smiled. "Ah," she said, "of course. I am a gentleman's daughter and you are a gentleman. No, my lord, you do not have to do the decent thing. I will not expose you, either, you see."

"It was your first time," he told her. "I could not expect you to understand. You had not the experience. Usually when sex is purchased, it is simply for pleasure, on the man's part at least. It was pleasing, was it not? For both of us? But it was more. In a sense it was my first time, too, you see. I had never made love before.

"What happened *was* love, Verity. I knew with my body while we loved, with my mind after it was over, that you had become the air I breathed, the life I lived, the soul I cherished. I thought you felt the same. It did not occur to me that perhaps you did not until I discovered that you had left me. Did you feel as much pain on that day, I wonder, as I did? I have never felt an agony more intense."

"I was a blacksmith's daughter," she said, "an opera dancer, and a whore. What you would have offered then would have been far less than marriage. I have not changed, my lord. I am the daughter of a clergyman, but I am still a whore. I will not be your mistress or your wife."

He possessed himself of both her hands. They were like ice. "You will scrape together the money," he said fiercely. "The fifty pounds. Every penny of it. I want it returned. And then I will hear you take back that ugly name you call yourself. Tell me something. And tell me the truth, *Verity*. Why did you allow me to bed you that night? Were you a working girl earning her pay? Or were you a woman making love, giving and receiving love without a thought to money? Which was it? *Look* at me."

She raised her eyes to his.

"Tell me." He was whispering, he realized. The whole of his future, the whole of his happiness depended upon her reply. He was far from sure of what it would be.

"How could I not love you?" she said. "They were magical days. And I was taken off guard. I went there with a cynical, arrogant rake. And I discovered there a warm, gentle, fun-loving, caring man. I have no experience with such situations, my lord. How could I not love you with my body and my heart and everything that is me? It did not once occur to me as *that* was happening that I was becoming a whore."

"You were not," he told her. "You were becoming mine as I was becoming yours. What we did was wrong. It should not have been done outside wedlock. But worse sins than that can be forgiven, I believe. Let me say one more thing before I plead with you again. I visited my father at Conway Hall after Christmas. He is the Earl of Grantham. Did you know that? I am his heir.

"He has been very eager for some time for me to marry and produce an heir since I have no brothers. I love my father, Verity. And I know my duty to him and to my position. But I told him that I could never marry anyone but you. That was when I still thought you the daughter of a blacksmith and an opera dancer. I *never* thought of you as a whore. What we did in bed together was love, not business."

"And how did your father reply?" she asked.

He smiled at her. "My father loves me, Verity. My happiness is important to him. In our family love has always been of more importance than duty. He would have given his blessing—a little reluctantly, it is true—to my marriage even to a blacksmith's daughter."

She dropped her glance again to stare down at their joined hands. He squeezed hers tightly and his heart hammered painfully against his chest.

"My love," he said. "Verity. Miss Ewing. Will you do me the great honor of marrying me?"

She kept her head down. "It was Christmas," she said. "Everything looks different at Christmas. More rosy, more possible, more unreal. This is a mistake. You should not have come. I do not know how you discovered who I am."

"I believe," he said, "the mistake is ours, Verity. We act as if Christmas is for one day of the year only, as if peace and hope and happiness can exist only then. It was not meant to be that way. Was all that business at Bethlehem intended to bring joy to the world for just one day of the year? What little trust we have in our religion. How little we demand of it and give to it. Why can it not be Christmas now, today, for you and me?"

"Because it is not," she said.

He released her hands then and reached into an inner pocket of his coat. "Yes, it is," he said. "It will be. How about this?" He held in his palm the linen handkerchief she had given him as a gift. He unfolded it carefully until she could see the gold star on its chain nestled within.

"Oh," she said softly.

"Do you remember what you said about it when I gave it to you?" he asked her.

She shook her head. "I hurt you."

"Yes," he said. "You did. You told me the Star of Bethlehem belonged in the heavens to bring hope, to guide its followers to wisdom and the meaning of their lives. Perhaps some power did not quite agree with you. Here it is, lying here between us. I believe we did follow it at Christmas, Verity, perhaps with as little understanding as the wise men themselves of where exactly it was leading us and to what. It led us to each other. To hope. To love. To a future that could hold companionship and love and happiness if we are willing to follow it to the end. Come with me. All the way. That one more irrevocable step. Please?"

Her eyes, when they looked up into his, were swimming with tears. "It can be Christmas today?" she said. "And every day?"

"But not in any *magical* sense," he said. "We can *make* every day Christmas. But only if we work hard at it. Only if we remember the miracle every day of our lives."

"Oh, my lord," she said.

"Julian."

"Julian." She gazed at him and he could feel his anxiety ease as she slowly smiled.

"Marry me," he whispered.

She lifted her hands then and framed his face with them. "I should have trusted my heart more than my head," she said. "My heart told me it was a shared love. My head told me how foolish I was. Julian." Her arms twined about his neck. "Oh, Julian, my love. Oh yes, if you are quite sure. But I know you are. And I am, too. I have loved you with so much pain, so much longing, so little trust. I *love* you."

He stopped her babbling with his mouth. He wrapped his arms about her and held her tightly to him. He held everything that was most dear in his life and vowed that he would never ever let her go, that he would never even for a single moment forget the strange, undeserved chance that had led him out into the desert to follow a star along an unknown route to an unknown destination. He would never cease marveling that he had been led, bored and cynical and arrogant, to peace and redemption and love.

In one palm, clasped tightly at her back as they kissed eagerly, joyfully, passionately, he held the linen handkerchief, which had been a treasured memento of her father, and the gold star, which he would hang about her neck in a few minutes' time.

The gifts of Christmas.

The gifts of love.

Dear Reader,

If you are like me, the first word that pops into your mind when someone mentions Christmas is *presents!* From the divine gift of love to the tokens of affection exchanged by lovers, families, friends and coworkers, the season is symbolized by the spirit of giving.

Edwina Denby, the heroine of my story, is called upon to offer a unique kind of gift to Miles Hampden, a young soldier she secretly admires. In exploring her life as a soldier's daughter growing up in India, I came upon the ancient legends every child there would have heard. Although the Ramayana stories are from a different culture a world away, I was struck by how the themes of honor, sacrifice, courage and duty still resonate, as they have since the legends were written over 2000 years ago.

Great and timeless as these virtues are, it is love, selfless and self-sacrificing, that is truly life's greatest gift. I hope you will enjoy watching as Miles and Edwina find and offer this gift to each other.

Julia Justiss

THE THREE GIFTS

Julia Justiss

To the men and women of our armed forces
who daily go into harm's way all over the world
so that we at home may be safe.

Chapter One

Outside Lisbon, Mid-November 1810

LIEUTENANT MILES HAMPDEN squinted into the setting sun at the twinkling of campfires that marked the enemy positions at the far side of the Lines of Torres Vedras. Fewer tonight, he noted. Having apparently accepted that he would not be able to lure Wellington out of his maze of defensive fortifications to do battle, it appeared General Messena was beginning to withdraw his troops.

So the French were leaving Portugal, as he would be shortly, Miles thought, shivering as a gust of November wind swirled over the barricade. With what little emotion remained to him, he could almost pity the half-starved enemy their long winter march through the barren countryside back to Spain.

He would be returning to the warmth and plenty of England, just in time for the beginning of the Christmas season. A prospect that, until the grim news that came last week, he would normally have greeted with gladness.

Instead of finding Hampden Glen decked in a festive array of holly and mistletoe, he would walk into a house wreathed in black. Instead of joining family and servants to haul in a Yule log, he would make a solitary pilgrimage to the family crypt that had held, for nearly a month by the time the letter reached him, the remains of his father and elder brother, killed in a carriage accident on their way home from a county fair.

The first raw blast of grief had faded, leaving him to go numbly through his duties for the few days remaining before he would catch a transport back to England. No longer simply Lieutenant Hampden of the Third Foot, but Viscount Hampden, head of the family and guardian to his widowed sister-in-law and her little daughter.

He would miss his comrades and the often dull, occasionally terrifying business of soldiering. But despite the fact that Wellington's army had not yet managed to drive the French out of the Peninsula, Miles had no choice but to resign his commission.

Not since, in the same cruel twist of fate that had

turned a second son into a viscount, the new heir to the Hampden title had become Miles's cousin Reginald—a debauched gamester of such ill repute that even Wellington, generally loathe to release a battle-tested officer, had gruffly observed when he gave Miles his condolences that 'twas nothing for it but for the new viscount to sell out.

Eyes still watching the campfires, Miles's mouth hardened as he thought of Reggie. Already known as a drunkard, a cheat and a bully at Oxford, after being expelled from the university, his cousin had settled in London, where he further tarnished the Hampden name with escapades of vice and high-stakes gaming.

No, Miles could not remain a soldier and risk having the fate of gentle Agnes and her little Beth fall into Reginald's soiled hands. Nor could he tolerate the prospect of his cousin squandering the assets of the estate that generations of Hampdens had carefully tended.

Of course, as Wellington had wryly observed, if Miles were quick enough about the business, he might find a wife from among the Marriage Mart lovelies in town for the season, breed himself an heir to secure the succession and be back in time for next summer's campaign.

His general's dry humor gave his dulled spirits a slight lift. With a soldier's uncertain life stretching before him, he'd never given much thought to the marriage that duty—and the looming threat of Reggie inheriting now made a matter of priority. Beyond the basics of good breeding, competence and compatibility, what sort of woman should he choose?

Hunching his shoulders against the cold, he replayed in memory the short catalog of ladies who'd impressed him. There was the sultry Portuguese contessa with the dark eyes and smoky voice, who would doubtless enliven the marriage bed. The cool blond beauty he'd imagined himself in love with his first year on the town—elegant, perfectly gowned, a charming hostess, but whose conversation concerned solely ton gossip or fashion. Lacy Standish, the neighbor he'd grown up with, practical, easygoing, an accomplished estate manager, but more a friend than a potential lover.

It seemed he'd never met anyone who possessed all the qualities he admired in a lady—which didn't augur well for finding a suitable life's partner on the double-quick.

Sighing, he concluded that he would have to do the best he could with the selection available when the time came. Since, mercifully, now was not that time, he put the matter out of mind.

'Twas nearly full dark, signaling the end of his watch. After exchanging pleasantries with the lieutenant who relieved him, Miles retrieved his horse and rode off, hoping his batman would have some hot tea waiting and perhaps have found a hare for the stew pot.

His ears had barely registered the loud report of a musket when a stunning, red-hot blow slammed into his back. And then he was falling, falling out of the saddle into the inky dusk.

FROM A MURKY HAZE, Miles fought back to consciousness, his eyes drawn to a flicker of light. *Enemy campfires.* Then he realized he was gazing not over the barricade, but at a lantern hung near where he lay propped upon a cot, agonizing pain radiating from his back and chest.

"Thank God, you're awake!"

Through the confusion and discomfort, Miles recognized the voice of his friend and fellow lieutenant, Allen, Lord Sanbrook and cautiously turned his head.

"Steady now!" Sanbrook admonished. "Wilson says you must remain as still as possible."

"What…happened?" Miles asked.

A different voice—another friend, Lieutenant William Wheaten—answered, "The trooper on duty says a sniper hit you just as you were leaving the barricade. And the bastards are supposed to be retreating! A pox on frogs and all things French."

"How…bad is it?" Miles asked.

There was an ominous pause before Sanbrook said, "You took a ball through the back of your shoulder. It appears to be still lodged in your chest, though with this cursed darkness and all the bleeding, Wilson says 'tis difficult to tell. The devil of it is that Dr. MacAndrews is away in Lisbon and not due back until tomorrow."

Miles fought to stay conscious. "Wilson is here?"

"Aye, sir, right here," the surgeon's assistant said.

"Can you…remove the ball?"

"That's the rub of it, sir. That ball mighta come to rest between your heart and your lung—or mayhap it broke into pieces. I'm no physician, you know, and I'm not about to go probing about in there, for seeing as little as I can see and knowing as little as I know, I'd kill you for sure. You'll just have to hang on until the surgeon gets back."

Even through his pain, Miles could discern the note of fear in the assistant's voice.

"Will I…make it…until morning?"

"We'll surely be praying that you do," Wilson replied.

He could be dying, Miles realized. It seemed ironic, after coming unscathed through a fistful of battles, and the bitter retreat to Corunna, that he might be snuffed by a sniper's bullet while practically on his way out of the country. He longed to give in to the throbbing demon biting at his chest and sink back into oblivion, but a nagging sense that there was something important, something vital he must do, made him fight the looming darkness.

Duty came to him in a cold sweat of awareness. Reginald.

"Can't let...Reggie inherit," he croaked, trying desperately to rally his strength.

"Damn, I'd forgotten the succession!" Sanbrook said.

"Nothing for it, old man," Wheaten said. "You'll just have to hold on until the sawbones can treat you.

"Could he will his estate to a comrade?" Wheaten asked. "Just for peace of mind," he added hastily.

"Probably not," Sanbrook answered. "If he tried to transfer assets to someone not kin by blood or marriage, Reginald would be sure to challenge it, and the courts would likely uphold the legal heir."

"If the matter is important," Wilson broke in, "he'd best do something about it now, while he's still conscious."

Sanbrook fixed Wilson with a look. "You think it's that critical?"

Wilson nodded. "Regret to say it, but I do."

The surgeon's assistant didn't think he'd see morning, Miles realized. For the first time, fear swept over him. He could accept his own death, but surely heaven would not let his brother's already bereaved family suffer further!

With his last reserves of strength, he clutched Sanbrook's hand. "Must…do something."

His friend regarded him steadily, then nodded and turned to the surgeon's assistant. "Wilson, you know Sergeant Riggins of the Second Regiment? He's a solicitor by trade, I believe. Have him fetched here as quickly as possible. So, Hampden," he said, looking back at Miles, "it appears William and I will have to find you a bride."

Chapter Two

EDWINA CROFTON DENBY was rolling bandages at the small wooden table in her father's billet when her mother looked up from her needlework and frowned. "Such a sad duty for a young woman on a fine fair night!" Mrs. Crofton observed. "You ought to tease Papa into taking you to Lisbon. With Christmas soon upon us, there's bound to parties honoring General Wellington where you could dine and dance and enjoy the company of his handsome officers."

Edwina gave her mama a fond smile. "You know my work with the wounded brings me solace, Mama. And you also know Papa wouldn't dare take me to Lisbon, for he would have to take you, too, and the admirers you always attract would drive him quite distracted with jealousy."

Mrs. Crofton laughed. "Nonsense! I may have been

a belle long ago, but 'tis you who would command their attention now." She hesitated, and Edwina braced herself for the advice sure to come.

Her mother continued, "'Tis more than a year since Talavera. I know you've said you have no wish to marry again, but you are still so young! You should pull your heart from the grave and look about you."

Despite her discomfort with her mother's well-meant advice, Edwina had no intention of putting a period to the argument by revealing it wasn't grief over her lost husband that made her disinclined to remarry. "I'm content to be here helping you and Papa."

"Yes, and we do love having you, but you deserve a home of your own. A husband, and children to delight you as you have delighted us."

A pang pierced her heart. If only Daniel could have given her a child, perhaps the disaster that had been her marriage would have been worth the pain. Damping down that old, familiar disappointment, she said, "Please, Mama, I don't wish to talk of it."

Tears brimming in her eyes, Mrs. Crofton came over to pat her daughter's hand. "I'm sorry, my dear, for broaching the matter again. Only you know how much your father and I long for you to find the happiness we have. The happiness you had with your dear Daniel."

Edwina swallowed the lump in her throat and

vowed anew never to reveal to her tenderhearted mama how great a lie that was. Nor did she wish to risk bringing on an attack of the vapors by revealing what she really intended to do once she'd seen Papa safely through this war: return to England and use the money she would inherit from grandfather to set up her own establishment.

Thanks to his bequest, the Lord be praised, she need not marry again.

A knock at the door pulled her from her thoughts. With the responsiveness of a combat officer of many years' experience, her papa, who'd been dozing in an armchair by the fire, jolted awoke and paced to the door.

He opened it to reveal two soldiers standing in the shadows, lamplight gleaming on their officer's lacing. "So sorry to disturb you, Major Crofton," one of them said. "We've come to beg an urgent favor."

"Enter, gentlemen, and warm yourselves by the fire," her father replied. "May I offer you both some port?"

"No, thank you, sir," replied the first. As they strode toward the hearth, Edwina recognized Lieutenant Wheaten and Lieutenant Lord Sanbrook from a neighboring regiment, the Third Foot. "We must be off immediately."

"How may I help you, then?" her father asked.

"One of our comrades was gravely wounded by

sniper fire a short time ago. As you may know, Dr. MacAndrews is not in camp at present. His assistant, Corporal Wilson, sent us to see if your daughter might come assist him."

Her father gestured to Edwina. "Ask her yourself."

Lord Sanbrook turned pleading eyes toward Edwina. "I know 'tis late, ma'am, but could you please come? Wilson says, except for the doctor himself, you have more experience than anyone in nursing the badly wounded and—" the two lieutenants exchanged an uneasy glance "—I'm afraid our friend's case is desperate."

"Who is the wounded soldier?" Edwina asked.

"Lieutenant Hampden."

Her mother gasped. "Oh, the poor man! Was he not supposed to leave for England in a few days?"

"Yes, ma'am," Wheaten confirmed.

Edwina drew in a shocked breath of her own. Though she didn't know the lieutenant well, she had been intensely aware of him every time he'd chanced to visit Papa's regiment. It was not just his handsome face and tall, commanding figure that drew her eye, but an aura of confidence and enthusiasm that lifted the spirits of everyone he met—even this rather shy widow of no particular beauty.

"Of course I will come," she replied. "Let me get my cloak."

A few minutes later, wrapped in that warm, fur-lined garment, she set off on horseback, her thoughts consumed with worried speculation about the lieutenant's condition. From the looks that passed between his friends and the grim lines into which their faces settled as they rode, she surmised that his condition was indeed perilous.

How sad it would be if such a vital, compelling young man were to lose his life tonight.

After a short ride, they reached the hospital tents. But to her surprise, after helping her down from the saddle, Lord Sanbrook put a restraining hand on her arm.

"Before you go in, I must explain the singular circumstances in which Lieutenant Hampden now finds himself. I beg you will hear the whole before you respond, even if some of it seems a bit…shocking."

Puzzled, Edwina answered, "Of course. Only tell me at once, that I might go assist Wilson."

"The ball that pierced Lieutenant Hampden's shoulder may have lodged in his chest. Wilson dares not probe for it and fears Hampden may not survive until the surgeon returns tomorrow. As I imagine you've heard, Miles recently became Viscount Hampden. As matters now stand, should he die, his cousin, a vice-ridden, debauched gamester, will inherit. He would also become guardian and trustee to the recently widowed Lady Hampden and her young daughter. I assure you, did you know Reginald Hampden as I do, you would realize the Devil himself would be more fit to have charge of such innocents."

"Then we must all hope Lieutenant Hampden confounds Wilson's expectations and survives."

"And so we do. But hindering Hampden's fight to survive is his great distress over what his kinswomen would suffer at his cousin's hands, should he succumb to his wounds. That, ma'am, is the matter with which we most need your assistance."

Edwina nodded. "I shall be happy to help in any way I can."

"The assistance we require is of a rather…personal nature. To state it baldly, ma'am, we propose to have you marry Lieutenant Hampden."

Edwina shook her head, sure she could not have heard him correctly. "You wish me to do what?"

Coloring faintly, Sanbrook cleared his throat. "Marry him," he repeated, more confidently this time. "You see, if Miles is married, he can will the guardianship of the widowed Lady Hampden, as well as all the assets of the estate which are not entailed, to his wife, with his solicitors as trustees, thereby protecting his niece and sister-in-law and at least some of the Hampden estate. The necessary paperwork is being completed as we speak and a chaplain is standing by to perform the ceremony. All we lack is a bride." He smiled at her. "We sincerely hope to persuade you to play that role."

Edwina stared at him for a full minute. "You must be mad," she said flatly, and turned back toward her horse.

Lord Sanbrook caught her shoulder. "Please, ma'am, don't go! I know 'tis an extraordinary request."

"Indeed," she said, shaking off his hand.

"Only consider! You'd be easing the last hours of a valiant soldier and—pray excuse me for putting the matter so crudely—saving the jointure and quite likely the person of a grieving widow from being ravished by a man who would hold her completely in his legal power. I beg you to think it over again before you refuse."

"I should dismiss it outright," Edwina retorted. The very notion that the handsome, titled Lieutenant Hampden would even consider taking to wife a non-descript widow of scant beauty and few family connections was ludicrous. Suddenly suspicious, she turned on Sanbrook. "This was your idea, wasn't it? Surely Lieutenant Hampden did not send you on such a mad scheme."

"It was indeed his wish, ma'am, which he will shortly confirm. He would, of course, have preferred to explain the whole to you himself, but Wilson and I thought it best for him to conserve what little strength he has left. Please, ma'am. We should not ask this of you were the situation not truly desperate."

Unbelievable as it all seemed, she could tell from his voice and manner that Lord Sanbrook was in deadly earnest. It still seemed outrageous—a clandestine midnight marriage to a dying nobleman—but if the heir to the Hampden title were as dissolute and unprincipled as Sanbrook painted him, the thought of a widow trapped in legal thrall to such a man was equally appalling. Despite her initial resistance, she felt compassion stir.

"I concede the situation appears grave. But what if I agree to your proposal and, by God's mercy, Lieutenant Hampden survives?"

"Then if you both wish it, you may tear up the contract and go your separate ways, with no one the wiser."

"Just like that?" Edwina angled her head to gaze up at him. "I cannot imagine any chaplain agreeing to marry us on such terms."

Sanbrook returned a rueful grin. "Were the circumstances not so extraordinary, I expect you would be correct. However, being well acquainted with the excellence of Hampden's character and realizing the gravity of his condition, Chaplain Darrow agreed to officiate, as long as you pledge that you are entering this…unusual union of your own free will. Should

Miles survive, a small gift in appreciation of your efforts could be arranged. Whereas, if our hopes for his recovery are not answered, you would of course receive a generous widow's competence."

Edwina stiffened. "If I agree to this, I will accept no reimbursement of any kind. I shall do it only to safeguard Lady Hampden and ease Lieutenant Hampden's suffering. But I shall not agree to anything until I hear this astounding proposal from Lieutenant Hampden's own lips."

Sanbrook nodded. "Then let us make haste while that is still possible."

Edwina wasn't sure what she expected, but from the sickly sweet odor of blood emanating from Hampden's cot and the panicky expression on Wilson's face, she realized Sanbrook had not overstated the gravity of his friend's condition.

"Thank heaven you be here at last!" Wilson said as he advanced to meet them. With a glance over his shoulder at his patient, he continued in softer tones, "Near half a dozen times, I feared I'd lost him."

Lord Sanbrook addressed a man in the uniform of a sergeant. "Is all the paperwork ready?"

"Aye, sir," the sergeant replied.

"You're sure it will withstand a possible court challenge?"

The sergeant gave Lord Sanbrook a chilly look.

"Before I signed on with Wellington, I was the best solicitor in Liverpool. Try as they might, not the fanciest of London lawyers will be able to find a loophole in these documents."

While the men talked, Edwina found her attention drawn to the man propped on the cot. Pain cut furrowed lines in his forehead as he exhaled shallow, panting breaths. From the fixed gaze of his eyes and the clench of his fists on the cot frame, she sensed that he was holding on to consciousness only by a ferocious effort.

Pity and regret for a life that appeared almost certain to be lost soon swelled in her breast.

Then Lieutenant Hampden saw her. The legal and social ramifications of the dilemma faded from mind as, in his fevered eyes, she read the desperate plea for help of a wounded being to the person he knew could ease his torment.

Without another thought, she walked over and took his hand. "Lieutenant, I was so sorry to hear of your injury."

"Thank you…for entertaining…so outrageous a proposition, Mrs. Denby."

His fingers, damp with sweat, barely returned the pressure of hers. "Hush, now, you must save your strength," she said, her heart contracting once more with pity. "Are you sure you wish to do this?"

"Would do me…utmost honor…if you consent…to become my wife," he said, panting a bit at the end.

Afterward she could not remember ever making a conscious decision. She simply heard herself saying, "I would be honored to accept your proposal."

"Excellent!" Sanbrook said. "Chaplain Darrow," he called, "The vows, if you please."

Emerging from the shadows at the far side of the tent, the reverend nodded to Sanbrook, then turned to address Edwina. "You are sure you wish to do this?"

For an instant, panic swept through her, but a single glance at Hampden's pain-lined face was sufficient to banish it. "Yes, Father Darrow. I am sure."

"Very well, my child. May God bless you for your compassion." Placing his hand over the limp fingers Edwina still held, the reverend began to read the familiar words of the wedding service.

As the proceedings went forward, Edwina had to suppress a hysterical giggle at the unreality of it all: the flickering red glow of the lantern, the wounded bridegroom gasping out his vows, his friend helping him place the heavy, bloodstained signet ring on her finger. Then it was over and the chaplain proclaimed them man and wife.

"Save the kiss…for later," her bridegroom whispered. His eyes fluttered shut and he sagged back, as if a great burden had been lifted.

For one charged moment, Edwina thought her new husband had expired, until her panicked eyes noted the slight rise and fall of the chest that indicated he remained, for the moment, among the living.

Sinking down on a stool, she numbly accepted the congratulations of the minister and the solicitor, who speedily withdrew. An awkward silence fell between her and the friends of the man on the cot to whom, apparently, she was now legally married.

"He shall be forever in your debt," Sanbrook said softly. "'Twas a truly noble and unselfish act."

"Indeed, ma'am," Wheaten echoed. "But this must be all quite a shock. May we escort you back to your father's billet now?"

Unreal as the wedding appeared, it seemed callous to vow to honor, cherish and obey and then ride back to her father's encampment while her titular husband lay dying. Nor, in truth, did she know yet what she would say to her parents about this night's odd business.

"Corporal Wilson, you did wish my assistance nursing…the lieutenant?" she asked, unable to get her lips around the word *husband*.

"Indeed, Mrs.—Lady Hampden. It would ease my mind."

Edwina shook off the little shiver—part apprehension, part something else she didn't wish to identify—at the sound of her new title on his lips. "Then I shall stay and tend him. You believe the ball may be lodged in his chest, I understand. Then I don't suppose we should move him."

"No, ma'am."

"If I might have some water, to cleanse the wound and cool his brow? And if either of you has some spirits, I can give him a sip to ease his pain, should he wake." She gave Sanbrook and Wheaten a slight smile. "I shall try my best to make his last hours as comfortable as possible."

Lord Sanbrook bowed. "Allow Wheaten and me to assist. As Darrow said, your compassion does you great credit."

Edwina waved off his praise. "Nonsense, 'tis only fitting. Since it appears that, however briefly, I am now his lordship's wife."

Chapter Three

LORD HAMPDEN'S WIFE. Edwina would have laughed, were the situation not so tragic. Once upon a time, she might have felt like the heroine in one of the gothic tales Mama so enjoyed, to find herself suddenly married to a handsome, titled, agreeable young man. Until Daniel, seemingly the embodiment of every girlish dream, had seared through her life and burned such childish ideas to ash.

Only in a tale as fantastical as the Hindu legends her ayah used to tell her when she was growing up would Viscount Hampden *choose* to marry Edwina Denby, daughter of a baron's younger son and a wealthy merchant's daughter. Not only was she far beneath his touch in the eyes of English society, she had seen him at regimental parties, surrounded by a cooing coterie of local ladies or dancing with the slender, doe-eyed Portuguese beauties he apparently favored. He would hardly pick a tall, plain, brown-haired English girl whose only notable attributes were a fine set of hazel eyes and the promise, several years hence, of inheriting a fortune. Particularly since, if the gossip being whispered about the encampment were accurate, the new viscount had no need of an Indian nabob's riches to refill the family coffers.

She sighed. If she had known when she first met him how badly Daniel *had* needed that wealth, how differently her life might have transpired!

At least she had entered this marriage mercifully free of illusions. And she could repay the trust Hampden had placed in her by capably tending her temporary husband.

At that moment, Lord Sanbrook returned with a basin of water. "Here you are, ma'am. After discussing the matter, Wilson and I thought that once you've done all you can for Hampden, Wheaten could escort you home. We'll stay with him the rest of the night."

They wished to spare her having to watch as Hampden breathed his last, Edwina thought. Not a tragedy she was keen to witness, yet part of her, illogically enough, resisted the idea of abandoning the man whose limp fingers she still retained in a light grasp. "I shall remain until I am fatigued, at which point I will gladly claim the lieutenant's escort. Ah, you found brandy."

After Sanbrook handed over the water and the spirits, Edwina set to work. She had thought Hampden unconscious, but as she gently eased his jacket open to wash his chest, he stirred under her touch. "Thank...you," he murmured.

Heartened to find him still responsive, she said, "Would you like some water? Wilson has propped you high enough that I believe you can drink, if I hold the cup."

The lieutenant returned a barely perceptible nod. A whistled inhale of breath after his first sip told her it must hurt him to swallow, but he persevered. After refusing her offer of spirits, he braced himself, only his gritted teeth revealing the cost of his silence as she finished cleansing his wounds.

Having done all she could to give Dr. MacAndrews a clear field on which to treat his patient if, by God's mercy, the lieutenant survived until his return, she sent Wilson away with a request for more clean water.

A feeble tug at her hand startled her. "Don't...go," Hampden whispered. "Please stay and...talk to me."

He must have overheard his friend's intention to bear her away. Once again, sadness and sympathy swelled in her breast, strengthening her resolve not to leave him. How many dying soldiers had she sat beside simply talking, filling their last hours with a feminine presence that soothed them with memories of home and family? Surely she could do no less for Hampden.

"Of course," she replied. "What shall I say?"

"Tell me…about you."

She supposed it was only natural that he would want to know more about the woman he'd so precipitously married, though her recent past wasn't something she enjoyed recounting. Best to summarize briefly and move on.

"Papa came to India in the army as a young man, where he met Mama, the daughter of a prosperous East India Company merchant. I was born and grew up in Bombay, living there until Papa's regiment was recalled here to the peninsula. Shortly before we were to leave, I met and married a young officer, Daniel Denby. He…he was killed at the battle of Talavera."

Hampden's eyes flickered. "Son of…Lord Alveney?"

Edwina stiffened. What had he heard? "Yes," she replied cautiously.

"Good family," Hampden said, closing his eyes again.

"Yes," Edwina returned drily, relaxing a trifle. Good family indeed. How many times had Daniel reminded her what rare good fortune it had been for one of her humble birth to snare a husband of such exalted lineage?

"After that, I felt I should remain and help Mama care for Papa until the war ends," she continued, hoping to forestall any inquiry he might make about why the widow had not returned to England and the shelter of her husband's family. "Mama has the sweetest of good natures and never complains, no matter how wretched the conditions, but she's not very... practical."

One blue eye opened. "You're...practical?"

"Oh, very," she confirmed. The only talent Daniel had grudgingly come to appreciate was her ability to create an oasis of comfort out of the chaos of an army on the march. "I've become quite an excellent campaigner, able to set up in anything from a hovel to a tent, and capable of coaxing a meal from the most unlikely ingredients. In addition to always having a fire blazing and a hot drink ready when Papa returns from duty."

"Excellent...skills for a wife," Hampden observed, his lips curving in the slightest of smiles.

Edwina felt herself flushing, unsure whether or not he was mocking her. "That's enough about me," she said, determined to turn the subject. "I should like to know more about you, too, but we'll save that for later. What else would you have me speak about?"

"Nursed a friend. Had...high praise...for your stories."

"Stories about India?" she asked, wondering if his comrade had been one of the wounded whom she'd distracted from his pain by recounting tales of valor, wisdom and treachery from the epic poems that had captivated her as a child.

"Yes. India," her husband whispered.

Relieved to escape more personal matters, after coaxing Hampden to take another sip of water, Edwina sat back. A pang of sadness and something else shot through her as his fingers moved on the cot, seeking hers.

Laying her hand on top of his larger one, she took a deep breath and began, "Long ago there lived a handsome prince named Rama. Sent by his father the king to a neighboring land whose ruler sought a strong and valiant prince to marry his daughter, Rama entered the competition for the hand of the beautiful Princess Sita.

Of all the noblemen assembled, only Rama succeeded at every challenge the ruler set before them. Sita soon fell in love with the resourceful prince, and he with her. The young lovers were married with great pomp and ceremony.

After the couple returned to Rama's home, his father announced his intention to turn over the throne to Rama. But the king's second wife objected. Reminding the king that he had once promised to grant her any two wishes, she told him that her first was to have her son rule instead of Rama. Her second was that Rama be banished.

Loyal and honorable as well as brave, Rama accepted that his father must keep his word. He meant to leave his beloved wife behind in the comfort of his father's kingdom, but Sita insisted on accompanying him into the wildness of the forest. 'As shadow is to substance, so a wife is to her husband,' she said, pleading that he let her walk before him and smooth his path....''

As Edwina narrated her story, Lieutenant Lord Sanbrook nodded off and Wheaten began to snore softly. Gradually the tenseness in Hampden's body eased, until finally he fell into a light sleep, his breathing growing fainter and more shallow.

He is slipping away, she thought, tears stinging her eyes. But when she paused, intending to wipe them away, she felt an almost imperceptible tightening on her fingers.

Hampden's blue eyes struggled open. "Don't... stop," he said, his voice the merest breath.

Edwina swallowed past the constriction in her throat. "I won't," she promised.

And so, through the rest of the long night, Edwina continued relating the adventures of Prince Rama and his bride. By the time the darkness outside the tent began to lighten with the approach of dawn, her throat was as hoarse and aching as her heart and she no longer tried to restrain the tears dripping down her cheeks.

This time when she raised a hand to swipe at her eyes, however, she found Lord Sanbrook awake, watching her.

"You've done far more than anyone had a right to expect," he whispered. "Miles is unconscious now. Let Wheaten take you home. I'll stay with him until…the end."

Exhausted, drained—and angry at being forced once again to witness the cost of war, for which the politicians back in England had no appreciation—she nodded. Gently she slipped her fingers from the lax but still warm hand in which they had rested through the night.

"I'll call upon you later," Sanbrook said as she rose.

Edwina turned to walk away, then paused. Though the thought of making such a gesture under the eyes of his friends brought hot color to her cheeks, she nevertheless felt compelled to bend down and brush her lips against Hampden's forehead. "Farewell, husband," she whispered.

"Go get some rest, Lady Hampden," Sanbrook said.

How astonished Mama would be to hear her called that, the thought struck Edwina as she followed Wheaten out of the tent.

SHE WAS WALTZING in the arms of a strong young man—her bridegroom. Giddy with happiness, she turned to wave at Mama and Papa, who beamed their approval from the head table under the tent erected on the grounds of Papa's quarters in the Bombay cantonment. Men in red-coated dress uniforms glittering with medals swirled past her, women in a butterfly hue of gowns clasped in their arms.

Her new husband pulled her scandalously closer, molding her against his well-muscled length. Her breasts tingled, her belly and thighs flamed as the movements of the dance brushed her against her husband's legs and abdomen…against the hard bulge in his breeches.

Soon enough they would steal away, and with sighs and kisses she would be free to shed his garments and explore every inch of the body that tantalized her, as he explored every inch of hers.

Laughing with the sheer wonder of it, she glanced up. Somehow the tented cantonment had vanished, replaced by the glitter of a Lisbon ballroom. Instead of Daniel's grim visage staring down at her, finely molded lips smiled in a face whose heated, intense blue eyes promised their owner, too, was anticipating the delights of the bedchamber.

Miles Hampden's face.

Edwina woke with a start to find her skin flushed and her breathing rapid. So vivid was the dream, it took her a moment to separate illusion from reality.

How had her mind gotten so muddled? she wondered, trying to still her pounding heart. She'd noticed Lieutenant Hampden as he came and went about his duties, of course—what woman could not? But from where had such scandalous thoughts about him sprung?

Suddenly she remembered—the midnight tent in a red glow of blood and candlelight, the hastily performed ceremony. Miles Hampden was now her husband.

He'd done nothing more amorous after the ceremony than squeeze her fingers, Edwina reminded herself. Nor, she felt certain, would he have been inclined to proceed further even had he not been gravely wounded. There was absolutely no reason that the memory of his hand holding hers should make her fingers tremble and burn.

As for her dream, she should dismiss it. After all, in the way of dreams, everything else about the images had been distorted. Certainly Daniel had never looked at her with such desire in his eyes. Even as early in their marriage as the morning of the wedding breakfast, she'd had to feign the aura of happiness.

Better that she rise and dress, figure out something to tell Mama and then go tend her new husband.

If he still lived.

She'd just thrown on her clothes and run a brush

through her rioting brown curls when a loud pounding on the house's outer door brought her rushing into the main room.

Standing on the threshold, obviously trying to coax Mama's Portuguese maid into allowing him entry, was Lieutenant Lord Sanbrook.

A glance at his ashen, hollow-eyed face sent Edwina's stomach plunging and she brought one hand to her chest. "Is he—" she asked in a voice gone suddenly faint.

Lord Sanbrook's face broke into a grin. "No! He's much improved. Come, you must see!"

Wearing a frilly dressing gown with a matching lace mobcap over her blond curls, Edwina's mother emerged from her bedchamber. "What's all the fuss?" Mrs. Crofton demanded. "Who has improved?"

Before Edwina could decide how best to answer that question, Sanbrook said, "Your daughter's husband."

Chapter Four

WHILE ASTONISHMENT registered on her mama's face, Edwina flashed Sanbrook a warning look before turning to the maid. "Bring coffee, please, Juanita?"

The girl nodded, her dark eyes alight with curiosity. Edwina suppressed an inward groan. Juanita's command of English might be less than perfect, but unless Edwina was much mistaken, whispers of a midnight marriage would begin to circulate within the camp as soon as the maid left to draw water.

Shrugging off that concern, Edwina continued, "Won't you both sit? After I tell Mama what happened, Lord Sanbrook, I will be happy to accompany you."

As they sipped the scalding brew, Edwina sketched for her mother the events of the previous night. "If Lieutenant Hampden is, as I sincerely hope, on the way to recovery," she concluded, "all that transpired will soon be reversed, so I beg you will mention this to no one but Papa. Please, dear Mama?"

"Married!" her mama exclaimed, shaking her head. "Edwina, how could you—and in such a havey-cavey fashion! Oh, 'tis most upsetting!"

"Do not worry, Mrs. Crofton, everything was quite properly done," Lord Sanbrook assured her. "Regardless of what transpires next, your daughter and her good name will be fully protected."

"Married," Mrs. Crofton repeated. Suddenly her face broke into a smile of pure delight. "And to such an excellent young man!"

"Now Mama, 'twas not a true wedding," Edwina cautioned.

"Well, married is married, to my way of thinking," Mrs. Crofton muttered, a gleam in her eye.

Edwina sighed. "I shall try to do better at explaining it all later, Mama, but now I must see Lieutenant Hampden. Has Dr. MacAndrews returned?" she asked Lord Sanbrook as she rose and fetched her cloak.

"Yes, earlier this morning," Sanbrook replied. "He was able to locate the remaining fragments of the ball just beneath Hampden's shoulder blade, which means—praise God—the injury is less serious than we originally feared. He will require careful tending, but it appears Miles has an excellent chance of making a full recovery."

"That *is* wonderful news," Edwina replied, genuinely happy for the lieutenant. She would much rather their hasty marriage be quietly reversed by its participants than terminated by her unexpected husband's death.

"Shall we go, then, Lady Hampden?" Lord Sanbrook said. "Miles has been asking for you."

"Lady Hampden—ooh, I like the sound of that!" Mrs. Crofton said, smiling again.

"Don't accustom yourself to it, Mama, for 'tis only temporary," Edwina advised, throwing a repressive look at Juanita, who carefully avoided her gaze. Her clandestine marriage and, if God smiled on the lieutenant's recovery, its subsequent cancellation would set tongues wagging, but the embarrassment would hopefully be short-lived.

At least she would not have to conceal the truth of this marriage from her parents, as she'd had to hide the travesty of her first one.

With that encouraging thought, she took the arm Lord Sanbrook offered and walked out of the house.

AS SOON AS THEY EXITED, Edwina said to Lord Sanbrook, "I assure you, despite Mama's...*romantical* notions, I am fully prepared to abide by the conditions of the bargain we made last night. I'm sure Lieutenant Hampden will wish to go about dissolving the union as quickly as possible, and I shall do all in my power to assist him."

Sanbrook gave her an approving nod. "I would imagine he does intend to do so, once his recovery progresses, but he told me this morning that for the present, he wished you to be treated with every courtesy as his wife. He specifically instructed me to insure you were addressed by your proper title. So," he added with a grin, "if I may help you to mount, my lady?"

Surprised, Edwina raised her eyebrows, mild resentment flashing through her as she accepted his assistance. Of course, an aristocrat like Hampden would want to have even a temporary possession marked as his own. He'd doubtless never considered that it might be easier for her if everything about their brief marriage were handled as discreetly as possible. Even under the best of circumstances, she'd have a great deal of unpleasant gossip to face down once he was gone and she returned to her former name and position.

A moment later she chastised herself for a lack of charity. It was most unfair for her to convict the lieutenant, about whose character she knew so little, of blind self-absorption. The concern for the fate of his sister-in-law and her child that had driven Hampden to embrace so drastic a means to protect them certainly spoke well of him.

Of course, those kinswomen were of his own rank. In the unflinching light of day, would he be embarrassed by his hastily acquired bride?

A wave of remembered humiliation washed through her, shaking the calm she'd resolved to display and making her clench her teeth to keep back tears. By the time they reached the hospital tents, her empty stomach was queasy.

Well, she was no longer an infatuated maid with a head full of empty dreams and a heart to be broken, she told herself. If she dealt with Hampden in a sensible, matter-of-fact manner, surely any embarrassment either of them felt would be of short duration and they could go about disentangling their lives with the cool dispatch that would be best for them both.

After they dismounted, Lord Sanbrook put out a hand to stay her advance. "Miles said he would like to speak with you privately, if you would permit."

Edwina damped down another wave of uneasiness. "Since in his current condition, the viscount could hardly overcome me with the force of his ardor, I imagine I shall be safe enough alone with him," she replied, trying for a light tone.

"Then I will leave you to him," Sanbrook replied,

clearly relieved to have been given permission to withdraw.

For a few more moments she tarried, watching Lord Sanbrook stride away. *Time to begin bearing the weight of last night's hasty decision*, she told herself. Then, squaring her shoulders and taking a deep breath, Edwina opened the makeshift door to the hospital tent. As she caught sight of her husband, her mouth dried and the words of greeting shriveled on her lips.

The man on the cot this morning, his big-framed body alert rather than slack-limbed, his face smiling rather than creased in pain, appeared to be mastering his injuries rather than succumbing to them. His color only a bit pale, Lieutenant Hampden watched her as she approached, his lips curved in a smile whose potent charm hit her right in the belly while his avid, blue-eyed gaze captured hers. "My lady wife! Please, do come in."

He looked, she thought, swallowing hard, somehow much…larger than he'd appeared last night. Larger and far more virile and commanding than a man who'd taken a shot through the shoulder only last evening had any right to look. It seemed unbelievable that this imposing man with the compelling eyes could truly be her husband.

For an instant, a vision from the dream that had

awakened her—Hampden's arms around her, his torso rubbing hers—flashed through her mind, setting her body aflame in all the appropriate places. She felt heat flush her face. Heart pounding, she forced herself to advance. Perhaps she ought to consider marrying again, she thought as she struggled to recapture her calm, if she were going to be prey to such lustful urges.

But not to a man as well-born and attractive as Viscount Hampden.

One such disaster of a marriage had been quite enough.

SO THIS WAS THE LADY he'd married, Miles thought. Of course, he'd known by reputation the woman Sanbrook had suggested to him as a bride, but his personal acquaintance with her had been slight.

Miles studied the tall, slender form and graceful carriage of the young woman walking toward him, taking in the pale oval face around which light brown curls peeped from beneath her bonnet. Her eyes met his appraising gaze squarely, he noted with approval, only a slight flush on her cheeks testifying to whatever chagrin or discomfort she might be feeling.

Those eyes—ah, yes, he remembered her eyes from the first time he'd met her in her father's camp. Her cheeks flushing then as they were now, she'd raised them to him shyly as she'd murmured a greeting. Large, lustrous eyes of a hue between green and blue that reminded him of the sparkling, aquamarine ocean off the Portuguese coast.

They were as mesmerizing as the husky, warm-as-melted-chocolate voice that had flowed over his agonized body through the night and brought him ease. Indeed, he was more than half-convinced that, worn down by pain, exhaustion and worry, he might have yielded his spirit to those demons of the night, had that beguiling voice not kept him tethered to earth.

To his surprise, she curtseyed before taking the stool beside his cot. "Good morning, my lord. I'm delighted to see you looking so much better."

So, she wished to be formal? Since he wasn't sure yet how to proceed, perhaps that was best.

"Thank you, Lady Hampden. I'm equally delighted to be feeling better. Though, given the extraordinary favor you have done me, might you consider calling me Miles?"

She smiled slightly. "I appreciate the honor, but since, the Lord be praised, it appears that last night's—arrangements—are no longer necessary, I would be more comfortable if we address each other as the mere acquaintances we shall shortly once again become. Indeed, if you wish, I am quite amenable to pretending the whole, ah, business never transpired."

A bit disconcerted by her seeming urgency to be quit of him, Miles shook his head. "I'm afraid it will not be so easy. At this distant remove from England, I expect we could probably get by with simply tearing up the wedding contract, but vows uttered before a minister of God, whatever the setting, are rather more binding."

Her green eyes blinked before she lowered her face. Butterfly wings, Miles thought, distracted by the play of the long lashes against her fair skin.

"I see," his wife said in small voice. "So we shall have to apply for an annulment through the church?"

"I'm not sure. Under normal circumstances, an annulment would be almost impossible to obtain. But," he added hastily when she looked back up at him, those lustrous eyes wide with alarm, "the circumstances being far from normal, I had hoped Chaplain Darrow might be persuaded to...disallow the proceedings. When I asked him about it this morning, though sympathizing with our situation, he informed me he did not feel he had the authority to do so and recommended that we consult the bishop's representative in Lisbon. I have every intention of fulfilling the hope that my wound will heal and the soil of Portugal will not, after all, be my final resting place, but until I am completely certain of that outcome, I would like to leave in place the legal protections for my family we were at such pains to construct. You understand my caution?"

She'd lowered her head again, her small even teeth worrying her lip—a rather lush lip, he noted with masculine appreciation. "How, then, do you wish to proceed?"

"I had intended to keep our compact secret—until the men in my company somehow learned about last night's wedding and came by this morning to either toast my survival or console my widow. I must beg your forgiveness for proceeding without first asking your approval, but I decided at that moment to confirm the news. I wish to show everyone I expect you to be treated with the same deference as if the wedding had taken place in your family's private chapel or at St. George's instead of in a tent."

"So there can be no slurs or innuendo attached to my name," she said after a moment. Again color came and went in her cheeks. "That was kind of you, my lord."

Pleased at her understanding of his motives, he gave her his most charming smile. "You do not think you could try *Miles?*"

She shook her head firmly. "*Lieutenant*, or *Hampden*, if you prefer, is more proper."

"I suppose for the present I must settle for *Hampden*. Until we sort this out, it might be more comfortable for you to avoid the curious or impertinent by spending much of your time here, as a new wife would be expected to tend her wounded husband. While I regain my strength and we become better acquainted, we can consider how best to resolve this matter."

"There is only one resolution that was ever contemplated if you survived, my lord—a complete dissolution of the agreement. Surely you can understand *my* concern about that."

Once again, Miles felt stung. Then, his usual good humor reasserting itself, he said wryly, "And here I was, considering that since I'm already a rather fine fellow, becoming a titled nobleman of means would render me an irresistible matrimonial prize! But now that the news has gotten out, you must realize the considerable harm your reputation might suffer if we disavow the proceedings. I'm not in habit of marrying ladies and then abandoning them."

She met his gaze steadily. "I didn't mean to be disparaging. But 'tis nonsense to consider yourself in any way beholden to me, nor am I in need of assistance. Since I intend to remain here with the army, where I am well-known and where the circumstances that prompted our bargain would be well-appreciated, I doubt my reputation will suffer. I thought I made it quite clear to Lord Sanbrook last night that I would not..." Her flush deepened and she looked away, avoiding his glance. "That is to say," she continued, "there is no question of any, ah, reimbursement, other than your thanks for my assisting you through a time of great anxiety."

"You certainly did that. Even more, you kept me alive when Wilson had all but despaired of my survival."

"Well, he may have been worried last night, but from what I understand Dr. MacAndrews discovered this morning, it appears you were never in peril of succumbing."

"We needn't dispute that now. May I ask you for one more favor—to tend me until I am well enough to proceed to Lisbon? Your excellent nursing shall ensure that I do recover, and we will have time to discuss ending our bargain in the manner you desire."

Again she hesitated. Miles found himself more strongly driven to obtain her agreement than he could have imagined. "I promise not to be too much of a burden," he coaxed. "And besides, I want more of your story."

Mercifully, that brought a smile to her face. "I can't believe you remember any of it."

"Of course I do! 'Twas a fascinating tale, about a valiant prince and his faithful bride and a banishment. You must tell me the rest."

She shook her head. "I can't imagine you are truly interested."

"But I am. The heroic scale of the saga you re-counted reminded me of the Greek epics I studied at Oxford."

Looking pleased, she nodded. "The Rama stories are nearly as old. My ayah made each tale so won-derfully vivid, she kindled in me a love of literature I still possess. Being a rather shy child, I naturally grav-itated to reading."

"Your brothers or sisters did not bedevil you into more active pursuits?"

"No. 'Tis a harsh climate, as you may know, and Mama's other three children died as babes. Growing up mostly alone, encouraged later by a governess who also loved the classics, I became what the ton would call a veritable bluestocking."

"What better occupation for a bluestocking than to use her erudition to entertain her recuperating husband?"

He was treated to a pointed glance from those sea-green eyes. "Her *temporary* husband."

Miles grinned. "We shall see. I have no intention of making you a widow just yet."

Those exquisite eyes flared wider. "'Twas not what I—oh, you're funning with me!"

He was still smiling at her indignation when Dr. MacAndrews walked in.

"Lieutenant, I'm pleased to find you well enough

to converse. And 'tis good you are here, Mrs. Denby. You can assist in my examination."

"Lady Hampden," Miles corrected gently.

Looking at him in surprise, the doctor opened his lips as if to make some light retort. At the hard gaze Miles fixed on him, he seemed to think better of it.

"Excuse me, I meant no offense. It is just that I've worked so long with Edwina—Lady Hampden, and with the circumstances so…odd, 'tis difficult for me to think of her as your… Well, no matter." Turning to Edwina, the doctor said, "Might I ask your aide, ma'am?"

By the time the surgeon had done probing, Miles was more than ready to accept his wife's help in sagging back against his cushions.

"Both wounds look good," the doctor said as he tightened the last bandage, "and I'm reasonably sure I got all the pieces of the ball that struck you. We'll know by day's end, for if I missed any, your fever will spike. You're bound to have some fever in any event. I understand you and your—" he raised his eyebrows and sent a faintly reproachful glance at Edwina "—wife hope to depart for Lisbon soon, but you'd best count on remaining here most of a week, to be sure that chest means to heal properly."

His head still woozy, Miles made no protest. "I…I am not as keen on departing as I thought I was."

"Are you feeling ill?" Edwina asked, touching her hand to his forehead, concern in her voice. "Let me fetch you some water."

Despite the nausea clamoring for his attention, before she turned to go, Miles caught her hand and brought it to his lips. "That would be most kind," he murmured.

After he released her, Edwina stood for a moment simply staring at her hand before turning on her heel to follow the doctor out of the tent.

With a sigh, Miles closed his eyes, which made the tent stop spinning and helped quell his queasiness. He'd done a good morning's work for a man who'd nearly stuck his spoon in the wall last night, he thought.

He'd convinced his reluctant bride to agree to nurse him. He felt deeply responsible for having led her into a dilemma of his making, and he wanted to be sure they had sufficient time to find a satisfactory way out.

He'd not been speaking lightly when he said he didn't marry a lady only to later abandon her. In full possession of his faculties, he'd made a vow before God, and though he may have thought when he'd pledged his troth that the span of time until death would part them would be measured in hours, still he had made a sacred promise.

His new wife was doubtless only being sensible in resisting the idea of remaining tied any longer than necessary to a man she hardly knew. Wounding as it was to his self-esteem, he was impressed by her independence and lack of concern for worldly consequence, for she surely realized that becoming a viscountess would mean a far easier, more privileged life than the one she now led.

Besides, assuming he survived, last evening's events only underlined the imperative that he marry and beget an heir. Since he'd already managed to acquire a wife, it might be wise to ascertain if they suited well enough for him to try to persuade her into making their temporary alliance permanent.

So HER HUSBAND was not as recovered as he'd first appeared, Edwina thought as she carried out the water bucket. He must convey that impression of strength through sheer force of personality, since it seemed he was capable of convincing one to do almost anything, whether it be persuading the doctor to let him ride off soon to Lisbon, or talking her into continuing to nurse him. Especially since, given the intensity of the reaction he evoked in her, remaining near him was probably a bad idea.

It wasn't just his physical attractiveness—although that was far too compelling. As a soldier's daughter, she had a natural admiration for an officer whose troopers considered him courageous and resourceful, for who knew better the character of their commander than the men he'd led under fire? In the short time she'd been connected with him, he'd shown himself a caring individual, too. Already he'd disarmed her resentment over his publicizing the wedding by explaining he wished to protect her from gossip.

She shook her head ruefully. 'Twas hard to be offended by such consideration. And this morning, rather than simply making conversation to smooth over the awkwardness of their situation, he'd seemed genuinely interested in her upbringing in India and the colorful stories that one of the regimental surgeons, chancing to overhear her relating them to some of the wounded, had pronounced "heathenish nonsense."

Edwina smiled. In the eyes of his society, she offered him nothing as a wife, but at least she did have an endless supply of legends with which to divert him. The smile faded as she considered how alarmingly engaging Lord Hampden was turning out to be. Given the fact that dissolving their marriage was going to take longer than she'd expected, she'd best take care, lest when he departed for England, she was left with something more painful than idle gossip to overcome.

Chapter Five

SEVERAL DAYS LATER, Miles awakened from a nap to find his wife gone and Allen Sanbrook sitting by his bed.

"How about some ale?" Sanbrook asked. "Nothing like a bit of home-brewed to speed you back to health."

Miles accepted a mug and took a long sip. "Ah, now that's the taste of England!"

"Indeed." Sanbrook downed a swallow of his own. "Have you consulted Sergeant Riggins yet? With you making such a fine recovery, I imagine you shall be released to travel soon, and you'll want to have made progress on unsnarling your legal tangles." He took another sip and sighed. "Probably have to wait until you reach Lisbon to sort out the religious ones."

"I don't plan to begin undoing anything just yet."

"Why not? Surely there's no longer any doubt that

you'll survive your injuries. And it will be better for the lady to undo the business quickly. I know you've tried to protect her, but the longer the marriage lasts before its dissolution, the more awkward her position is likely to be afterward. And she does mean to remain here. When I spoke with her yesterday, hinting that she might wish to accept a settlement and return to England, she froze me completely."

Miles chuckled. "That I can believe."

Sanbrook shook his head and laughed. "You'd think I'd accused her of entering into this arrangement with the intentions of a grave-robber! She frostily informed me that the matter of remuneration had been settled the night of your injury and she would thank me never to mention it again. Delivered the whole speech in such a top-lofty manner, she put me in mind of your grandmother. Now there was a tartar! But as I said, if she's determined to stay with the army, it's bound to be damned awkward when you leave here without her."

Miles put down his mug. "At the moment, I have no intention of leaving here without her."

Sanbrook's eyes widened in surprise. "You can't intend…that is, I don't mean to disparage Mrs. Denby, but—"

"Lady Hampden, if you please," Miles interrupted, his tone mild but his voice holding an edge of warning.

Sanbrook colored. "Um, yes, Lady Hampden. Ah, I see! You will have her accompany you to Lisbon to make working out the details of the annulment easier. Probably wise."

"You mistake me, Allen. I'm not at all sure I wish to proceed with an annulment."

"Not proceed?" Sanbrook echoed, frowning. "I know you appreciate her coming to your aid, Miles, but that's carrying gratitude a bit far, don't you think? Her father is naught but the younger son of some obscure baron and I understand her late husband's family doesn't even recognize her. She's a fine, courageous lady, I'll grant you, but she could never be considered a suitable wife for a viscount. Only think what your grandmother would say were you to bring home such a bride for Christmas!"

Miles smiled. "I expect she'd say I should do what I like, and the rest of the family be damned. It is *my* wife we are discussing, not some theoretical lineage out of Debrett's. And if I am to see the same woman over the breakfast table for the rest of my days, I should prefer her to be one I like and respect. Besides, recognized by the Alveneys or not, she's said to a nabob's granddaughter. Nose it about that she has inherited great wealth, and all but the highest of sticklers will accept her."

Sanbrook angled his head, considering, then nodded. "Since there's no taint of the shop about her, that might answer. Luckily for you, the Hampden estate is well-breeched enough that you have no need of her supposed fortune to buttress such a claim."

"Neither encroaching nor a shopkeeper, but a wonderful cook," Miles added, a grin breaking out as he lifted the cover from an iron pot on the table beside them, releasing a mouth-watering aroma. "Only see what an excellent stew she brought me. Savory chicken and vegetables, here on the siege lines outside Lisbon in November! The best my batman has been able to manage of late is a few dried carrots. She told me she was a good campaigner, but I swear, the woman's a wizard."

"I hardly think ferreting out chickens in a war-ravaged countryside is a skill your family will appreciate."

Miles's smile faded. "If they don't, they should. Come now, Allen, you know I wasn't bred to be viscount, nor do I have any inclination to spend my life in London, like some of the macaroni merchants we saw when we came up from Oxford. Indeed, her complete absorption with the trivia of the ton was what convinced me I wasn't in love with the blond chit I met that Season."

"The Magnificent Millicent," Sanbrook said drily. "Still the most exquisite creature I've ever beheld."

Miles shrugged. "I'll wager she couldn't wring a chicken's neck and make her recuperating husband the best stew he'd ever tasted."

Sanbrook broke into a reluctant laugh. "No, I'm quite certain she could not. But once you get back to Hampden Glen, you'll have servants aplenty to cook and forage. Your wife will be expected to occupy herself with very different duties—duties the new Lady Hampden may be ill-prepared to handle."

"I sincerely doubt there's anything she couldn't handle. What's more, I *like* her, Allen. She's the quickest study I've met in a female, understanding my meaning without my having to explain every point. Far from turning missish when her good deed devolved into this cursed coil, she's remained calm and reasonable. And in her own way, she's quite attractive, though she never resorts to feminine wiles to try to win her point. I think we could deal as well together as any couple who've made a marriage of convenience, and better than most."

"You *think*," Sanbrook echoed. "But you're not sure yet what you mean to do. Remember, then, that you'll shortly be back in London, where you'll have a wealth of more suitable women eager for your attentions. Since the lady in question has indicated from the outset that she is perfectly willing to release you, 'tis not a matter of honor to uphold the agreement.

Please, Miles, consider carefully before you make irrevocable an arrangement you may later come to regret."

"Since I know you speak out of genuine concern, I'll take no offense at the advice," Miles replied tightly, surprised by the depth of the anger evoked by his friend's disparagement of Edwina Denby. "But I'm becoming surer by the day that the current arrangement will suit me best. I'm less sure whether she'll agree to keep me."

Sanbrook looked at Miles incredulously, then burst out laughing. "Not keep you? A piece of that ball must have lodged in your brain!" He picked up his mug and stood. "I've got watch, so I must go. Enjoy the ale—and your exemplary stew."

Miles stared thoughtfully at his friend's retreating back. He was reasonably certain that if he did decide he wanted Edwina Denby to remain his wife, persuading her to agree was going to be a challenge.

After nodding to Lieutenant Lord Sanbrook, who bowed as she passed him in the brilliant winter sunlight, Edwina entered the dim hospital tent. As her eyes adjusted, she found her temporary husband lounging on his cot.

"Ah, my lady wife! Let me tell you again how excellent a stew you made," he said as he waved her to a seat. "My batman practically wept with jealousy."

Edwina felt herself flush with pleasure at Hampden's praise. "I'm glad you enjoyed it."

"I did indeed. But now that I've stuffed myself, how about another story?"

"You would not rather have a game of chess? Papa said you may keep the board as long as you like."

Hampden shook his head and gave her that warmly intimate smile that always seemed to make her stomach flutter—fool that she was. "No, I'm feeling so lazy after that excellent meal, you'd trounce me for sure. The humiliation of being beaten twice in a row might severely set back my recovery."

Edwina chuckled. "Considering by how narrow a margin I won, I imagine there's little chance of you suffering so horrid a fate. But if you prefer, of course I shall give you a story. Where did I leave off?"

"Prince Rama had been exiled to the forest, where his wife Sita insisted on accompanying him," Miles replied.

"Ah, yes. One day Prince Rama went off to hunt, but first warning Sita to stay inside a protective circle he'd constructed for her. But an evil ogre, ruler of a neighboring land, saw her all alone and was overcome by her beauty. The ogre, who could quite conveniently change his shape, turned himself into a beggar seeking alms. Sita, moved by pity for his plight, was tricked into leaving the circle to assist him, upon which the ogre prince captured her and carried her away."

"Sometimes performing a selfless deed can have unforeseen and life-changing consequences," Hampden said.

Edwina opened her lips to agree, but something focused and fervent in his gaze stopped the breath in her throat. She knew the moment he said it that his comment concerned far more than her story, but was he referring to the sense of honor he felt made it imperative that he not abandon his chance-given wife? Or that the circumstances which brought two improbably matched individuals together had sparked something that was changing how he looked at the situation—and her?

As it was changing the way she felt about him.

She moistened her lips, held captive by the intensity in his eyes, not sure whether to ask him what he meant or to once again ignore his remarks and proceed with the story. Before she could decide, he smiled, easing the tension, and said, "Please, continue."

"N-naturally," she began, her pulse still hammering hard enough to make her stumble a bit over the words, "Concerned when he returned to find his wife gone, Prince Rama became distraught. He could discover neither any trace of her nor find anyone who knew what had befallen her."

"Having one's wife disappear would be most up-setting."

Hampden inclined toward her as he spoke, his voice nearly a whisper, the blue of his eyes deepening with a heat she recognized but could hardly believe she was seeing—in *his* eyes as he looked at *her.*

Her whole body went tense, flooded with a sweet urgency that compelled her to lean toward him even as he leaned toward her. His lips hovered at her cheek, the soft exhale of his breath carrying the scents of ale and spices. Her lips tingled, burned as she angled her mouth up to his.

"Good, you're here, Lady Hampden," the surgeon's voice announced from the doorway, severing the peculiar force that held her spellbound. Feeling color flood her face, Edwina jerked away as the doctor advanced toward them. "You can assist while I examine his wound."

Thank heaven the doctor had interrupted! she thought. The situation—and her emotions—were tangled enough without further complicating them by allowing her attraction to Hampden to have free rein. She'd best keep such urges in check, lest she give the strong-principled viscount greater cause to feel honor-bound not to release her.

Still, she thought wistfully as she helped Mac-Andrews rebandage the wound he'd pronounced as healing nicely, Hampden had meant to kiss her, she was nearly certain. Much as she deplored the feeling, she could not suppress the warm glow that suffused her at discovering the attraction she felt for him was apparently reciprocated.

Too unsettled by the experience to wish to remain alone with him, she said, "Since your visits always tire the lieutenant, doctor, I shall leave him to rest."

The doctor chuckled. "I seem to have that effect on many of my patients. Rest is a good prescription if you've a mind to be on your way to Lisbon shortly. Which, I believe, you may safely be in a day or so."

Edwina followed in McAndrew's wake. "Can I assist you with any other patients, Doctor? I'm afraid I've not been much use to you of late."

MacAndrews shook his head. "I've had only the odd accident to tend. With winter coming on and the enemy departing, there are few wounded, thank the Lord."

"Lady Hampden," her husband called as she reached the doorway. As she glanced back, he gave her a reproachful look, as if fully aware of the reason behind her hasty retreat. "I'll rest now as you suggest, but please come back soon. If the doctor means to give me permission to travel in just a few days, we have much to discuss."

"I'll return in an hour," she promised, finding it hard to meet his gaze. With a quick smile, she escaped.

At least she'd have a short reprieve in which to regain her composure. If she took up her story immediately upon her return, maybe she could stave off the polite argument about their future she sensed was coming.

She'd been surprised at first to find he truly enjoyed her stories. But, it seemed their minds often ran along parallel paths, just as his dry, understated humor frequently amused her.

Perhaps that was one of the reasons she found herself liking him so much. The deep-seated sense of responsibility that made him beloved of his men spilled over into the rest of his life, whether it be expressed in his feelings of obligation to her, for the welfare of the estate he'd unexpectedly inherited or for his dead brother's dependent family.

While that intense blue-eyed stare affected her in quite another manner. Just recalling it triggered an ache deep within her body that had no prospect of being eased.

She put a hand over the quivering warmth in her belly. Oh, this was bad.

She'd made a special effort to find that chicken and prepare him that stew. She'd wanted him to enjoy it. Worse, she'd wanted to impress him with her resourcefulness, and had derived far too much pleasure from his praise.

There was no point trying to make him think well of her. They were different sorts, and the sort she was did not belong in the world to which he was returning.

Even if, duty-bound, he felt obligated to take her with him, even if he held her in some affection, that would not stop the snide whispers and sidelong glances from his peers, who would look down on so woefully underbred a wife. The affection he felt for her would not change the fact that remaining his wife would mean a permanent exile from her loving, but socially inferior family.

Worse yet, she must face the unwelcome truth that she was already halfway to falling in love with him.

When Daniel had blazed into her life with his fair-haired brilliance and easy charm, she'd thought him a prince as perfect as the one in her nurse's stories. Not until too late had she learned he was but the pasteboard image of royalty, no more substantial than the face cards in a game of whist.

Miles Hampden, however, was showing himself to be the genuine article.

The longer she knew him, the more she admired him. After they'd been apart, she couldn't stop the little jump in her pulse when she walked into the hospital tent and saw him again.

Lest she indulge the increasingly appealing temptation of encouraging him to honor the vows they'd sworn, she'd better recognize the danger her deepening emotions for him would mean, should their temporary marriage of convenience be made permanent.

Quite simply, living with his polite affection could devastate her more thoroughly than the most cold and haughty indifference Daniel had shown her. For Daniel, after a searing view of his true character brought her infatuation to a sudden end, had never truly touched her heart.

The heart that, she realized with a hollow feeling in the pit of her stomach, Miles Hampden had already come dangerously close to capturing.

Chapter Six

As Edwina came into the common room of their billet after a nap, her mother looked up from her needlework. "I'm glad you rested, my dear. How is your husband?"

"Sleeping, at the moment. He must gather his strength, since Dr. MacAndrews said this morning that Hampden may soon be well enough to leave for Lisbon."

"Excellent! You will accompany him, of course."

The pang she felt at refuting that assumption was far stronger than she'd like. "No, Mama, I don't expect so. You know we plan to seek an annulment. I can sign whatever documents are needed here before he leaves. It is better to begin going our separate ways sooner rather than later."

"Why should you separate?" her mother countered. "Only consider, my dear! Hampden is handsome, titled, wealthy, congenial—at your age and in this place, you can hardly expect to encounter a more attractive prospective husband! He married you of his own free will, and I think you should hold him to it."

"Certainly not, Mama! Our agreement was meant to protect his family under very specific circumstances. Should I insist on his honoring the bargain after those circumstances have changed, I am certain he would do so, but he would have to despise me for cheating him of the opportunities a man of his rank should have to choose a more suitable bride. Indeed, I should despise myself should I play him so low a trick."

Her mother raised her eyebrows. "So you say, but I think you have both gone beyond the bargain you made that night. Oh, I know he isn't your beloved Daniel, but I don't believe you would have consented to wed Hampden in the first place if you hadn't, whether you realized it or not, harbored some warm feelings for him. My dear, 'tis time to let go the past and look to your future! Besides, it seemed to me when I spoke with him that he was nearly convinced to let the marriage stand."

"You've spoken to him?" Edwina replied, torn between resentment and alarm. "About me and our—situation? When? What did you say?"

"I've visited him several times while you were resting," her mother replied. "What could be more natural than my looking in on my daughter's new husband? I know your feelings for Daniel may have blinded you to other men's attractions, but truth be told, I find Lord Hampden to be the more engaging. Not that Daniel wasn't handsome and his manners very correct. But your Lieutenant Hampden is much more approachable."

Searching for some appropriate response while she frantically tried to construct a plausible but unrevealing argument, she replied, "He isn't *my* lieutenant, Mama. He never was."

That much was true enough, she thought with a pang.

"I believe he could be, if you'd make but a push to secure his affections," her mother replied. "If you could only hear with what warmth and admiration he speaks of you! And he's been so flatteringly anxious to hear every detail I could relate about your life."

Color rose to her face as Edwina envisioned half a dozen potentially embarrassing scenarios her mother might have revealed. "Oh, Mama, how could you?"

"I told him nothing but the truth," her mother protested. "What a dear child you were, and so brave, like the time you saved your ayah from that snake by bashing it with a club. How kind and sweet you've always been to your mother, who isn't nearly as clever as her daughter and whom you must often find very silly. How deeply you loved your first husband, how long you've grieved over him, and how grateful I am to Lord Hampden for awakening you to a future when I had began to despair of your ever moving beyond the past. You do care for Hampden, don't you, my dearest?"

Her mama had always been able to sense how Edwina thought and felt—which was why Edwina had been forced to distance herself from her parents during her troubled marriage. To admit that her strong feelings for Hampden were the primary reason for insisting this marriage be dissolved might raise uncomfortable questions about how, given her supposedly unshakable devotion to Daniel's memory, she could have suddenly have developed such a deep affection for her new husband.

Facing Hampden now seemed preferable to continuing this discussion with her far-too-perceptive mother.

"I do care for him, Mama," Edwina admitted at last. "I'm sure we'll work matters out to a mutually satisfactory conclusion. But now I should get back to him."

The knowing look in her mama's eye as she made a hasty exit left her feeling distinctly uneasy.

THANKING HEAVEN Hampden didn't know her as well as Mama did, Edwina walked toward the hospital tent. Even if he insisted on talking about their future, she should be able to return the appropriate answers without his suspecting her growing attachment to him.

She halted on the threshold in surprise, however, as she found her husband out of bed, pacing about the tent.

"Are you sure you should be up walking?" she asked.

He gave her the special smile that sent her pulse racing, even as she damned herself for the reaction. "I hope that means you're worried about me, my lady wife. But I need to build my stamina, if we are to ride to Lisbon shortly. I must say, it feels good to be upright again."

Still smiling, he came over and kissed her hand. Feeling her face flush, she tried not to snatch it back. Of course, he couldn't feel the jolt that raced through her at his touch, nor could he know the deplorable rush of joy she derived from that simple, courtly gesture. As if she truly were his lady, and he found pleasure in seeing her.

Edwina, who was usually of a height with the men she encountered, was equally unsettled by having Hampden tower over her. 'Twas absurd to let his superior size make her feel somehow feminine, delicate—

and tempted to surrender herself into his care like some spineless heroine out of a Minerva Press novel.

Keep your dealings straightforward and unemotional, she told herself. "Won't you sit?" she asked, anxious to restore the equilibrium between them. "You don't want to chance setting back your recovery. Then I'll continue my story, as you requested."

"Perhaps you are right," he agreed, obediently returning to his cot. "Though I'm anxious to hear what happens next, first I'd rather we talk about *our* story."

Avoiding that too-mesmerizing gaze, she said, "Yes, we should finalize matters. I'm prepared to sign whatever papers you need to begin the annulment process."

For a moment he hesitated, and she thought with a flare of mingled alarm and gratification that he meant to ask again whether she still felt an annulment was necessary. "I suppose you could dictate a statement here, with the chaplain as a witness," he said at last. "But I'd feel more confident of the matter being successfully resolved if you would accompany me to Lisbon. Indeed, the bishop's representative may insist upon speaking with you."

'Twas ridiculous to feel let down. Had she truly expected he would now beg her to continue so unequal a union, simply because she made a superior stew and could match him at chess?

"I expect that would be prudent," she said, relieved that her voice betrayed none of the agitation she felt.

"Good, that's settled. If you would feel more comfortable, I would be happy to have Mrs. Crofton accompany us. With Christmas approaching, she might enjoy some shopping in Lisbon."

The last thing Edwina wanted, on what would doubtless be a heart-wrenching journey, was her perceptive mother close at hand. "I'm sure Mama would be reluctant to leave Papa. I can bring her maid, Juanita, as a chaperone."

"As you wish," he replied. "If you could both be ready to travel in two days, I believe MacAndrews can be persuaded to release me. Now, I should like that story."

He certainly was clever, Edwina thought resentfully as she seated herself. Within a few sentences, he'd surprised her into agreeing to accompany him to Lisbon when every sense warned that bidding farewell to him here, where she had work to throw herself into to ease the pain of parting, would be far preferable. "Where did I stop?"

"The prince's wife, Sita, had been abducted by the evil ogre who ruled the neighboring kingdom."

"Ah, yes," she said, ready to escape from the muddle of her life into the safe realm of fantasy. "The ogre prince tried alternately to woo and threaten Sita into yielding to him, but she refused to think of anyone but her beloved Rama."

Smiling faintly, Miles watched his wife's expression as she wove her story. Strange that when he'd first met her, though he'd admired her fine eyes, he'd thought her otherwise rather plain. Probably because she'd been so shy, her voice low and her eyes downcast. But now, with her face animated, her hands gesturing and the sultry richness of her voice flowing over him, he found her as enchanting as the Indian princess in her story.

Every day spent in her company made him surer that continuing this marriage would be the best solution for them both. Given what he knew of London society, he figured his chances of meeting a lady who would make him a more congenial life's partner than Edwina Denby were slim. In turn, he could offer her respect, friendship, material comfort and a life of purpose overseeing the welfare of his numerous properties and tenants.

Still, when she'd given him a perfect opportunity to declare himself, he'd been unable to take it. Though he sensed in her a growing affection for him, he'd been afraid to ask her to continue their relationship and risk a flat-out refusal. Better instead, he reasoned, to lure her to Lisbon on the pretext of consulting the experts and give himself more time to beguile Edwina into agreeing to make their temporary marriage permanent.

Unease stirred as he recalled her mother describing her continuing grief over her lost husband. An irrational and surprisingly intense spurt of jealousy followed. She was *his* wife now and he wished her to remain so. As his body recovered, so too strengthened the desire to make her his in every way. If he could lure her into his bed and please her there, he could put a stop to this talk of annulment and perhaps loosen the hold her late husband still exerted over her.

Making love to her should also rid her of the notion that he wished to continue their marriage merely out of duty. He certainly hoped so, for sometime over the last few days he'd gone irretrievably beyond that point. He now found himself very fond of his chance-given bride and determined to build a future together.

The sensual possibilities shimmered in his mind. Grinning, he told himself he'd best make sure he was recovered enough by the time they reached Lisbon to seduce her into sharing his vision.

Chapter Seven

THREE EVENINGS LATER, Edwina lounged in the sitting room of the suite her husband had engaged upon their arrival in Lisbon. She was hard put not to pace the room while she awaited Miles's return from the British embassy.

At least, to her relief, their journey did not seem to have set back Hampden's recovery. Though to her discerning eye, he'd been fatigued by the time they arrived, he'd still managed to present quite the commanding figure of the wealthy viscount, awing the staff of the hotel he selected into a flurry of obsequious bowing.

Judging by the sumptuous nature of the rooms they occupied and the lavish meals brought them, Hampden must be dropping quite a lot of blunt. She glanced toward the door, thinking ruefully that the servants hovering outside would treat her quite differently, did they know how soon "Lady Hampden" would become once again plain Mrs. Denby.

By now she just wished to have it done with. It had become increasingly difficult to maintain a calm and disinterested facade when spending so much time in Hampden's constant and engaging company, especially with the landlord and all the world treating her as his wife.

Last night, thinking it best to bring to an end the sort of enchanted intimacy they'd shared while she spun her stories, she declined when he asked that she embellish the shortened version she'd given him of the Ramayana saga. She'd asked instead that, now that he could speak at length without distress, he tell her about his home in England.

She'd hoped an echo of the themes of lineage and duty upon which Daniel had condescendingly pontificated would help distance him. Unfortunately, Hampden had shown he, too, was a gifted storyteller, making her laugh with tales of his exploits as a boy and painting so vivid a picture of Hampden Glen, his friends and family, that she could nearly imagine herself there. Rather than being put off, she found herself filled with a wistful longing to meet his gentle sister-in-law and the niece upon whom he doted. To see the rolling hills and green groves of his home, so different from the India in which she'd grown up.

Perhaps after he returned home, she could write to him, inquire about his own and his family's well-being. They had grown to be friends over these past few days; surely he would agree to them remaining so.

It required little further reflection for her to realize the impossible nature of her wish. His first duty, surely, would be to find a wife, and it would be no more easy for her to envision him with another woman in his arms than it would for that lucky lady to tolerate her new bridegroom's correspondence with a former, if temporary, wife.

No, she could play no further part in his life once he returned to Hampden Glen, even from a distance.

The one topic they'd carefully avoided during dinner last evening was the subject of the annulment.

After visiting the bankers this morning and sending her off to shop, Hampden had gone to his appointment at the embassy. And so she waited with fraying patience to discover what he'd found out about the process of bringing to an end, once and for all, the bargain between them.

Resolutely she swallowed the lump of sadness rising in her throat. Truly, the break could not come soon enough. Each day, as Hampden recovered more of his health and strength, he drew her further into the cocoon of his protective care. Having been forced after her marriage to Daniel to rely completely upon herself, it was far too sweet a luxury to have someone else with whom to share managing all myriad small details of daily life.

More insidious still were the increasing small courtesies he extended her—handing her out of carriage, gripping her elbow as they went up or down the stairs, kissing her fingers when he left her or returned—affectionate touches she ached to reciprocate. She shivered as she recalled how, last evening as he bid her good-night at the door to her chamber, rather than simply kiss her fingertips, he'd drawn her close and rested his lips against her forehead.

Desire had ignited within her at his nearness, heating her belly, making the tips of her breasts tingle, and requiring her to dig her nails into her palms to keep from raising her head so her lips could meet his.

Heat flamed anew in her body, just remembering it. Please, Lord, she prayed, let him bring back papers for her to sign tonight. Let her begin her sad and solitary return to the encampment tomorrow, that she might escape the temptation of his closeness before the ever-strengthening urge to caress him led her to do something that would make him feel honor-bound to make their union permanent.

'Twas pain enough that when he left, he'd take her heart with him.

So on edge were her nerves, she jumped when the door finally opened and her husband walked in. Guiltily, greedily, she offered him her hand, then closed her eyes to savor each touch as he brushed his lips across the knuckles. Her heart rate sped and she drew in an involuntary breath when, instead of releasing her hand, he turned it over and nuzzled her palm.

When he finally let go, she was so giddy she caught only one word in three of the apology for his tardy return.

"I hope you had a…useful meeting," she managed. *Pull yourself together, Edwina.*

"I've asked Manuelo to serve dinner in half an hour, if that is agreeable? We can have a glass of wine first."

A servant knocked even as he finished speaking. The several minutes required for the wine to be poured allowed her to settle her nerves before the footman withdrew, leaving them once again alone.

"Did you have a pleasant afternoon?" Hampden asked. "I'd half expected you to be sporting a new gown, though you look very charming in that one. Did you find what you required in the shops?"

"Yes, the linens here are very fine. I obtained some handkerchiefs for Papa, lacework for Mama and the toy you asked me to purchase for your niece's Christmas gift. I hope it will be suitable."

"I'm sure Beth will love it. But did you get nothing for yourself?"

"I require very little," she replied honestly.

He gave her a reproachful look. "I wish you had purchased at least a few fripperies for yourself. Only imagine the enormous drop in consequence I shall suffer among the hotel staff if they begin to think I'm the sort of nip-parsing Englishman who begrudges his wife a new dress!"

Edwina gestured around the gold brocade and mahogany-appointed sitting room. "I'm quite certain you are already spending enough for this suite to escape so lowering a fate." Resisting the little voice that whispered for her to put off the discussion until after dinner, she made herself ask, "And what did you discover?"

He took a sip of wine before giving her a wry smile. "Well you might ask, given how patient you've been, even if your anxiety to be rid of me is painful to my self-esteem."

"I'm not anxious to be 'rid' of you!" she protested, feeling as always the unwelcome blush on her cheeks. "It's just that, since we both know a union between us is not...suitable, it would be wiser to terminate it before..."

She made the mistake of looking up into his eyes, as he watched her with a heated intensity she'd found at first astonishing and which, over the last few days, had grown thrillingly familiar. An intensity that set off the familiar ache of need and desire.

She cleared her throat and continued, "Before we grow more...entangled than we already are."

His smile faded. "I'm sorry you think so, for undoing our bargain is proving to be as difficult as I feared. After reading the explanation provided by Chaplain Darrow and expressing his severe disapproval of the haste that prompted the marriage, the bishop's representative declined to judge its validity. I must file a petition with the Archbishop's office in England, he said."

He took her hand and began stroking it. "I'm afraid you will be burdened with me a bit longer."

His fingers traced a lazy pattern from her knuckles up across her wrist to just under the sleeve of her gown. Scarcely able to breathe, her attention captivated by the shiver of sensation he was evoking, it took a moment for his words to register.

"Nothing can be done here?" she asked, conscious of both dismay and a guilty surge of gladness. He would leave as he must, but the ties between them would not have to be severed just yet.

Even better, she realized, it would have to be easier to say their final goodbyes by letter rather than in a gut-wrenching few moments on the dock. *Thank You, Lord*, she whispered silently.

Then he banished all ability to think by raising her hand to his lips and kissing each fingertip in turn. "'Twill be such a bother to untangle everything. Are you sure we cannot simply leave things as they are?" He raised her chin, forcing her to look into his eyes. "I flatter myself you've grown a little fond of me."

"Y-yes. You've become a very good friend."

"Then don't you think we could rub along well enough together—at least as well as most married couples? I understand you loved your first husband deeply. Knowing what it is to lose someone so dear, might it not be more…comfortable to be married to a 'very good friend'?"

The mention of Daniel conjured up memories bitter enough to dispel some of his sensual sway and stiffen her resolve. Though the inequities in their respective stations would make a union between them uncertain enough, it was precisely because she couldn't live with his "comfortable" affection that she must end this.

Gently she tried to pull her fingers free, but before she could speak, dismay filled his face and he said, "Pray, forgive me! 'Twas presumptuous and insensitive to speak of him, for now I have made you sad again, which was the last thing I wished. Indeed, I was hoping that our…friendship might help you move beyond your grief. We do have much in common, and though I can't offer you anything as wonderful as the stories you've spun me or the exotic appeal of a life on campaign or in India, I can promise you a future of important, useful work. The Hampden lands are extensive and require a dedicated, capable mistress to oversee their well-being. You insist you are not part of the world to which I'm returning, but the truth is, nor was I bred to the role I must now play. You could help me as I learn to assume my responsibilities."

Edwina had to smile. "Yes, but having been neither born to that world, as you were, nor bred to its tasks, I hardly think there is much I could do to smooth your path."

He smiled back. "You could teach my cook to make a superior stew."

In an instant she was transported to the awful afternoon when she'd learned the truth about her appeal to Daniel. Furious upon discovering that she would not receive for several more years the inheritance upon which, it turned out, he'd been counting, he'd snapped, "What other benefit do you think a wife like you could offer me, besides her fortune? I already have a cook and an estate agent to haggle over trade."

That old wound reopened, without thinking she flashed back at Hampden, "Perhaps I could also help your manager barter for a better price on wheat?"

Aghast, she damned her hasty tongue as a look of puzzled distress appeared on Hampden's face. "I'm sorry," he quickly replied, "that was clumsily put. I did not mean to infer that I intended to put you to work—"

"No, of course you did not," she interrupted, casting about for something to soften her remark. "I—I only meant that, what I've learned about directing servants on campaign or in India is unlikely to be of much assistance in England, so I could be of little use to you. That is—your estate is already prosperous, or so I've heard."

Mercifully, the frown left his face and he smiled at her. "The little I've been able to induce my wife to spend should make no serious inroads on my capital."

She smiled back a bit nervously. "That is fortunate. I stand to inherit a large amount from my grandfather, but not until I am five-and-twenty. So at present, I could not even offer you the advantage one would expect to derive by wedding an India nabob's heiress."

"The sole advantage I hope for is to keep close by me the lady who has become my very dearest friend."

As Hampden accompanied that softly voiced rejoinder with a look both heated and tender, fortunately for her sanity, at that moment, a knock sounded at the door. A procession of servants entered bearing trays. While a half dozen attentive footman attended them for the remainder of the lavish meal, their conversation turned to a discussion of the political situation in England and the army gossip Hampden had picked up at the embassy.

After the servants left them to their glasses of port, Edwina said, "I haven't eaten so well since I last visited Grandpapa's compound, where he lives quite like a raja!"

"I thought we would both appreciate a change from rabbit stew and scrounged vegetables. Won't you join me?" Hampden indicated a place on the sofa.

Edwina eyed the spot to which he invited her. Sitting next to him was definitely not wise. But unable to produce a plausible reason to refuse, she came to perch gingerly beside him, all too acutely aware of him so close she could feel the heat emanating from his body and inhale the spicy scent of port on his breath.

"We can book passage on a ship leaving tomorrow," he told her as, senses already beginning to swim at his nearness, she tried to concentrate on his words. "Will you not come with me? Bringing home a bride would do much to restore to a grieving family the joy that should be theirs at Christmas. If you still insist upon nullifying our bargain, I swear I will do all in my power to accomplish that, but I expect the matter would proceed more quickly if you were present to give testimony and sign documents."

The point was valid, and it tempted her. But could she remain in his company and still resist him?

While she pondered that question, he set down his port and slid closer. "It might be prudent to spend more time together. I believe our friendship would only deepen, so if we discovered after returning to England that abolishing the marriage proved difficult, we might grow more amenable to letting it continue. You do consider us friends."

She ought to scoot away from him—but she couldn't. *Savor it*, the little voice in her head whispered. *He'll be leaving tomorrow.*

"Y-yes," she said, struggling to ignore his lips and concentrate instead on his words. "We are…friends."

"We work well together—and laugh together, too. It's important to be able to laugh together, don't you think?"

He began caressing her hand from her wrist down to her fingers. Exhaling a long sigh of delight, barely able to follow his argument, she murmured, "Yes."

He moved his other hand to brush her cheek, then continued down her neck, across the long plane of her collarbone and lower, until the tips of fingers rested at the edge of her bodice, touching the top swell of her breast. "We could share even more," he murmured. "You find me attractive, do you not?"

Without waiting for a reply—which was fortunate, for she was by now beyond speech—he bent his head and kissed her neck. With a wordless gasp, she closed her eyes and focused on the sensation as his lips slowly traced the path of his fingers from her throat down her chest to the edge of her bodice, until she could feel the warmth of his breath against her breasts. Just below where his lips rested, her nipples swelled and burned.

"I could please you," he whispered against her skin. "Let me show you how well we suit. If I fail to…satisfy, I promise to let you go and implore you no longer."

Please. Satisfy. He wanted to make love to her.

With every nerve aroused, she battled to heed the faint warning in her brain that to yield would mean catastrophe, for she had no doubt that he would please her. And then she would be lost.

"I'm sure you could please us both. But…I cannot."

"Why not?" he persisted, once again closing the distance between them and putting a persuasive arm on her shoulder. "You've admitted we share a deep affection. Why should we not pursue its natural extension?"

It was ludicrous to try protesting that she didn't find him attractive. But she simply couldn't confess that she had fallen top over tail in love with him.

She must invent some excuse to set him at a distance before her senses overwhelmed her judgment and his powerful appeal triumphed over her rapidly weakening resistance.

With her last bits of self-control, she threw off his hand, forced herself up and staggered to the hearth.

Breathing heavily, Hampden leaned back against the sofa. "Again, I must beg your pardon," he said after a moment of fraught silence. "I've repelled you with my forwardness."

"No, it isn't that!" she said, turning away from the fire to face him. "You must know I find you attractive. It's just that acting upon that attraction would be…" *Disastrous. Irreversible.* She thought frantically, trying to hit upon an appropriate word.

Then, suddenly, a means of escape flashed into her mind. "Unsuitable," she finished.

"Unsuitable?" he echoed, frowning. "In what way?"

"You see, though we share a…a fond friendship, you force me to confess that my emotions are already engaged."

She watched his face as he straightened, digesting her comment. "To some other man? Not your late husband?"

"Yes. To someone else," she said, relieved by his reaction and inventing her story as she went.

His frown deepened. "Indeed? Is this a recent attachment? Your mother gave me no hint of it."

"She knows nothing about it. The gentleman in question hasn't made me a declaration yet, and though I am—or I was—in hopes that he might soon do so, until I was sure he reciprocated my esteem, I thought it best not to hint of anything to Mama."

"I see." Eyes narrowing, he regarded her with suspicion. "And who is this lucky gentleman, if I may be so bold as to inquire?"

Edwina took a deep breath. She'd hoped to avoid having to mention a name, but though Hampden seemed to have recovered from the embarrassment of having his attempt at seduction rebuffed, he was clearly not ready to let her off with less than a complete confession.

Uttering a swift silent prayer that both the Lord and the surgeon would forgive her the falsehood, she replied, "Dr. MacAndrews. I've worked closely with him for more than a year now, you see, and a mutual respect and affection has ripened between us that, until your unfortunate accident, I felt might lead to our union."

She made herself stand unflinching under his steady regard.

"You believe yourself in love with Dr. Mac-Andrews?" Hampden asked.

"I am very much in love with the man I would hope to marry," she replied carefully.

"I see," he said again, rather stiffly. "And he reciprocates your sentiments?"

"I'm not sure. I have hopes that he might."

"And you would prefer to pass up the certainty of the affection we share on the *hope* that MacAndrews might in time reciprocate your stronger feelings for him?"

"I would prefer to retain that option, yes," she replied even more carefully.

Hampden jumped up and poured himself another glass of port before turning back to her. "Why did you not inform me of this attachment earlier?"

"Well, you must remember that, at first, you were not expected to survive until the doctor's return. So under what was, you must admit, considerable pressure from your friends, I agreed to our bargain, anticipating there would be no awkwardness with Dr. MacAndrews that I could not later explain away."

His eyes narrowed. "And when I did not obligingly die? Did you talk with him then?"

"No, of course not. It would not have been fitting to discuss such a thing until the bargain between us was resolved. I thought that as your health improved, you would become as conscious as I of the unsuitability of the arrangement and be anxious to go about dissolving it. Since the matter regarding Dr. MacAndrews is rather delicate, I hoped to avoid speaking of it. I only do so now because you've forced me."

He took another sip and nodded. "With my boorish and forward behavior. For which, once again, I apologize."

He was angry, she thought, stifling the desire to try to mollify him. Well, she'd wanted to put distance between them. With him believing she cared for another man, the honor that had forced him to uphold their bargain would now compel him instead to find the means to let her go.

Silly to feel so dangerously close to tears, when she was near to achieving precisely what she'd attempted. And if the odd scenario she'd invented gave him a disgust of her, so much the better. "I accept your apology," she said with as much spinsterly primness as she could muster, what with her senses still in rebellion and her heart feeling as battered as a shuttlecock. "Perhaps now I'd better retire. You plan to take that ship tomorrow, you said?"

"I said we—I—could do so if I chose."

"You should get some rest, as well. Thank you again for a lovely dinner, and good night."

Abruptly he paced forward and seized her chin in

one hand. "I will see you again in the morning. You'll not try to slip away in the night?"

"No, I won't go away," she answered, jerking her chin free and stepping back before he could notice that her knees were shaking and her hands trembling from the force of the battle raging within her between what she desired and what she knew she must do. So close were the tears brimming at her lashes that she would have agreed to almost anything to escape. "I'll see you in the morning."

He gave her a short, brusque nod, his face now shuttered. "Then, may you sleep well, Lady Hampden."

Chapter Eight

SLEEP WELL. Slim chance of it, Miles thought, watching Edwina walk with her usual calm to the door of her chamber. The door before which last night he'd kissed her, hoping to receive the invitation he craved to accompany her within.

Again tonight, he'd felt her trembling on the edge of succumbing to the attraction that, he felt sure, throbbed in her veins as it coursed through his. Until, clever fellow that he was, he'd brought up the memory of her sainted first husband and spoiled everything.

But that wasn't his worst error—or the greatest surprise. What a presumptuous fool he'd been, thinking he could convince Edwina that friendship was a strong enough base on which to continue their marriage. He should have guessed that, having loved her precious Daniel, she would want no less than a complete commitment if she wed again.

Surely there could be no other reason for her to prefer a man like Dr. MacAndrews—a man who hadn't yet even declared himself!

Which made Miles twice the fool. He'd come dangerously close to nearly coercing her to accept his advances. Cringing at the memory, he downed his port in one swallow.

If he felt ashamed and angry at having made an idiot of himself, it was his own fault. True, Edwina Denby hadn't repulsed the steadily increasing intimacy of his advances, but neither had she actively encouraged him. He'd thought her major objection to their continued union to be the same farradiddle about the difference in their stations that had concerned Sanbrook. He'd simply never considered the possibility, coxcomb that he was, that another man might have also perceived the qualities he found so attractive in her and made a push to engage her affections.

The fact that her mother didn't know about MacAndrews made him feel a bit better. Prudent lady that she was, it seemed entirely reasonable that Edwina would not have confided in Mrs. Crofton until she'd received a formal offer, since, after arousing expectations in her mother, it would be rather awkward to continue working with MacAndrews if those hopes were never realized.

Of course, the man would have to be an imbecile to earn the affection of a woman like Edwina and not capitalize upon it. No wonder MacAndrews had given him such a strange look when he found they were wed.

As his anger and embarrassment faded, Miles had to admit that beyond the shock of her revelations lay a deep disappointment—and more than a little jealousy.

As for the keenness of that disappointment, after having considered Edwina *his* for the last few days, it was only natural to feel like a blow the discovery that his plans for the future would be unrealized.

At least he'd had the wit to remain a gentleman, if barely. Upon learning that his lady's heart was set upon another, however strong his dismay—or jealousy, he could not in honor stand in her way. Especially after all she had sacrificed to assist him.

Miles poured himself yet another port, threw himself onto the sofa and glared into the flickering fire. What good was it having survived to return home a wealthy viscount with beautiful ancestral lands if he couldn't compete for the affections of his wife with an untitled, limb-hacking surgeon who offered his bride life in a tent?

Sanbrook and his friends, of course, would say he'd

had a lucky escape. He now had a legitimate reason to return to England and petition to dissolve their marriage—which, contrary to what he'd told Edwina, he could probably proceed to do without her accompanying him.

He flinched again, recalling how, if not precisely lying, he'd stretched beyond its original meaning the prelate's simple statement that it might be wise to have Edwina present, should the archbishop wish to question her.

If Edwina remained adamant about the marriage's dissolution, somehow he must make it happen. He'd then be forced to trade his uniform for the togs of a London Tulip while this year's pack of proud ton mamas paraded before him a procession of overly perfumed, melody-screeching, harp-twanging virgins of impeccable lineage, all eager to acquire his name, title and blunt.

Unlike Edwina—proud, thrifty Edwina—who had disdained a new gown and purchased only handkerchiefs, some bits of lace and the gift for his own niece he'd asked her to buy.

Something uncomfortable twisted in chest. But Edwina had made her choice clear. Despite their friendship and even admitting the physical pull between them, Edwina preferred returning to the army to beguile her surgeon.

While he must go to London, end their marriage and try to beguile a new bride.

An appalling sense of loss welled up from deep within. He doubted he'd find another lady with lustrous eyes like Edwina's, which had never flinched from the pain and horrors of the field hospital. One whose hands could effectively soothe a wounded man's agony, or whose warm velvet voice had kept a dying man tethered to life.

Despite the blow to his self-esteem, 'twas good that he hadn't succeeded in seducing her. For then, despite his pledge to contrary, he'd never have let her go.

Sighing, he sought out the decanter. Time for a good bit more of that port. Though he told himself 'twas his shoulder that ached, he knew in truth that the pain nagging at him was centered lower, on the left side of his chest.

EDWINA CLOSED the door to her chamber and leaned her trembling body against it. She could have no doubt now that Hampden wanted her.

An insistent little voice asked her why desire and mutual affection could not be enough. Why was it so essential that she hold all her husband's heart, as long as she commanded his respect, upheld his name and, in time, bore his children?

If she did not capture his whole heart, she answered, 'twas unlikely she could retain even that affection he now felt for her, once they returned to a world that would disapprove of their union. Even Lord Sanbrook, whom she knew liked and respected her, had made no secret of his opinion that the bonds should be dissolved. She might have entered this marriage without her husband feeling the scorn Daniel had directed at her, but with all his friends and relations ranged against her, in time Miles would come to despise her as well.

Neither her pride nor her heart could tolerate that. Forcing herself to deny the temptation to go back to him, she wandered to the window.

The stars twinkling overhead promised fair skies and a good breeze for the ship that would carry Hampden away tomorrow. She placed a hand over her breast, where she could almost feel the imprint of his kiss still burning against her skin. Never in the worst days of Daniel's casual cruelty had she ached like this.

If only she could have taken his gift and still have been able to set him free! Knowing that if she had succumbed, Hampden would consider them irrevocably bound, did not quell the longing.

She'd experienced physical union during her marriage when Daniel had condescended to take her, no more attractive bed-sport being available. But she'd never been intimately joined with a man she loved, who touched her with affection rather than idle lust.

Now she never would.

A tear slipped down her cheek. It seemed so monstrously unfair that she be denied experiencing that joy just once, when she was already doomed to living the rest of her life without him.

Maybe you can capture joy—just once.

The daring, dangerous thought startled her, made her hand clutch on the rich brocade of the curtain. Though she tried to dismiss it, the idea gained momentum, sweeping through her mind with the irresistible force of tomorrow morning's tide.

If she had the temerity to proceed, Hampden might reject her as she had him. But if he chose not to—they could steal one night together, a night of ecstasy without consequences or regrets.

Of what significance was a bit of humiliation compared to the chance of winning that?

Her decision made, she rushed to the wardrobe. Already the moon was high in the sky, and if one night was all she would ever have, she didn't want to lose another moment.

MILES WAS SEATED on the bed, shirt off and trousers half-unbuttoned, when a knock sounded at the door.

Excitement lanced through him, swiftly smothered by a dose of reality.

It could not be Edwina...or rather if it was, she would doubtless want to consult him about some trifling matter of business—passports or passage money or some such.

She didn't really want him. As husband or lover.

Irritated anew by that truth, he called out, "Go back to bed! We can settle whatever is necessary in the morning."

He didn't like admitting that if he allowed her into his room on any pretext, he knew he'd not be able to let her go without attempting once again to seduce her.

"Please, señor, mistress says I must see you."

The muffled voice speaking in halting English sounded like that of the Crofton's maid, Juanita.

Alarm succeeded his irritation. Had something happened to Edwina?

Snagging his shirt and refastening his trousers as he went, he trotted over to open the door. As he'd suspected, the maid stood on the threshold.

"What is it? What's amiss?" he demanded.

"My mistress sends me," the girl said, dropping him a curtsy. "She says milord's shoulder gives him pain. She sends me with salve to ease it, to help him sleep."

Only one thing would give him ease, he thought

sardonically. "Tell your mistress I'm gratified by her concern, but 'tis unnecessary. My sleeping does not depend on ease for my shoulder."

As he started to close the door, the maid raised a hand. "Please, señor, Mistress will be angry if I do not obey."

The poor girl did indeed appear to be trembling, in addition to having swathed herself in that veil all the local women wore—probably to protect her maidenly eyes from the shocking sight of a gentleman half-undressed. "I promise your mistress won't beat you, child. Go to bed."

Instead of retreating, though, the girl stepped closer. "Please, *señor*. It will bring you...pleasure."

His senses were a bit wine-soaked, but suddenly it dawned upon him that the figure of the girl looked startlingly familiar. Leaning forward, he caught a whiff of jasmine—the scent to which his mind had clung on the awful night of his injury, blocking out the stench of blood and fear.

Edwina! He was certain 'twas his erstwhile wife, not her mother's maid, seeking entrance to his chamber.

She must have changed her mind—so why the deception?

"Please, *señor*, may I come in? It will take little

time to soothe you. Then you may sleep undisturbed."

A slow grin formed on his face. Whatever her reasons for this charade, he was more than happy to accommodate her. He'd be a fool if he didn't ensure the "soothing" lasted until dawn—and he had no intention of being a fool twice tonight.

Chapter Nine

"VERY WELL, if your mistress insists." Still smiling, Miles stood aside to let the veiled figure enter, his fatigue and melancholy vanishing in a heat of erotic anticipation. "What would you have me do?" he asked, trying to keep the amusement out of his voice.

"Sit there, on the bed, milord. I will do all."

That sounded promising. The mere thought of what she *might* do made his body harden while he deposited himself as instructed.

She came over to stand beside him, unbuttoned his shirt and carefully drew it off his injured shoulder. Breathing in again her scent of jasmine, Miles grew even surer his midnight visitor must be Edwina.

The flickering light of the single bedside candle outlined the swell of her breasts straining against the too-tight bodice of the maid's gown. He felt himself harden further, his fingers itching to release the taut garment. He wanted to bury his face between the soft jasmine-scented mounds, let his eager tongue tease her nipples to swollen peaks while his fingers delved lower....

Shifting on the bed in his now uncomfortably confining trousers, he bit back a groan and stilled the hands already reaching toward her. For now, he would restrain himself and see what she would do next.

First she folded his shirt—oh, his tidy Edwina—and set it aside. Then she extracted a small bottle from her apron pocket, poured onto her hands a scented liquid and gently applied it to his shoulder.

Warmed by her body, the oil flowed smoothly over his skin. She began massaging it into his shoulders, the top of his neck, down his back. After a few moments, his eyes fell shut and a sigh of sheer rapture escaped his lips. So exquisite was her touch, it almost competed with the desire throbbing in his breeches.

But not quite. Mustering up words with an effort, he said, "Would you rub also...my lower back?"

Her hands obligingly descended, extending the magic of her massaging fingers down his back and flanks. After another few timeless moments of bliss, however, she paused.

As he scraped together wits enough to wonder if her mission had indeed been merely medical, she poured more oil on her fingers and applied them once again to his shoulder. But instead of working the muscles of his back, she inched down his chest, circling closer and closer until her fingers almost touched his nipples, teasing them as he'd envisioned teasing hers. He stifled a groan, his arms going rigid as he struggled to keep himself motionless. Just as he thought he could stand no more, she captured the sensitive peaks and rolled them in her oil-slick thumbs.

A blast of lust roared through him. He wanted to sweep up her skirts, toss her onto the bed and take her that instant. But with his pulse and every other part of him throbbing, he dug his fingernails into the bed linen and made himself remain still.

A mission that became increasingly difficult as her fingers resumed their slow descent, tracing along his ribs and stroking the upper curve of his belly. He thought her breathing grew more rapid and uneven, but it might be only the thunder of his own heartbeat in his ears.

Her fingers paused at the top of his trousers, then dipped beneath, coming oh-so-close to what he badly wanted her to stroke.

Retreating instead, she tugged at his waistband. "Remove these, please," she said, her voice breathless and the accent less pronounced. "Then I can…finish."

Before she had time to step aside, he had the buttons of the trousers undone. In one motion he shucked them and his drawers onto the floor and sat back on the bed.

This time, he knew he was not mistaken about hearing her long, slow exhale of breath, followed by a charged silence as, from behind her veil, she stared at his naked, completely aroused body. Excited by the idea of her watching him, he leaned back to give her a fuller view.

"What would you have me do next?" he asked.

Without answering, she whirled around and paced to the bedside table. "'Tis not…modest for a maid to see you so," she said, and extinguished the single candle.

Miles chuckled softly. Modest or not, she'd taken time to look her fill before remembering her maidservant's role. What next would she desire?

"Lie down, milord, that I might ease your back."

'Twas the tightness in front he most wanted eased, but again, obedient to whatever fantasy she wished to play out, he lay facedown. "Now that darkness preserves your modesty, will you not remove your veil?" he asked over his shoulder. "So when you… minister to me it does not come loose and become stained by the oil."

To his delight, a faint rustling told him she'd taken his suggestion. Hard as he tried, though, he could make out nothing in the inky darkness that cloaked the chamber.

Then she began massaging him again, and all thought drowned in a tidal rush of sensation.

As if freed from restraint by the darkness, the motion of her hands became frankly sensual. Her fingers outlined his ribs, rounded and molded his buttocks, circled over the tops of his thighs and down between his legs, which he parted, encouraging her to stroke lower still, where his buried cock pulsed in anticipation of her touch.

He groaned when she followed his lead, tracing the juncture of his thigh until her fingers fondled him, igniting another bolt of sensation and ripping a cry from his throat.

As if pleased by his response, she stroked him there again and again, until unable to lie still any longer, he rolled to his back and seized her wrists. "Ease me... here," he gasped, curling her fingers around his swollen length.

For an instant he feared he'd been too bold, for as he released her wrists, she pulled her hands away. Before he could gather enough words for either protest or apology, he heard the faint clink of the glass container, then the sibilant sound of pouring liquid. As he waited, barely breathing, she wrapped her oil-slick hands around him and slowly massaged his entire length.

Sweat beaded on his chest, his forehead as his hands fisted on the sheets and his legs and torso clenched, arching into her touch. She began to stroke him rhythmically and he moved with her, caught up in an erotic trance of her making.

He knew his control was swiftly eroding. As wonderful as this was, he wanted more, wanted his sweat and oil-slick body sliding against her as he buried himself in her warm depths, wanted her bare breasts free to his mouth and tongue, wanted to feel her spasm around him as he exploded within her.

Past reason or speech, he grabbed the material of her skirt, bunching it up to seek the skin beneath. An instant later, she yanked the cloth free and in a rustle of skirts, climbed onto the bed and straddled him.

A single thrust of her hips plunged his oiled cock in to its full length. He wanted her to pause so he could rip loose the bodice imprisoning her breasts, dispose of the skirts that barred his way to bare skin. But she leaned forward and found his mouth, her tongue seeking his urgently, her slippery hands biting into his shoulders as she arched into him and withdrew, arched and withdrew.

And then there was no time for anything but meeting her thrust for thrust as she rode him, her breathing a gasp that rose to a sob and then sharp cry as she tensed and shattered around him. An instant later, keening with her, he followed her into oblivion.

When his brain finally resumed functioning several minutes later, Edwina lay collapsed atop him. A wave of affection swelling his chest, he hugged her close, content to listen to their ragged, panting breaths.

'Twas unaccountably erotic to lie there, still intimately joined, the prim, proper lady who had nursed him so devotedly now stretched against his naked body while she remained almost entirely clothed, her modest maid's gown buttoned up to her chin. Indeed, he could already feel his spent member begin to stir.

Stroking the damp curls off her face, her kissed her. "Thank you for giving me…ease. But I need still more."

She stirred and he felt the butterfly-light brush of her lashes against his chin. "More?" she asked, surprise in her voice.

He chuckled, setting off vibrations in his torso that brought him into pleasing contact with her moist, tight depths. "Yes, more. Soon. But the material of this gown scratches. You must remove it."

He felt her smile against his fingertips. "Mistress said to obey you in all things." With the lazy ease of a cat she stretched and then sat astride him, reaching behind her to undo the bodice, as if unconscious of how each rocking movement made him harden within her.

At last she unhooked the final fastening and tossed the garment aside. Her breasts bounced free into his waiting hands and he moved eagerly to caress them, his mouth thirsting for their taste.

The skirts would have to wait. Quickening his pace within her as he pulled her down to him, he wished he'd not drawn the curtains against the moonlight, for he burned to watch the rosy tips of her nipples stiffen as he licked them. Next time, he promised himself as he fastened his mouth on one and sucked greedily.

A shudder passed through her and she cried out, sparking an answering throb in his cock.

Threading his hands under her disheveled skirts to cup her bottom and pull her more firmly against him, he released the hard pebbled tip and whispered, "Now, sweeting, let us both seek ease."

HOURS LATER Miles woke to find the sun a halo of gold against the still-drawn curtains. Sighing with glorious repletion, he turned over in a tangle of sheets, not surprised to find his audacious Edwina gone.

He glanced about the chamber but, tidy as ever, she'd left no trace of her midnight intrusion. To be fair, he thought, chuckling, that maid's gown was probably fit now for nothing but to be hurled into the fire.

No matter. He would gladly buy the maid a dozen gowns to replace the one that had emboldened his surprising wife to pleasure him.

After last night, there could be no more twaddle of annulments and unequal stations in life and duplicitous, unworthy surgeons. In her ministering angel disguise, Edwina had bound them inextricably together, surpassing in the bargain his lustiest imaginings.

Suddenly he was filled with the need to see her. Would his mere presence remind her of the bold caresses she'd given him in the darkness and bring that endearing blush to her cheeks?

Too impatient to deal with neckcloths and buttons, he threw on a dressing gown and went out. Surprised at the intensity of the joy that swelled his chest as he walked over to kiss her cheek, he said, "Good morning, dear wife."

Keeping her eyes downcast, she turned her face away while—yes—a blush rose to her cheeks. "Good morning. As it seemed you wished to sleep late, I instructed Manuelo to wait on breakfast. Shall I ring for it now?"

He slipped beside her on the sofa. "Yes, I found last night's activities wonderfully fatiguing. I'm surprised you are not still resting, as well." He picked up her hand, intending to kiss it, but she quickly snatched it back.

"I had much to complete—packing, the disposition of your kit. When must you be at the ship?"

"Mid-morning. We shall have time to breakfast and settle with the hotel before we set off." The faint warning bells in his head rose in volume as she sidled away from him.

"I…I rather thought we would say our goodbyes here," she said, not meeting his glance. "Not on the docks amid a throng of onlookers."

Despite the inner voice warning something was wrong, it took a moment for the meaning of her words to penetrate. "Say our goodbyes?" he repeated, halting in the act of pouring himself coffee. "I understand you wish to inform your family of our departure, but surely they were expecting it. Could you not write a note?"

She shook her head. "I'm not leaving with you."

He set the cup down with a thunk, an odd flutter in his chest, still trying to deny what her words seemed to indicate. "If you simply must see your family again, I suppose I can delay my departure a few more days, though I do need to proceed home as quickly as possible."

"There's no need to delay. I meant I'm not returning with you at all. It may take a bit longer to process the annulment without my being present, but I promise to sign and return the papers the instant I receive them. I thought…I thought we settled all of this last night."

"So did I—when you came to my chamber!" he barked, anger rising in turn with his dismay. Surely she didn't mean to deny what they'd shared!

Her blush deepened. "You are mistaken. 'Twas mama's maid I sent to massage your shoulder last night. I've already chastised her for her...enthusiasm. If you please, I don't wish to speak of it further."

He could almost believe her an outraged spinster whose maid he'd unthinkingly debauched. Almost.

Except for the scent of jasmine that teased his nose and the fact that she would not meet his eyes.

He took her chin and forced her to look at him. "Edwina, what nonsense is this? I didn't understand last night why you felt it necessary to come to me in disguise, but 'twas no maid who spent the night in my bed. Why are you trying to deny 'twas you?"

Her color still high, she shook his hand free and met his gaze calmly, a chill in her eyes. "It most certainly was the maid. After confessing to you my intentions about Dr. MacAndrews, how could you insinuate that I would indulge in bed-sport with a man I did not love? 'Tis a grave offense against my honor."

He could only stare at her, uncomprehending. "You do mean to deny it," he said slowly. "And send me back to England alone, to dissolve our marriage? How can you claim to have honor and do that?"

Her chin rose a notch higher, her gaze growing frostier still. "If we have but a short while longer to be together, my lord, let us not spend it insulting each other." She turned from him to her coffee cup.

A caustic mix of incredulity, outrage, anger and hurt roiled in his belly. "So this is how you mean to end it? We'll break our fast, you'll bid me goodbye and send me to the ship while you return to Torres Vedras?"

"Yes. 'Tis what I expected to do from the first. 'Tis what we agreed upon."

'Twas not what *I* agreed to, he thought, and then suddenly realized she was correct—the myth of her returning with him had ever been solely a creation of his own mind. The sharp edge of his anger blunted against the hard certainty of impending separation.

"You expect me to depart and simply forget the woman who saved my life?" Forget the woman who had surprised and shocked and captivated him through the whole of one long splendid night, he added silently.

"Preserving your life was God's gift, not mine," she countered. "Now I'll go give Manuelo his instructions."

Before he could think how to stop her, she rose from the sofa and went out the door.

Incomprehension turned to frustration and a rapidly reviving anger. Why would she share his bed and complete their union, then turn her back and seek to pull them asunder? It made no sense.

'Twas an insult—almost a betrayal of what he thought they'd shared. A raw sense of loss bubbled up from his gut, stinging like acid on his already flayed feelings. With a curse, he seized the coffee cup and hurled it into the hearth, where it shattered into a hundred fragments.

Rather like his heart.

THREE HOURS LATER, Miles clomped up the gangway of the merchant frigate *Reliant*, scheduled to set sail on the afternoon tide for England. Would that the sharp sea breeze of the journey might succeed in blowing out of his heart and head all thought of Edwina and the pain of her leaving him.

He didn't think it likely.

He hadn't, after a rather desultory effort, managed to persuade her to see him as far as the ship. Instead, after allowing him a single kiss of her cheek, she had bid him goodbye in their rooms at the hotel.

In the hours since Edwina's shocking denial, he'd found himself going over and over last night's incredible encounter. As wonderful as it might otherwise have been to discover so deliciously wanton a side to Edwina, he supposed he should congratulate himself on what now looked like a providential escape from spending his life as a cuckold. A fate that surely would have been his, if Edwina were so free with her favors that she could blithely seduce him while intending to marry another man. Still, Edwina behaving in such a way seemed completely out of character for the woman he'd come to know.

As he reached the main deck, he saw a group of wounded soldiers, some limping, some being carried on litters.

Grateful for the diversion, he thrust his gloomy thoughts aside and went to lend them assistance.

He'd almost reached the small group when he recognized, leaning over one of the litters, the unmistakable figure of the surgeon, Dr. MacAndrews.

Miles skidded to a halt. His first instinct was to change direction and avoid the man. Then again, if he were being forced to relinquish his wife, he could at least discover if the man she preferred returned her regard.

Not that finding out would do much good. But as he hesitated, intending to walk away, memories from last night attacked his senses. The sound of oil pouring into warm palms... The scent of it and her as she massaged it into his skin... The feel of her drawing his length between her fingers and thrusting him deep into her body.

While desire and despair and fury warred for dominance in his brain, his feet began moving. A moment later, he found himself at MacAndrew's side.

The doctor spied him before he could speak. "Going home at last, Lord Hampden? Congratulations!"

"I understand good wishes are due you, as well— if the happy event Edwina hinted about is soon to occur?"

The surgeon stopped short, his face coloring. "Edwina mentioned it, did she? Well, the good wishes are a tad early, but 'twill not be too much longer now, I trust!"

At that avowal, Miles's last, secret hope that Edwina might have been dissembling crumbled. Apparently Mrs. Denby *had* trifled with his affections and lured him to bed, giving him a tantalizing glimpse of a future the doctor's words had just confirmed to be a lie.

He hadn't felt such a sickness in his gut since a horse kicked him at Talavera. Hurt and fury suffusing him in equal measure, though he'd meant to choke out a goodbye and turn away, he found himself compelled to speak.

Perhaps the doctor needed a pointed, if veiled, warning about the woman he intended to wed.

"I sincerely hope your marriage will be as blissful as you anticipate—given the character of your intended bride."

Dr. MacAndrews stiffened. "Just what do you mean, sir?"

"Only that your prospective fiancée's desire to succor the wounded sometimes carries her to, shall we say, excessive lengths," Miles retorted, glorious memories of Edwina's midnight ministrations again filling his head.

The surgeon's offended look turned puzzled. "Succor the wounded?" he repeated. "Are you still in pain, my lord?"

"No, I am much recovered." *In body, if not spirit.*

"You've not taken laudanum? Your memories must be muddled, then, for you seem to have confused the time you lay wounded with what Edwina told you of my plans. I love my Alicia dearly, but she faints at the mention of blood."

Miles grew still. "Alicia?"

"Alicia," the surgeon repeated, a bit impatiently. "The young lady Edwina told you I intend to marry."

Miles took a deep breath, wild hope emerging from his initial confusion. "Apparently I *have* muddled it. Your Alicia is not a nurse at the camp?"

The doctor laughed. "Good heavens, no! I'd never allow her within a mile of such a place. No, she's at home with her family in Kent, longing for my return as deeply as I long to return to her, I hope."

"I see. An excellent young lady, Edwina said." *You*

scheming little minx, he thought as the doctor rattled on about his beloved.

He didn't know why Edwina had concocted such a Banbury tale, but he did know he wasn't leaving Portugal until he found out. After excusing himself to the surgeon, Miles loped to the gangway.

He'd have to hurry if he wanted to catch his exasperating, infuriating, baffling wife before she left for Torres Vedras.

Chapter Ten

BACK AT THE HOTEL, Edwina paced from her elegant chamber out onto the balcony. Her baggage had been carried downstairs, but still she lingered, gazing over the Lisbon rooftops toward the harbor.

She would wait just a bit longer, until the ship bearing Miles to England sailed by. If he chanced to be on deck, she might catch one last glimpse of him.

Their chilly parting earlier this morning had extinguished the last tiny spark of hope that Miles might declare he truly loved her and beg her to honor their vows, despite her supposed attachment to the surgeon. At which point, she would reveal she loved him as well.

She shook her head. Surely the bitter past should have taught her better than to indulge in such fairy tales.

What was she to do with herself after the end of this short-lived marriage? Despite the desire Miles had awakened in her, the incredible rapture of last night's intimacies had bound her so closely to him she now found it difficult to imagine giving herself to any other man. Perhaps it would be better to hold with her original plan of setting up her own establishment.

Perhaps the indelible memories of that single night with the man she loved would be enough to help her endure a lifetime of emptiness without him.

A knock at the door roused her from her contemplations. Probably it was Manuelo, asking if she were ready to depart. Her eyes still fixed on the view of the harbor, she walked over to open the door. And then stood astounded to find Miles Hampden on the threshold.

"Y-you're not on the ship?" she stuttered.

His unsmiling gaze pinioned her in place. "I found I had unfinished business here. If I might enter?"

She simply couldn't bear playing their parting scene again. "Please, there can be nothing further to say."

Ignoring her outstretched hand, he strode past her into the room. "I thought I could leave, just like that," he said, turning to face her. "But I found I could not. At least, not until I ask you about what I learned this morning from Dr. MacAndrews."

"Dr. MacAndrews!" she echoed, belatedly closing the door and following him to the sofa.

"Yes. I met him just now on the ship, evacuating some of the wounded. By the way, I told him to send our compliments to his fiancée, Miss Alicia Wentworth, who resides with her family back in Kent."

Damn and blast! He'd discovered her deception, she thought, then realized she should have immediately pleaded ignorance of the engagement and expressed a feigned outrage at the doctor for leading her on. Well, perhaps 'twas not yet too late. "I...I had no idea! To think that he—"

"Edwina, enough. Admit it, you fabricated that story about MacAndrews out of whole cloth."

Edwina hesitated. She might try to bluff her way out of this tangle, but she didn't think she was that good a liar. Perhaps if she served up just a portion of the truth, it would be enough to get him quickly out of this room—before her yearning for him shredded what was left of her good intentions and she begged him to stay.

"I knew you felt honor-bound to uphold the bargain, all the more so as our...friendship grew. I needed a reason for you to release me that would leave you feeling truly free to return home and find another wife, a more suitable lady, of whom your family would approve."

"Perhaps the highest sticklers in society will consider the match between us shockingly unequal, but I expect many will envy me. Snagging an India nabob's heiress for your wife is always good ton."

"Don't you see? It would never suit!"

"But *we* suit, Edwina. Have the last ten days not demonstrated how well-matched we are in preferences, perceptions, wit? Did last night not show how even better we suit in delightfully intimate ways? So why persist in trying to send me away? I think you owe me some better explanation. After all, 'tis an insult to *my* honor that, despite my protestations to the contrary, you seem to think I'm not capable of upholding the vows I made to you."

"'Tis not that!" she protested, trying to come up with some other plausible explanation. "'Tis just…"

"Is it because of what happened between you and Denby? Because he wooed you into wedding him, assuming you were already in possession of a fortune, and was furious when he discovered he had to wait for it?"

For an instant, shock like a dunking in the icy waters of the Douro stole her breath. "Who told you that?"

He shrugged. "'Tis the conclusion I came to just now, on my way back from the docks. It simply wasn't reasonable for you to be so opposed to our union because of the disparity in our stations when you'd already been married to a man of similar standing. Unless, despite what everyone seems to believe, the union wasn't a happy one." His voice softened. "It wasn't happy, was it?"

At that unexpected question, all the aching sorrow she worked so hard to contain seem to burst free of its restraints. For a moment, she struggled to keep the tears back and halt the flow of painful memories.

Perhaps, after all they had shared, he deserved the complete truth—since he'd stumbled upon most of it anyway.

"No," she admitted. "The union was not a happy one."

"Denby dissembled to you about his feelings, didn't he? I cannot imagine you agreeing to wed a man who wanted only your inheritance, no matter how much in love you may have been. But if it was the fortune he wanted so badly, why did he not discover the terms of it before you wed? For neither can I imagine you deceiving him."

After all the half truths she'd fed him, she felt gratified that he still believed she possessed that much honor. "I didn't. The first time he mentioned my fortune, I hastened to inform him of its conditions."

"And yet he wed you anyway, thinking it worth the wait? And in time you discerned his true feelings?"

She smiled, a bitter twist of the lips. "It happened sooner than that." She looked away, the humiliation of the memory making her unable to meet his concerned gaze. "Several weeks after he began courting me, he took me walking in the Queen's Gardens. I was mad for him, too young and stupid to realize what he truly desired of me, and delirious with joy when he kissed me and said he wanted me for his bride—his very rich little bride. His ardor began to cool when I had confessed I wouldn't become an heiress for several years, but just then two of his friends burst out of the shrubbery and caught me still in his arms. Having been found in that compromising situation, my reputation would be destroyed, he told me, if we did not become engaged."

"So you felt compelled to marry him?"

"No—at least, not at first. After he called on Papa and, I imagine, had confirmed what I'd tried to tell him about my fortune, he was furious. He avoided me for days. Having by then had time to realize his true sentiments, when he finally did call, I told him there was no reason to continue the engagement. I would cry off. He informed me that was impossible—for a Denby of Alvaney Court to be jilted by a provincial nobody would make him a laughingstock. Besides, having determined in the interim that my eventual fortune would be all he'd hoped, he knew his papa would agree to pay off his debts—which, it turned out, were massive—and fund him until I received my inheritance.

Distasteful as it was for him to marry so far beneath him, he would make the best of it, and so must I."

Miles uttered an oath. "You were still so in his thrall you settled for that?"

"I thanked him for the honor of his offer and told him I considered our engagement over. He warned me if I insisted on crying off and ruining his plans, he would tell my parents he was relieved that honor no longer compelled him to marry the daughter of a man of mediocre family serving in a third-rate regiment, whose mother was the vulgar offspring of a jumped-up Cit. That his friends had seen how I'd lured him into the garden to trap him into making me an offer, and soon the whole cantonment would know I was an ill-bred girl of questionable morals."

"Your papa should have shot him."

"I suppose I should have found another way out, but Mama was so delighted with my excellent match, Papa so proud and happy for me that I couldn't bear to think of the hurt and embarrassment they would suffer if Denby carried out his threat. So I married him."

"Bastard! You are a thousand times too good for him."

Edwina smiled wryly. "'Tis certainly not what he believed."

"How did you endure it?" Miles asked softly, reaching out to stroke her cheek.

She closed her eyes at his touch, the painful memories somehow eased in the telling. "As one does anything unpleasant. And by vowing I would never allow myself to be placed in so untenable a position again. I hope now you understand why you must let me keep that pledge."

"I understand why you've been so insistent on ending our agreement. But do I have no say in a matter that concerns me so nearly? Am I not permitted to plead to keep the companionship of a woman whose courage, intelligence and resourcefulness fill me with admiration? Who has come to occupy such a central place in my life that I cannot imagine living without her? Do you care for me so little?"

She opened her mouth, closed it, that last, most dangerous confession trembling on her lips. The one she dare not make. "I do care for you," she said instead.

"How much, Edwina?" he demanded. Then, before she could imagine what he meant to do, he pulled her close, his mouth coming down hard on hers.

She might resist his words, but to pull away from the touch she yearned for so desperately was beyond her power. With a moan of despair and need, she clutched him fiercely, opened her lips to the invasion of his tongue, pursued it with her own, putting into the last kiss she would ever have from him all the passion she'd been denying, and the love that consumed her soul.

When at last he broke the kiss and cradled her against his chest, she could not bear to look at him. Knowing she was close to losing the battle to restrain her tears, she tried to pull away.

He refused to free her. Tilting her chin up, he demanded again, "How much do you care for me?"

It was too much; her nerves and will were worn past resisting. "All right, I admit it—I love you! And so I cannot subject myself to the misery of remaining wed to a man who holds me in a merely familial affection. Please, let us keep the bargain we made. Take the freedom I offer you and find a woman you can truly love."

His gaze grew fiercer, more insistent. "If that is how you feel, let me propose a new bargain. It may have taken a French sniper's bullet to get my attention, but I've now had two weeks to discover what a treasure was waiting right before my eyes. I love you, too, Edwina. Will you agree to remain my wife—not for my title or fortune or even to bless my family with your caring presence—but so that I may hold forever the woman who has completely captured my affections? I must warn you, I'm not prepared to let you go unless you swear to me that you cannot give me your heart, as I have yielded you mine."

For a moment she forgot to breathe as she took in the enormity of the declaration he'd just made. "Oh, Miles, I gave you mine long ago."

"Then let us share our first Christmas together, my dear wife, while we plan for our future. The Lord gave back me life—you offer me freedom. Now I would freely pledge my life and love to you. And is love not the greatest gift of all?"

He loved her, loved *her* with the same passion she felt for him. Though she could still scarcely believe it, she had no doubt how priceless was that pledge.

Miles let her go and dropped to one knee. "Edwina Denby, will you do me the honor of remaining my wife, to love and to cherish until we are parted by death? Oh, and I promise to furnish an endless supply of scented oil."

Over the burst of joy swelling her chest, Edwina could feel the blush suffusing her cheeks. "When you phrase it thus, I suppose I must say yes."

With a whoop of triumph, Miles bounded to his feet and captured her in a hug. "Excellent!" he cried as he released her. "Now, what with nearly forcing the man who loves you to sail out of your life, you've had a distressing morning. I believe it must be time for some *soothing*—at my hands." With a wicked grin, he tugged her toward his chamber.

Edwina couldn't help but smile back. "Let me place myself in your hands, now and forever, my dearest love." And with that, she willingly let him lead her away.

Dear Reader,

When I think of a Regency Christmas I think of the family celebrations described in Jane Austen's letters—ice-skating, caroling, impromptu dancing, playing charades and sitting around a roaring log fire telling stories. In *The Season for Suitors* my hero, Sebastian Fleet, has forsaken the pleasures of a family Christmas after a terrible tragedy. Can Carla Davencourt, who has loved Seb for years, open his heart to the comfort and joy of the Christmas season?

This story is especially for all those readers who wrote to me after Seb first appeared in my books and asked when he would have a story—and a love—of his own.

I wish you all a very happy and peaceful Christmas season.

With love from

Nicola Cornick

THE SEASON
FOR SUITORS

Nicola Cornick

Chapter One

THE LETTER arrived with his breakfast.

It was written in an unmistakably feminine hand and it smelled faintly of jasmine perfume.

Sebastian, Duke of Fleet, was not pleased to see it. Letters from ladies, especially those that arrived early in the morning, usually presaged bad news. Either some misguided woman was threatening to sue him for breach of promise, or his great aunt was coming to stay, and he welcomed neither.

"Perch, what is this?" the Duke asked, tapping the parchment with his finger.

His butler continued to unload the breakfast from the silver tray, placing the coffeepot at an exact degree from the cup, and the milk jug at the perfect angle from both. Perch was a butler of precision.

"It is a letter from a lady, your grace."

The duke's brows drew together in an intimidating frown. He had spent much of the previous night at Whites; both the drink and the play had been heavy, and this morning his mind was not very clear. At least he had had the sense to reject the amorous advances of one of London's latest courtesans. He had had no wish to wake up with her painted face beside him.

He had an unwelcome suspicion that he was getting too old for drinking and debauchery, a superannuated rake. Once he started to wear a wig and use face paint to cover the ravages of age, he would have to ask Perch to shoot him.

He pushed aside the dispiriting thought. Without the wine and the gambling and the women there was little left for him, except a rambling old mausoleum of a house that, on this December day, was particularly difficult to heat. Indeed, his hot water bottle had burst in the night, adding another unpleasant dimension to his night's slumber.

"I *perceive* it is from a lady," he said coldly. "I simply wondered which lady was attempting to communicate with me?"

Perch's expression suggested that his master might consider breaking open the seal in order to find out, but after a moment he answered him.

"The letter was delivered by a man in the Davencourt livery, your grace."

The duke reached thoughtfully for the coffeepot and poured for himself, then he slid his knife under the seal, scattering little bits of wax across the table, where they mixed with the crumbs from the toast. Perch winced at the mess. Seb ignored him. What benefit was there in being a Duke if one could not scatter crumbs as one pleased? After all, he attended to his ducal responsibilities in exemplary fashion. He had improved the family seat at Fleet Castle, he was generous to his tenants, he had even been known to attend the House of Lords if there was a particularly important debate taking place. His days were perfectly ordered—and damnably boring. Life was hard when one had done everything there was to do.

He unfolded the letter and looked at the signature.

Yours sincerely, Miss Clara Davencourt.

He was aware of rather more pleasure than seemed quite appropriate. He had not seen Clara Davencourt for almost eighteen months and had not known she was currently in London. He sipped his coffee, rested the letter on the table and swiftly scanned the contents.

Your Grace…

That was rather more formal than some of the things Miss Davencourt had called him during their last encounter. Arrogant, conceited and rude were the words that sprang immediately to his memory.

I find myself in something of a dilemma...

Seb's blue eyes narrowed. The combination of Miss Davencourt and a dilemma was sufficient to strike dread into the strongest constitution.

I find that I need some paternal advice...

A smile curled the corner of Seb's firm mouth. Paternal advice, indeed! If Miss Clara Davencourt had deliberately set out to depress his pretensions as the most notorious rake in Town she could not have done a better job. He was only twelve years her senior and had not begun his life of dissipation at so young an age that he was qualified to be her father.

My brother is preoccupied with affairs of state and all the more suitable of his friends are unavailable at present, which only leaves you...

Seb winced. The minx. She knew how to deliver a neat insult.

I therefore have no alternative than to beg your help. If you would call at Davencourt House at the earliest opportunity I should be most grateful.

Seb sat back in his chair. Calling on young ladies in order to play the role of paternal confidant was so foreign to him as to be ludicrous. He could not imagine what had possessed Clara even to ask. Of course, he would not comply. It was out of the question. If she needed advice she should be sending for a female friend, not the greatest rake in London.

He glanced out the window. The winter morning looked crisp and bright. There was a dusting of frost on the rooftops. There were so many possibilities for a clear Yuletide morning. He could go riding. He could go to Tattersalls and spend more money on horses. He could go to Whites and read the paper, chat with his cronies, drink some more fine brandy. He yawned.

He could go to Collett Square and call upon Miss Clara Davencourt.

It would be something to do. He could teach her that summoning rakes to one's drawing room was in every way a poor idea.

He folded the letter and slid it into his pocket. Draining his coffee cup, he stood up and stretched. He was aware of a most unfamiliar feeling, a lifting of the spirits, a sense of anticipation. He took the stairs two at a time, calling for his valet as he went.

MISS CLARA DAVENCOURT was sitting in the library of the house in Collett Square, listening with a quarter of an ear while her companion, Mrs. Boyce, read to her from the *Female Spectator*. She checked the little marble clock on the mantelpiece. The Duke of Fleet would surely have received her letter by now. She wondered when he might call. Then she was struck by the thought that perhaps he might not call at all. Given that they had parted on the worst possible terms eighteen months before, she supposed it was quite possible he would not wish to see her again. She fidgeted with the material of her skirt, smoothing away imaginary creases. Seb Fleet was a rogue, but on this occasion that was what she needed. A gentleman simply would not do.

Clara wrinkled her nose slightly as she recalled their last meeting. She had called Fleet a callous, coldhearted scoundrel when he had rejected her admittedly unconventional but honest offer of marriage. It had taken all her courage to propose in the first place, and to be turned down had been a dreadful blow. In her pride and unhappiness she had told him that she never wished to see him again so she could understand if he chose not to respond to her plea now.

"The Duke of Fleet, ma'am." Segsbury, the Davencourt butler, was bowing in the doorway. Clara jumped. Despite the fact that she had been half-expecting him, she felt shock skitter along her nerves. Mrs. Boyce jumped, too. She dropped the newspaper and her hand fluttered to her throat. Clara noted the pink color that swept up her companion's neck to stain her cheeks, and the brightness that lit Mrs. Boyce's eyes. She bit her lip, hiding a smile. She had seen Sebastian Fleet have this effect on many ladies, no matter their age.

The duke was bowing to Mrs. Boyce and smiling at her in a way that made the woman's hands flutter like nervous moths. Clara watched with a certain cynicism. Charm was as effortless to Fleet as breathing.

Nevertheless, as he turned toward her she could not quite repress the flicker of awareness that he kindled inside her. She had assured herself that the previous eighteen months had taught her indifference where the Duke of Fleet was concerned. Now she knew that she lied.

It was impossible to be indifferent to Sebastian Fleet. He was a big man, both tall and broad, and his command of any room and any situation appeared natural. Despite his size he moved with a nonchalant grace that compelled the gaze. Clara reminded herself not to stare. She dropped her eyes to the embroidery that rested in her lap. She hated embroidering and would leave the material sitting around for months with absolutely no work done on it at all, but at a time like this it was a useful subterfuge.

Fleet was standing before her now. She could see the high polish of his boots. She resisted the urge to look up sharply. Instead she raised her chin slowly, composedly, every inch a lady of quality.

His eyes were very blue and lit with a devilry that told her more clearly than words that he was remembering their last meeting. Her heart thumped once with a mixture of nostalgia and relief. Now, she was sure, they could behave as mere acquaintances.

She saw the look in his eyes and amended the thought. She was far too aware of his physical presence to be comfortable with him. She felt her color rise and silently cursed him. He had taken her hand although she had not offered it. Neither of them were wearing gloves, and his fingers were warm and strong against hers, sending a shiver along her nerves.

"It is a great pleasure to see you again, Miss Davencourt." He held her hand for a moment longer than was quite respectable. A rakish smile curved his firm mouth. "I was afraid we might never meet again."

Clara cast her gaze down. "I regret there was no other course open to me, your grace."

The Duke's smile grew. He turned to Mrs. Boyce. "I wondered whether I might have a little time alone with Miss Davencourt, ma'am? We are old friends."

For a moment Clara thought her companion was so swept away by Fleet's charm that she was actually going to agree. Then the happy light died from Mrs. Boyce's eyes. Clara had impressed upon her many times that she was not to leave her alone with any gentleman, least of all a certified scoundrel. This, the one time Clara *did* wish to be left alone, was the first occasion on which Mrs. Bryce had remembered what her duty entailed.

"I am sorry, your grace, but that would not be in the least proper of me."

Mrs. Boyce sat up straighter, looking fully prepared to take up residence on the gold sofa until the Duke had departed.

It took more than a mere refusal to stop Seb Fleet. "I had actually intended to take Miss Davencourt driving, ma'am," he said. "It is such a beautiful day."

Mrs. Boyce's face cleared. "Driving! Oh, I see. Well, in that case there can be no objection. Nothing untoward could possibly take place in a curricle."

Fleet smiled broadly. Clara knew with an instant's insight that he was thinking of all the disreputable things that *could* happen in a curricle. No doubt he had indulged in them all at one time or another. But he spoke quite gravely.

"I assure you that Miss Davencourt will be completely safe with me, ma'am. I view her in a strictly paternal fashion."

Clara cast him a demure, sideways glance, which he met with his bland blue gaze. She had hoped that her reference to his paternal advice in the letter would vex him, since he had spent so much time at their last meeting telling her that he was too old for her.

"Then I shall fetch my cloak," she said, dropping a slight curtsey. "Thank you, your grace."

The flash of amusement in Fleet's eyes told her that he was not fooled by this show of meekness. She felt his gaze follow her out and almost shivered under the cool blue intensity of it.

She kept him waiting only a few minutes and he was openly appreciative when she rejoined him in the hall.

"It is a rare woman who does not take an hour over her preparations, Miss Davencourt."

"I was concerned not to keep your horses waiting in the cold, your grace," Clara said, with an expressive lift of the brows.

"Rather than not wishing to inconvenience me? I take the snub, but your concern for my team is still admirable."

Clara gave him a little smile and accepted the arm that he offered. He handed her up into the curricle, tucked a thick rug about her and offered her a hot brick for her feet. Despite the chill of the day she felt snug. Fleet leapt up beside her and took up the reins. Clara noticed immediately that they did not travel with a groom and prayed that Mrs. Boyce had not observed the fact from her vantage point behind the drawing room curtains. It certainly made matters easier for her, for she wished to have no eavesdropper on their conversation; on the other hand it also made her a little nervous. She could not expect standard decorum from Fleet. In fact, she never knew what to expect from him. That was half the trouble.

"I confess I was a little surprised to hear from you, Miss Davencourt," Fleet said with a quizzical smile, as he moved the horses off at a brisk trot. "The terms of our parting left me in no doubt that you wished never to see me again."

Clara smiled back with dazzling sweetness. "You are quite correct, your grace. As I intimated in my letter, only the direst need led me to contact you. I hoped that out of the friendship you have for my brother, you would agree."

Fleet sketched an ironic bow. "And here I am, Miss Davencourt, at your service. How comforting it must be to know that you may appeal to my sense of honor and know that I will respond immediately."

Clara's lips twitched. "You are all generosity, your grace." She looked up and met the intense blue of his eyes. "I hope," she added politely, determined to get the awkward part out of the way as soon as possible, "that we may put the past behind us. I am older and wiser now, and you—"

"Yes?"

"You, I suspect, are exactly as you were two years ago."

Fleet inclined his head. "I suspect that I am."

"So we may understand each other and be friends?" Clara finished.

There was a pause before Fleet spoke, as though he were weighing her words and found them lacking in some way she could not quite understand. "If you say so, Miss Davencourt," he said slowly.

He shot her another look. Clara felt her nerves tingle. She had always known Sebastian Fleet to be shrewd; those members of the ton who declared the duke to be nothing more than an easygoing rake did not understand him at all. The sharpness of mind behind those cool blue eyes had been one of the things that had attracted Clara to him in the first place. But she should not be thinking on that now. Dwelling on his attractions was foolish. She was no longer a green girl of one and twenty to fall in love with the most unobtainable duke in society.

The breeze ruffled Seb Fleet's dark golden hair, and he raised a hand absentmindedly from the reins to smooth back the lock that fell across his forehead. Contrary to both fashion and common sense, he wore no hat. The very familiarity of his gesture jolted Clara with a strange pang of memory. They had been in company a great deal together at one time but it was illusory to imagine that they had ever been close. Fleet had squashed that aspiration very firmly when he had rejected her proposal of marriage. No one ever got close to Sebastian Fleet. He did not permit it.

She knew she should not raise old memories but Clara had never done as she should. "When I proposed to you…" she began.

Fleet's brows snapped down in a thoroughly intimidating way. "I thought we were not speaking of the past, Miss Davencourt."

Clara frowned. "I would like to say my piece first."

Fleet sighed with resigned amusement. "I was under the impression you said your piece when we parted. *Arrogant, proud, rude, vain* and *self-satisfied* were all epithets I took to heart at the time and have not forgotten since."

"And," Clara said, "I imagine you have not altered your behavior one whit as a result."

"Of course not." Fleet flashed her a glance. "Naturally I was flattered by your proposal but I made it clear I am not the marrying kind."

"Being too much of a rake."

"Precisely."

"I thought it was worth asking you anyway," Clara said, with a small sigh.

Seb smiled at her, a dangerously attractive smile. "I know," he said. "It is one of the reasons I like you so much, Miss Davencourt."

Clara glared at him. "You like me—but not enough to marry me."

"You are mistaken. I like you far too much to marry you. I would be the devil of a husband."

They looked at each other for a moment. Clara sighed. She knew he liked her, which was half the trouble. They liked each other very much and it was a perilous form of friendship, forever in danger of toppling over into forbidden attraction.

Fleet turned the conversation decisively. "Tell me what I may do to help you, Miss Davencourt."

Clara hesitated. "I suppose it was unorthodox of me to write to you."

Fleet glanced at her. There was a smile in his eyes. "In so many ways. Most young ladies, particularly with the history that is between us, would think twice before pursuing so rash a course."

They had turned in to the park. It was too cold a morning for there to be many people about, but Clara found it pleasantly fresh, if chilly. Autumn leaves and twigs, turned white with frost, crunched beneath the horses' hooves. The sky was a pale, cloudy blue with faint sunshine trying to break through. Clara's cheeks stung with the cold and she burrowed her gloved hands deeper under the fur-lined rug.

Fleet slowed the curricle to a pace that required little concentration and turned his head to look at her directly. "Perhaps," he added dryly, "you will satisfy my curiosity when the time is right?"

Clara's throat was suddenly dry. Feeling nervous was an unusual experience for her.

"I have a proposition for you." Clara looked at him out of the corner of her eye. He was starting to look a little exasperated.

"You are dissembling, Miss Davencourt," he said. "Could you be more specific?"

Clara swallowed hard.

"I need a rake," she said bluntly, "so I sent for you."

It was impossible to shock the Duke of Fleet. He was far too experienced to show any reaction to such a statement. After a pause, he said, equally bluntly, "Why do you need a rake?"

Clara drew a deep breath. "I need a rake to teach me how to outwit all the other rakes and scoundrels," she said. "I used to think I was up to all the tricks that a rogue might play, but I am sadly outwitted. I was almost abducted in broad daylight by Lord Walton the other day, and at the theater Sir Peter Petrie tried to back me into a dark corner and kiss me. If I am not careful I shall find myself compromised and married off to save the scandal before I have even realized it. It is intolerable to be so beset!"

Fleet gave a crack of laughter. "You are a sensible girl, Miss Davencourt. I cannot believe you unable to depress the pretensions of the worst scoundrels in town! Surely you exaggerate?"

"Sir, I do not," Clara said crossly. "Do you think I should be asking you for help were it not absolutely necessary? Now that I am an heiress, matters are threatening to get out of hand."

"How thoughtless of your godmother to die and leave you so much money," Fleet said sardonically. He dropped his hand lightly over her gloved ones. "If only you were not so pretty and so rich, Miss Davencourt. You have become irresistible!"

Clara turned her shoulder to him. "Oh, I should have known better than to ask you for help! You always laugh at me. But you know it is true that one is seldom the toast of society if one's parents are poor."

Fleet's grip tightened for a moment and she looked up to meet his eyes. "I do understand," he said. "Your situation is not so different from being a duke subject to the wiles of matchmaking mamas and their daughters. You would be astounded at the number of young ladies who have twisted their ankles outside the portals of Fleet House," he added ruefully. "The pavement must be unconscionably uneven."

Clara stifled a giggle. "I do recall that you are unsympathetically inclined toward twisted ankles. When I sprained mine that day we had the picnic at Strawberry Hill you refused to believe me, and I was left to hop back to the carriage!"

She thought Fleet looked suitably contrite. "I apologize. That was very uncivil of me."

Clara sensed a moment of weakness. "So you see the difficulty I face," she said, spreading her hands in a gesture of pleading. "Will you help me?"

The weakness had evidently been an illusion. Fleet gave a decisive shake of the head. "Certainly not. This is nothing more than a blatant attempt to trap me into marriage."

Clara was outraged. Her lavender blue eyes flashed. "I might have known you could not disabuse yourself of the idea that I might *still* wish to marry you, your grace! Despite everything I have said you cannot believe yourself resistible! Of all the arrogant, conceited, vain and self-satisfied *old* roués!"

There was a look in his eyes that suggested he admired the spirited nature of her outburst—but it was clear that the word "old" had stung him.

"That is most unfair of you," he said. "I am only three and thirty. Hardly in my dotage!"

Clara gave an exaggerated sigh. "Let us ignore your tragic obsession with age for a moment, your grace. The whole point of what I am asking is for you to teach me how to outwit a rake, not fall into his arms. You need have no concerns that I intend to importune you. I have no romantic feelings for you whatsoever!"

There was a heavy silence between them. The horses had slowed to a standstill beneath the bare branches of an oak tree as Seb Fleet turned his full attention toward her. Despite the cold air, Clara felt a fizzing warmth inside her that was not merely irritation. Under his slow and thorough scrutiny the color rushed to her face in an even hotter tide. Breathing seemed unconscionably difficult.

"No feelings for me," he drawled. "Can that be true?"

"No," Clara said, gulping down a breath. "I lied. I feel exasperated and infuriated and downright annoyed and you are the cause of all of those feelings."

"Strong emotions indeed."

"But not of the warmer sort." Clara evaded his

gaze and picked at the threads of the tartan rug. "I have everything I desire in life at the moment. Why should I wish to marry anyone, least of all you?"

She saw the flash of something hot and disturbing in his eyes and added hastily, "Do not answer that! It was a rhetorical question!"

"Of course." Fleet's smile was wicked. "I doubt that you would appreciate my answer anyway."

"Very likely not. It is bound to be improper."

"What do you expect when you are talking to a rake? You cannot have it both ways, Miss Davencourt."

Clara sighed sharply. "Which is exactly why you would be the perfect person to help me," she said. "You are an out-and-out rogue. When we met, you took my hand before I was even aware of what you were doing. You charmed my companion into giving you time alone in my company. Those are precisely the things I wish to learn to avoid."

Fleet shook his head. "The answer is still no, I am afraid."

"Why?" Clara felt indignant.

"Because, my very dear Miss Davencourt, it would not serve," Fleet said. "You may not have realized it—" he turned toward her and his knee brushed against hers "—but I am behaving very much against type in refusing your request. Your average rake would accept, with no intention of keeping matters theoretical and every intention of seducing you."

Clara looked at him skeptically. "You actually claim to be acting from honorable motives?"

"The very purest, I assure you. But then, I am no average rake."

Clara did not need to be told. Sebastian Fleet was not average in any way. The languid arrogance, the dangerous edge, the sheer masculine power of him—all of these things made him exceptional. She shivered deep within her cloak.

To ask him to help her had been a reckless idea from the first; she recognized that. But her need had been genuine. She had been under siege and she was tired of it. She was also very stubborn.

"Can I not persuade you otherwise?" she begged. "I am not asking you to escort me about town, merely to tell me those dangerous behaviors to guard against."

She saw him shake his head decisively.

"To do so would be extremely perilous, Miss Davencourt. I might forget I was a gentleman and a friend of your brother and act on instinct. And I do not mean a paternal instinct."

Clara looked into his eyes. The instinct was there, masculine, primitive, wholly dangerous. She felt her senses spin under the impact of his gaze. She knew that he wanted to kiss her. Right here. Right now. He had never pretended he did not find her attractive. She knew that had their circumstances been different he would have tried to seduce her without a qualm.

He had been ruthlessly open with her in the past, telling her he intended never to marry, did not wish for the responsibility, and that he was incapable of being faithful. It had been her disillusion and disappointment that had led her to rail at him for not being the man she had wanted him to be. And now he was rejecting her again, albeit for a very different proposal, and once again she could recognize his reasons and even appreciate them, in a way.

She cleared her throat and made a little gesture of acceptance. "Very well. I understand what you are saying and...I admire your honesty."

His eyes opened wider with surprise and then, echoing her thoughts, he said, "It is no difficulty to admit I find you very attractive, Miss Davencourt. I would have the most dishonorable intentions toward you if matters had fallen out differently."

He sighed, picked up the reins and gave the horses a curt word of encouragement. The curricle picked up speed.

It was a moment or two before Fleet broke the slightly uncomfortable silence between them. "Do you truly intend never to marry?"

Clara raised her brows. "I cannot say never, but for now I am very happy as I am."

"It would be a tragic waste for you to remain single."

Clara felt a sharp stab of anger then that he could appreciate the qualities that might make her a good wife—for someone else.

"I doubt you are a good judge of that," she said. The words came out more sharply than she had intended and, although his face did not register any emotion, she sensed he was hurt. He did not pursue the point, however, and once again a silence fell.

She was on the point of apologizing when he said abruptly, "You are genuinely happy as you are?" There was an odd note in his voice. "By which I mean to ask if you truly have everything you wish for?"

Clara ignored the small voice that told her she had everything she wished for *except him.*

"Of course," she said firmly. "I have my family and my friends and plenty to occupy myself. I am very happy." She fixed him with a direct look. "Aren't you?"

She saw him hesitate. "Not precisely. Happiness is a very acute sensation. I suppose you could say I am content."

"Content." Clara thought about it. There was a comfortable feeling to the word but no high excitement about it. "That is good."

"It is good enough, certainly." Fleet had turned his

face away from hers and as a result she could not read his expression. He was difficult to read at the best of times, with that bland blue gaze and those open features. He appeared to be straightforward when in fact the reverse was true. Frustration stirred in her at how opaque he was, how difficult to reach. But then she had no reason to try to reach him. She had tried before and been rebuffed. She reminded herself that no one ever got close to the Duke of Fleet. This difficult friendship was as good as she would get. She had to decide whether it was worth it or not.

"If your rakes and fortune hunters are causing such a problem, I would suggest that you appeal to your sister-in-law, Lady Juliana, for help," Fleet said, breaking into her thoughts. "I doubt there is a rake in town who can out-maneuver her."

Clara shook her head sadly. "That would be the ideal solution but Juliana is entirely engrossed with the babies at present. That was really why I contacted you. We are to go to Davencourt for Christmas in a couple of weeks, but until then I imagine I am very much left to fend for myself."

"With the help of the redoubtable Mrs. Boyce, of course."

"Yes, and you have seen how much use she is!" Clara laughed. "I love her dearly but she conceives that she will have failed in her duty if she does not marry me off, and so makes a present of me to every passing rake and fortune hunter. I believe they view me as the ideal Christmas gift."

Fleet looked at her. His blue gaze was warm enough to curl her toes.

"I can imagine why, and it is nothing to do with your money."

Clara raised her chin.

"Since you are not to give me the benefit of your theoretical experience, your grace, I refuse to permit you to flirt with me. Rather I suggest you take me home." She looked around. "Indeed, I have no notion where we are!"

The path was narrow here and wended its way through thick shrubbery. Even in winter the trees and bushes grew dark and close overhead, enclosing them in a private world. It was a little disconcerting to discover just how alone they were in this frosty, frozen wilderness.

Fleet was smiling gently. "Take this as a free piece of advice, Miss Davencourt," he said. "Always pay attention to your surroundings. The aim of the rake will always be to separate you from company so that he may compromise you."

He put up a hand and touched one gloved finger lightly to her cheek. Her gaze flew to his as the feather-light touch burned like a brand.

"And once he has you to himself," the duke continued softly, "a rake will waste no time in kissing you, Miss Davencourt."

For what seemed like an age they stared into each other's eyes. Clara's heart twisted with longing and regret. Could he look at her like that if he did not care for her? He would deny it of course. Lust was easy for him to admit, love impossible.

Her body ached for him with a sudden, fierce fire. His presence engulfed her. She felt shaky, hot with longing. She raised her hand and brushed his away. Her fingers were not quite steady.

"Your point is well made, your grace." Her voice was husky and she cleared her throat. "I shall guard against that possibility."

Fleet's hand fell and he straightened up in his seat. Clara breathed again, a little unevenly.

"Take me home," she said again, and there was more than a little entreaty in her voice.

They came out from under the trees and joined the main path. A gentleman on a very frisky bay rode past, touched his hat to Clara and bowed slightly to Fleet, then pirouetted away with a fine display of horsemanship.

"Coxcomb," Fleet said.

His face was set in grim planes, the line of his mouth hard. Clara's sore heart shrank to see it.

The next barouche to pass them contained a gentleman and two painted ladies, who smiled and ogled in their direction, the gentleman in particular giving Clara a thorough scrutiny through his quizzing glass. Fleet cut them dead.

"Friends of yours?" Clara enquired politely.

"Not of the type that I would acknowledge when I am escorting you." Fleet paused perforce to avoid several young blades who had deliberately blocked their path in order to pay their respects to Clara.

"Walton, Jeffers, Ancrum and Tarver," Fleet said, when they had moved on. "I begin to see your difficulty, Miss Davencourt." He paused. "Perhaps if people see me squiring you about, that may dissuade the gazetted fortune hunters from pursuing you."

"I doubt that will dissuade anyone," Clara said. "It is well known that you have no intention of marrying, your grace, so it is more likely to encourage them if they think that I am prepared to spend time with a notorious rake."

Fleet cast her a look. "Nevertheless, Miss Davencourt," he said slowly, "perhaps I could help you."

Clara looked hopeful. "You have reconsidered?"

Fleet shook his head. "Not at all. I will not teach you about rakes. That would be foolhardy. But as it is only for a few weeks I *will* act as your escort while you remain in town and keep the gentlemen from troubling you." He smiled. "All in the most perfect and irreproachably paternal fashion, of course."

There was a thread of steel beneath his courteous tone, as though he would brook no refusal, and it brought Clara's chin up in defiance.

"Pray, do not conceive it to be your duty to help me, your grace," she said sharply. "I would detest the thought that I was a burden to you."

Fleet smiled a challenge. "If I cannot help you in one way, why not accept my assistance in another, Miss Davencourt?" he said persuasively. "I will protect you from unwanted attention and, since you have no wish to marry, I shall not be getting in the way of any gentleman you would consider a genuine suitor."

Clara bit her lip. In some ways it was a tempting proposition since it would free her from the odious attentions of insincere suitors. In other ways, though, his suggestion was sheer madness. To spend time in Fleet's company would only remind her of all the things she had loved about him, all the things she could not have. The cure had been hard enough last time. To invite trouble again now was plain foolish.

"No," she said, unequivocally.

Fleet shrugged and her heart shrivelled that she meant so little to him one way or another.

"Very well, then." His tone was careless. "I shall take you home."

Chapter Two

FLEET REFUSED to leave Clara at the door as she would have wished, but escorted her into the hall. There was high color in her face, both from the cold air and from their quarrel, and she refused to meet his eye. Her chin was raised and her whole body was stiff with haughtiness. Fleet found it amusing, provocative and downright seductive. He wanted to kiss the hauteur from her lips until her face was flushed with passion, rather than pride. He wanted to feel that voluptuous body softening, responding, under his hands. He shifted uncomfortably. He had always wanted Clara Davencourt in the most simple and fundamental way. It was unfortunate he simply could not have her and he had to learn to live with that. Under the circumstances it was probably the most foolish idea to offer her his escort and he should be grateful she had turned him down. He was uncomfortably aware that it had been the interest of Tarver and Walton and half a score others that had made him wish to keep her close. Allowing Miss Clara Davencourt to arouse his possessive instincts was a mistake. For that matter, allowing her to arouse any instincts at all was totally unsafe.

Lady Juliana Davencourt was in the hall, which broke the rather difficult silence between them. Juliana was dressed in an old striped gown and Fleet, remembering the wayward widow of the past, would never have believed she could have anything half so frumpish in her wardrobe. She was cradling a tiny baby in each arm and looked up with a smile as they came in at the door. Fleet thought she looked young and vibrant and alive with happiness. It was most odd. He had known Juliana Davencourt since she was a debutante, had once even thought that her particular brand of cynicism might be the perfect match for his, yet here she was transformed into someone he barely recognized. And why was she carrying the babies herself? Surely Davencourt was rich enough to employ a dozen nursemaids? This modern trend toward caring for one's children oneself made him shudder.

"Sebastian. How delightful to see you again!" Juliana did not offer him her hand, for which he could only be grateful since he was certain it was not clean. She turned to Clara, drawing them both with her into the warmth of the library, where a fire burned bright in the grate. Clara removed the enveloping cloak that she had been wearing, affording Fleet the opportunity to admire the luscious curves accentuated by her fashionable gown. It was all that he could do to keep his mind on the conversation.

"Did you enjoy your drive?" Juliana asked.

"Yes, thank you, Ju," Clara said. "I think it will snow later, though. It is most unconscionably cold. How is little Rose's croup this morning?" She had taken one of the babies from her sister-in-law with a competence that both beguiled and appalled Fleet. He watched as the child opened its tiny pink mouth in an enormous yawn, then gave an equally enormous burp. Its eyes flew open in an expression of extreme surprise. Clara gave a delighted laugh.

"She is taking her food well enough, it seems!"

Fleet watched as Clara raised a gentle finger to trace the curve of the baby's cheek. She was smiling now, her face pink from the nip of the chill air outside, her hair mussed up by the hood of the cloak, escaping in soft curls about her face. Fleet stared, unable to look away. Something tightly wound within him seemed to give a little. He felt very odd, almost light-headed. It was as though he was seeing Clara in a different way and yet the revelation made her appear even more seductive. Clara with her own child in her arms…

Then he realized that Juliana was addressing him, and had been doing so for some time. He had no idea what she was talking about.

"We would be very pleased, Sebastian, although if you felt that you could not we would understand…"

"Of course," Fleet said automatically, forcing his gaze from Clara. "It will be my pleasure."

"You will?" Juliana sounded pleased, relieved and surprised at the same time. "But that is wonderful! Martin will be delighted!"

It was her tone that helped to focus his thoughts. What had he agreed to do? Juliana sounded far too excited for this to be a simple dinner invitation. He looked up to meet Clara's quizzical blue gaze. "You have surprised me," she said slowly, "but I, too, am delighted, your grace."

She gave him a smile so radiant that Fleet felt shaken and aroused. The fire seemed extremely hot and he was feeling very odd. He wondered if he had caught an ague.

Clara dropped a kiss on the baby's forehead.

"I think it is appropriate for your new godfather to hold you now," she murmured, moving towards him.

Understanding hit Fleet in a monstrous wave of

feeling. He had just agreed to be the baby's *godfather!* He cast a terrified look at the little bundle Clara was holding out to him. Juliana was approaching in a flanking maneuver, murmuring something about him taking a seat so he could hold both babies at once. Both babies? Had he agreed to be godfather to the *pair* of them? He opened his mouth to protest, then closed it again, aware of the enormity of the situation in which he found himself. He could not in all conscience back out of the arrangement now. Juliana and Clara were both looking at him with shining eyes; it made him feel like a hero. He would have to wait until later—get Martin Davencourt alone over a glass of brandy, explain he had made a mistake, had thought he was being offered something much simpler, like a cup of tea or an invitation to a ball. He was certain he could sort the matter out, but in the meantime he would have to play along.

He sank into the big armchair before the fire and sat as still as a statue while the infants were placed in his arms. If he moved he might drop them. Worse, they might vomit on his coat of blue superfine. He had heard babies were prone to do such things although he had never been near one in his life.

They smelled faintly of a milky sickness that turned his stomach, and yet at the same time they were the softest and sweetest things he had ever touched. He lowered his nose gently and sniffed the top of Rose's head. She moved a little and made a small mewing sound. The other baby opened his eyes suddenly and stared at him. He realized he did not even know the boy's name.

"What…" His voice had come out huskily. He cleared his throat. "What is his name?"

"Rory," Juliana said. She was smiling. "They are called Rory and Rose."

Fleet looked down on the tiny bodies nestling close. He felt as though they had fastened their little hands about his heart and were squeezing tightly. A whole wash of emotions threatened to drown him.

He had to escape, and quickly. He looked at Juliana, then Clara, in mute appeal.

"Well, I…"

"You have done very well for a first attempt," Clara said, sounding like his childhood nanny, "although you do look utterly terrified."

To his inexpressible relief, she lifted Rory from his arms. Once Juliana had retrieved Rose he was free to stand, although his legs felt a little shaky. He made somewhat blindly for the door as though he could smell the fresh air and freedom.

"Thank you for the drive, your grace," Clara called after him. "Shall we see you tonight at Lady Cardace's Snow Ball?"

Fleet stared at her, trying to work out if he had heard the question correctly. He did not want to find himself accidentally agreeing to be godfather to yet more children or to something even more terrifying. He saw a tiny frown touch Clara's forehead at the length of time it was taking him to answer.

"Had you not been invited?" she inquired.

"Yes." Fleet took a grip on himself. "Yes, I shall be there."

Clara gave him another of her melting smiles. Much more of this and he would be quite undone. Clara and the twins between them had unmanned him.

"Good," she said. "I shall look forward to seeing you tonight."

FLEET TURNED the horses toward home. Some of the light seemed to have gone out of the day. Clara's vivid personality had set the air between them humming with life. Without her, everything seemed more dull and grey. He dismissed the thought as fanciful. It was simply that the weather had turned. Dark clouds were massing on the horizon, promising snow. The wind was sharper now, with a cutting edge. Despite the fact that he told himself it was just the effect of the weather, he found he missed Clara's warmth.

He remembered the twins with a shudder. He was

not cut out to be anyone's godfather. He was scarcely an example for the younger generation. If it had simply been a matter of presenting suitably large gifts on birthdays and Christmases then he might have fulfilled the requirements, but he was depressingly aware that the role of godfather asked much more of him. It was a pity—Clara probably thought more highly of him now than she had ever done in their acquaintance. That should not be permitted to sway him, however. He did not seek her good opinion. Nevertheless, it would be a shame to lose it so swiftly.

The snow was starting to fall. In London it fell with sooty edges, to lie in a dirty slush on the streets. For a moment he recalled the pure brightness of Fleet in the snow, the way the icicles hung from the branches and the river froze over in intricate icy patterns and the snowdrifts lay ten foot deep in the lee of the hedges. He ached to be there.

The panic was rising in his throat, as it sometimes did when he thought of Fleet in the winter. He dashed the snowflakes from his eyes and tried to think of something else. The twins… No, that was a bad idea. His panic heightened. Suppose something happened to Martin and Juliana? If he did not rescind his role as godfather he could conceivably end up with the care of two small children. The images crowded his mind. Babies crying, nursemaids fussing around… By the time he turned in to the stables at Fleet House he had got as far as redecorating one of the bedrooms as a nursery. He handed the curricle over to the grooms, hurrying inside, away from his fears.

The house was warm and quiet. The day's newspapers were waiting for him in the library. He sat down, but instead of picking up the *Morning Post* his hand strayed idly toward the bookcase. His eyes fell upon an ancient copy of Sterne's *Tristram Shandy* and he picked it up without thought. The book fell open at the title page, where there was an inscription in childish letters:

Oliver Fleet.

He shut the book with a sudden, violent snap that raised the dust from the pages. It had been about this time of year that his brother's accident occurred. He hated Christmas. He had never passed the holiday at Fleet since Oliver's death.

He settled back in his chair. The silence was almost oppressive. He could hear the brush of the snow against the windowpane. It was nine hours until Lady Cardace's rout. Then he would see Clara again. He tried not to feel too pleased and failed singularly. He liked Clara Davencourt immensely and that was his weakness; he found her hopelessly seductive and that was his danger. With her corn-gold hair, huge blue eyes and voluptuous curves, Clara was ridiculously pretty and the embodiment of every masculine fantasy in which he had ever indulged. He suspected he was not the only gentleman to have had such musings, but he was fairly certain he was the only man who admired Clara for the shrewd intelligence that lurked beneath her charming exterior. She had a sharp mind, and most men would dislike that; Seb Fleet adored it. He loved their conversations. Such admiration had proved his downfall two years before when he had nearly fallen in love with her.

He must guard against falling in love with Clara Davencourt now. He had no desire to marry and he could not have her any other way. And yet the day did seem darker without her presence. He had an unnerving feeling that he was lost in some way and Clara was the only one who could save him. Total foolishness, of course. The business with the infant Davencourt twins had affected his judgment. He would regain his calm with strong coffee and the *Morning Post*. And when he saw Clara Davencourt that evening she would be just another debutante. A pretty debutante, a rich debutante, but like all the other pretty little rich girls. He rang for the coffee. He reached for the paper. But he could not banish Clara from his mind.

THE SNOW WAS ALREADY a foot deep by the time the Davencourt carriage turned onto the sweep in front of Cardace House that evening. The glare of the lanterns was muted by the swirling flakes and the guests were hurrying within to escape the bracing cold.

"Our slippers will be soaked," Juliana grumbled, gingerly accepting Martin's hand to help her down onto the damp red carpet that led up to the door. "If it were not that this is the most important ball of the season and I am on tenterhooks to see what Lady Cardace has in store for us, I would rather be curled up in the library at home with a cup of hot chocolate and a good book!"

Clara shivered as the icy wind found its way beneath her cloak and raised goose bumps on her arms. Her evening gown was so flimsy it felt as though the wind were cutting through it like a knife. She hoped Lady Cardace's arrangements for her guests included both a hot drink and a roaring fire. There was nothing worse than a cold ballroom in winter.

Lady Cardace was the leading hostess of the Little Season, and invitations to her Snow Ball were the most eagerly sought tickets of the year. Each winter she arranged something truly original and each year the lesser hostesses would copy her, driving Lady Cardace to ever more outrageous forms of entertainment the next time.

"Ah," Martin said, looking about them as they hastened into the house, "I think this year's theme is the traditional Christmas. How charming!"

They surrendered their coats to a footman and accepted the hot cup of negus proffered by another servant. Clara gratefully inhaled the richly alcoholic fumes and warmed her hands on the crystal glass. Lady Cardace had exceeded herself this year. Sprays of holly and mistletoe adorned the ballroom walls, the deep green of the leaves contrasting richly with the red and white berries. The ceiling was hung with clouds of white gauze and sparkling snowflakes, a huge fire glowed behind the grates at each end of the hall, and the orchestra was already striking up for the first dance of the night. From the refreshment room wafted the enticing scent of a richly warming beef soup. Martin immediately headed in that direction to fetch a bowl for each of them.

Despite the festive atmosphere, Clara felt bluedevilled. It was nearing midnight and a surreptitious first—and second—scan of the ballroom told her the Duke of Fleet was not in attendance.

She glanced about her a third time, taking pains to conceal the maneuver. It seemed that every other accredited member of the ton was pressed into Lady Cardace's mansion. The evening was a dreadful crush. But the only man Clara secretly wanted to be crushed against was absent.

She wished now that she had not written to Sebastian Fleet. She had managed perfectly well without seeing him for the past eighteen months. Now she had stirred up those old feelings once again and a part of her ached for his presence.

"You look as though you have chewed on a piece of lemon peel," Juliana said, slipping her arm through Clara's and guiding her toward the rout chairs at the end of the room. "It is Sebastian Fleet, I suppose. You never quite managed to cure yourself of that affliction, did you, Clara?"

Clara bit her lip. She had not realized her preference for Fleet's company was still so obvious after she had spent so much time and effort in trying to appear indifferent. But Juliana's eyes were kind so Clara shook her head ruefully and admitted the problem. "I fear not. I have tried, but I cannot help my feelings."

"Ah, feelings." Juliana's lips curved into a smile and Clara knew she was thinking of Martin. "What a blight they can be. No, there is absolutely no point in fighting how you feel."

"I thought," Clara said, "that you disapproved of my tendre for the Duke of Fleet?"

"I did," Juliana said cheerfully. "I do. One cannot approve of Fleet. He is too old for you, he is too experienced and he is too much of a rake."

Clara sighed. She knew Juliana was right, but in some deep and stubbornly instinctive way she believed that she was the right woman for Sebastian

Fleet. She had always believed it, but his rejection of her had made her falter and question her conviction.

"I do not wish you to be hurt, Clara," Juliana said. "Fleet has had years of practice in keeping intimacy at bay. I understand because I did the same thing myself."

"And Martin helped you to see that it need not be so," Clara reasoned.

"That is true. But that does not mean the same thing will happen for you." Juliana touched her hand briefly. "I am sorry, Clara. I want to help you—to save you the hurt." She shot a glance over Clara's shoulder. "Fleet is here now. Do you need a little time?"

Clara cast one swift glance toward the door then shook her head rapidly. "I am very well. I know you only mean to help me, Ju."

Juliana nodded and squeezed her arm, then they both turned to watch the Duke of Fleet approach. There was a prickle along Clara's skin, a mixture of fear and anticipation. He looked so autocratic, so easily in command.

Fleet had bumped into Martin in his journey across the room. Clara observed that Martin had managed to forget the refreshments. No doubt he had been distracted by some political discussion and had completely forgotten his original errand. She shook her head slightly.

The two men were coming toward them, deep in conversation. Juliana was beaming with a smile of warm pleasure as her husband approached her and Clara felt a pang of envy that she could not repress. She longed for such intimacy with Sebastian, but that was much more than he was prepared to give her.

Even so, she was scarcely indifferent to him. There was something about the way he moved that made the breath lock in her chest. She could swear her knees were trembling a little.

The duke had seen her now. He had also apparently noticed that a couple of gentlemen were hastening toward her, determined to get there before he did. A smile touched the corner of his mouth. The expression in his blue eyes made Clara feel ridiculously hot and bothered. She felt as though his gaze were stripping her naked. Damn the man. How could he work such mischief across a crowded ballroom?

Fleet had caught up to the two young men, Lords Elton and Tarver, and had diverted them from their original course toward Clara by grasping their arms, bending to have a word in their ears and then sending them packing in no uncertain terms. Clara's lips thinned. Though she had not particularly wished to be importuned by either Elton or Tarver, nor had she a need for Fleet to play the high-handed protector. Especially when she had earlier rejected his offer of help.

Fleet was upon them now. He bowed, first to Lady Juliana, then to Clara.

"How do you do, Lady Juliana, Miss Davencourt? It is a pleasure to see you this evening."

A faint smile curved Juliana's lips. "Thank you, Fleet. How pretty of you. Now, I sense you want something. How may we help you?"

Clara could sense Fleet watching her. She turned away and pretended a complete lack of interest. Surely there was some fascinating event occurring on the other side of the dance floor that she could focus upon.... Fleet took her hand. Her pulse jumped. He was smiling, very sure of himself.

"I was hoping you would grant me the pleasure of a dance, Miss Davencourt."

Lady Juliana was looking pointedly at their clasped hands. Fleet let go of Clara and she gave him a look of limpid innocence.

"I beg your pardon, your grace, but I do not dance this evening."

Both Fleet and Juliana looked startled.

"You do not dance tonight!" Fleet sounded thoughtful and not in the least put out. "How very dull for you to attend a ball and not indulge in the dancing."

Clara smiled. "I have no wish to indulge with you, your grace. You must forgive me. Pleasant as it is to see you, I told you earlier that I was not in need of your escort."

She sensed both Juliana's amusement and Fleet's chagrin, although he did not permit any expression to mar his features. Instead, he turned to Lady Juliana.

"If you were to recommend me as a suitable partner, ma'am, Miss Davencourt might be persuaded to relent."

Clara's lips twitched. She had to concede that it was clever of him to try an approach through Juliana but she was fairly certain her sister-in-law would not let her down.

Juliana laughed. "I cannot recommend you as suitable in any way, Fleet, at least not to a respectable young lady."

Fleet gave Clara a rueful smile that nevertheless held a hint of some other, more disturbing emotion in its depths. It promised retribution.

"Then if you will not consider me suitable, Lady Juliana," Fleet continued, "pray take pity on me."

Juliana flicked an imaginary speck from her skirts with disdainful fingers. "Pointless to appeal to my sense of pity, Fleet. You know I have none."

"I know your husband intends to dance with you, Lady Juliana," Fleet said, watching Martin finish his conversation with an acquaintance and make haste to join them. "A pity that Miss Davencourt denies herself—and me—a like privilege."

Juliana's whole face lit up at the sight of her husband. "When you are married, Fleet, then you may have the privilege of dancing with your wife. For now it is Miss Davencourt's right to deny a suitor if she chooses and she is weary of rakes. I suggest that you nurse your disappointment in the card room. Clara?"

Clara inclined her head. "Lady Juliana is in the right of it, your grace. I shall bid you good evening."

Fleet bowed gracefully. "Then I shall take you at your word. Good night, Lady Juliana, Miss Davencourt."

He went without a backward glance.

Clara watched him go. The lowering thing was that he radiated such indifference. She wished she had not given in to the childish impulse to thwart him. It was not that she wished to dance with either Lord Elton or Lord Tarver, but she had wanted to make that choice for herself. Once Fleet had dismissed them and presented himself as substitute she had vowed to reject him.

"A word of warning," Juliana said, turning back to Clara for a moment as Martin urged her toward the dancing. "Do not make a habit of playing these games with the Duke of Fleet. He *made* the game when you were still in the schoolroom."

"I think Clara was quite right to turn Fleet down," Martin said unexpectedly. "He can do nothing to enhance a lady's reputation."

"No, dear," Juliana said with an affectionate smile, "but as usual you have no notion of what is really going on." She led her spouse away to join the set that was forming for the quadrille.

He made the game...

Clara shivered a little. Fleet had told her that very morning he was no ordinary rake. She must be mad.

Everyone else was dancing and Clara realized she was the only girl left sitting out. It was not something that happened often, but whatever Fleet said to Elton and Tarver had evidently made the rounds, for although plenty of gentlemen were looking in her direction, none were making any move to engage her. How exceedingly annoying. Clara's exasperation with the Duke of Fleet grew stronger. Some of the debutantes were smiling behind their fans, clearly delighted the prettiest girl in the room was partnerless for once. Clara gritted her teeth. She would not stay to be laughed at. She would have to make a strategic retreat to the ladies' withdrawing room.

It felt like an unconscionably long time that she lurked in the shadows, pinning and repinning her silver brooch, tidying her already immaculate hair and smoothing her dress. Eventually she was so bored she could bear it no longer. She stalked out into the corridor wondering whether Juliana and Martin had concluded their dance and would provide her with some company.

The corridor was dark and quiet. Sprigs of holly and mistletoe adorned the walls here, as well, between the flaring lanterns. There was a scent of pine and citrus in the air, a smell so nostalgic of Christmases past that Clara paused for a moment and breathed in the heady scent, smiling. She was thinking of Christmas at Davencourt, when a door on her right opened abruptly and the Duke of Fleet stepped out directly in front of her.

"At last," he said. "I have been waiting for you."

SEB FLEET HAD BROKEN both his resolutions for the evening within two minutes of stepping inside Lady Cardace's ballroom. His plan to tell Martin he had changed his mind about being godfather to the twins fell at the first hurdle when his friend greeted him with such delight that Fleet found himself unable to disappoint him. He might have despised himself for such sentimental weakness—it was an affliction that he had not suffered previously—but then he caught sight of Clara and all other thoughts fled his mind.

Clara had long ago ceased to wear the white muslin of the very young debutante and tonight she was in a gown of delicate pale green. It swathed her soft curves with the sort of cunning elegance that accentuated rather than hid the body beneath. Her fine, blond hair was swept up to reveal the tender line of her neck. She was smiling at something Juliana was saying. She looked radiant; Fleet felt it like a punch in the stomach. He vaguely remembered that he had resolved to avoid Clara that evening.

He had stopped, stared, and barely been able to conceal from Martin the fact that he was profoundly, outrageously, attracted to his sister. Then he had seen Elton and Tarver heading in the same direction with seemingly much the same thoughts as his own, and had ruthlessly stepped in to tell them that he was Miss Davencourt's escort that night unless they wished to challenge his right. Neither of them had done so.

He felt an almost uncontrollable compulsion to kiss her, to claim her, before the assembled company. The impulse appalled and excited him more than any other emotion he had ever experienced. Only the thinnest shred of self-control prevented him. Public response to such behavior would be to hound him into marriage or be cast out. So his desire for Miss Clara Davencourt would remain unslaked. Except…

Except that he could not resist. Part of a successful rake's strategy, of course, was cold calculation. He needed to be in control at all times. Seb Fleet had lost his control where Clara Davencourt was concerned. And now he had her where he wanted her.

Clara had stopped dead when she saw him. In the second it took for her to recover from her surprise, Fleet leaned one hand against the wall, pinning her between his body and the door.

This was dangerous and foolhardy, but he felt an exhilaration that brooked no refusal. A strand of honey-colored hair had loosened from its clasp and lay against her cheek, heavy and smooth. He raised one hand to touch it and felt her jump. Her eyes were huge and dark in the shadows of the hall. When she spoke her voice was shaky and he felt a powerful rush of conquest.

"What do you mean when you say that you were waiting for me? You were playing cards."

Fleet shook his head. "I merely wanted you to think that."

There was silence between them. He kept her trapped between him and the door, so close he could feel the warmth of her body through the thin muslin of her gown. He leaned forward and brushed his lips against her ear. She jumped again and the response caused a jolt through his own body.

"Do not…" Her words were a whisper.

"I was intending to have you all to myself," Fleet said softly. "I knew you would not stay alone in the ballroom when you were devoid of admirers—what lady would expose herself to such humiliation? So I merely waited for you here."

He saw her expression change to anger.

"How conceited you are!" she exclaimed. "First you abandon me in the ballroom and then you presume you may pick up with me again whenever it suits you!"

Again she saw him smile. "I did not abandon you, Miss Davencourt. You rejected me."

She bit her lip. "Most gentlemen can comprehend a simple refusal, your grace."

"Alas, I have always been slower to understand than most." His breath stirred a tendril of her hair. The curve of her cheek was achingly sweet and the pure line of her jaw so tempting that he wanted to bury his face in its curve and breathe in the warm, feminine scent of her skin. His body tightened unbearably.

She turned her head slightly toward him. Their lips were no more than an inch apart now.

She whispered, "I have something to tell you, your grace."

Excitement kicked through his body. He could feel the caress of her breath against his cheek. She moistened her lips with the tip of her tongue and he almost groaned aloud to see it.

"You told me this morning that a lady should always be aware of her surroundings in order to thwart the evil plans of a rake." She raised her gaze to meet his. "I wanted to show you that I have taken you at your word. Good night."

He thought he had her trapped, but now he realized she had one hand behind her back from the very beginning of their encounter. Indeed, he could read the triumph in her eyes. There was the softest of clicks as the doorknob turned in her palm. She gave him a smile that was pure provocation, stepped back into the ballroom and closed the door gently in his face.

Chapter Three

SEB FLEET caught himself just before he slammed the palm of his hand against the panels of the closed door in sheer frustration. So, Clara Davencourt had out-played him for a second time that evening. He, on the other hand, had been taking his own game entirely too seriously. The constriction in his breeches told him just how desperately he wanted her. The physical ache was only matched by the aching disappointment of denial.

He shook his head slowly. He had been seduced by his own seduction. He had assumed he could outwit Clara and steal a kiss. But he wanted so much more from her; he could not pretend otherwise. He felt trapped between a rock and a very hard place.

"Are you all right, old fellow?"

Fleet straightened up. His host, Lord Cardace, had

come out of the library further down the passage and was looking at him with concern and no little curiosity. He realized he must have looked very odd, half-slumped against the wall.

"I am very well, thank you, Cardace," Fleet said. "Just a trifle winded. The gout, you know. In my toes. Damnably painful when I try to dance."

Lord Cardace grimaced sympathetically. "The trials of age, eh, Fleet?"

"And of the bottle," Fleet agreed.

Cardace clapped him on the shoulder. "Then I'd find a seat if I were you. My wife has arranged for the mummers to entertain us. Can't abide all that old-fashioned singing and dancing myself and it's not for the old and infirm."

"Thank you for the advice," Fleet said with suitable gratitude.

He allowed Cardace to escort him with solicitude into the ballroom, then slipped away to the shelter of an alcove not, as his host assumed, to sit down and rest his aging bones, but to observe Clara without being observed. She was sitting between her brother and Lady Juliana in the demure pose of the perfect debutante. Fleet's lips twitched. She looked entirely composed. There was no hint that a few minutes before she had been within an ace of being ravished in a corridor by an out-and-out rake. The suitors were swarming around her again and Fleet felt the familiar wave of primitive possessiveness swamp him at the way the men were fawning, kissing her hand, whispering in her ear, smiling, toadying.

Until that moment, he had promised himself he would walk away. Clara Davencourt was not for him and well he knew it. He was full of good intentions. Then she gave her hand to Lord Elton to lead her into the dance, and a powerful wash of jealousy swept through Fleet. He started toward her.

One kiss. He would take one kiss and then he would leave her alone forever. He promised himself that.

He noted the precise moment she saw his approach. Her blue eyes narrowed with a disbelief she could not quite conceal. She caught her full lower lip between her teeth for a second before she turned aside to respond to something Elton was saying. The same honey-colored curl he had touched earlier in the darkness now curled in the hollow of her throat. She looked both fragile and determined. He could sense defiance.

Elton was no lady's champion. He saw Fleet approaching, turned pale, babbled something to Clara and shot away across the floor as though his coat were on fire. Clara turned on Fleet, ignoring the set that was forming around them, the curious ladies and gentlemen who had seen her abandoned before the dance even started.

"What on earth did you do to Lord Elton?" she hissed.

"I did nothing." Fleet was all innocence as he gained her side and took her arm.

"You know what I mean!" Clara's face was flushed with annoyance. "You spoke to him earlier! What did you say?"

"I warned him not to pester you with his false protestations of affection."

Clara snorted. "So that you could pester me instead?"

"You injure me."

"And you infuriate me!" Clara's blue eyes flashed. "Twice now I have bid you good-night."

"I am sorry. I never retire early from a ball."

"Oh!" Clara let go of her breath on an angry sigh. "Your high-handed interference first left me without partners and now has me standing alone in the middle of a set."

"I would offer to dance with you," Fleet said, "but you have already refused me and I do not wish to put my fate to the touch again."

Clara gave him a dark look and turned to stride off the floor. Her back was ramrod straight, her entire figure stiff with outrage. She ignored the raised brows and titters of amusement.

Fleet followed. Clara was standing with her back to him. He put a hand on her arm, leaned closer and spoke for her ears only.

"Do not be too complacent about escaping me earlier. I shall kiss you before the night is out. I swear it."

He felt her tremble. She spun around to face him. Her gaze was uncertain now, but behind her eyes he saw the flicker of something else: she was intrigued against her will, unwillingly fascinated, tempted… His blood fired at the thought.

"I do not believe you," she said, summoning all her will to steady herself.

"Believe me," Fleet said.

He had timed the matter to perfection. There was a shout that the mummers were coming and then a tide of people swept them to the edges of the ballroom as the dance broke up. The door was flung wide and the mummers marched in to the beat of the drum. The orchestra took up the tune with gusto and the crowd shifted and split as the dancing started again. Gone was the decorous elegance of the waltz. This music was fast and wild and, for a moment in the flickering fire and candlelight, amid the boughs of holly and mistletoe, it seemed as though they were in a medieval hall surrounded by all the pageantry and joy of Christmas.

Fleet grabbed Clara's wrist and drew her into his

arms. Her body was soft against his and she came to him without demur. Perhaps she imagined they were to dance, for the strains of the music filled the air, mingled with laughter and voices.

Instead he drew her into the shadowed darkness of the window recess. It was colder here. Snow brushed the panes and the reflection of the candlelight shone in the glass. Without another moment's delay he bent his head and covered her mouth with his.

She stiffened with shock, but only for a moment. He felt her body soften against his, felt the instinctive response she could not hide. Her mouth opened beneath his and his mind spun even as a vise closed about his body, the desire he could barely control rampaging through him like wildfire.

He reined in his urgency and slid his tongue gently, caressingly, along the inside of her lower lip, teasing a response from her. He must be gentle; this was not the time and the place for anything else. She made a small sound in her throat at the invasion of his tongue and he was shot through with lust so hot and primitive he was suddenly within an ace of tangling his hand in her hair, and slamming her back against the cold stone wall to kiss her within an inch of her life.

The beat of the music was in his blood now, primeval and intense. His mouth crushed hers again, his tongue sweeping deep. He wanted her naked in his bed. He wanted to strip away the layers of clothing between them and take her with an urgency and desire that made no concession to gentleness. He had wanted her for such a long time. He had denied that need and now he could deny it no longer. "Clara…"

He said her name on a ragged whisper as his lips met hers for a third time. Her eyes were closed, the lashes a dark sweep against her cheek. Her lips were swollen from the ruthless demands of his. She was trembling.

So was he. His emotions were frighteningly adrift. The way Clara was clutching at his jacket to pull him closer, the taste of her, the fusion of sweetness and desire, kindled in him sensations never previously experienced. She was his and his alone; he would never let her go.

He pressed her closer to him, one hand coming up very gently to caress her breast. He could feel the nipple harden through the muslin of her dress against the palm of his hand. The heat ripped through him.

Their lips parted slowly, reluctantly, one last time and he felt as though he were losing something. He felt cold.

She was looking at him with such dazed sensuality in her eyes that his heart turned over. He could not speak. A moment later she blinked and her expression warmed from bemusement into anger.

"When I asked for your help this morning," she said sharply, "I was *not* requesting lessons in kissing."

Sebastian, shaken by the unexpected intensity of the experience and by achieving the one thing he had dreamed of doing for the past two years, was rocked back.

"You scarcely need lessons, my dear," he said. Did she not understand her own power? If she could do that to him with one kiss he shuddered to think what would happen when he took her to bed. *When?* He forced his wild thoughts to slow down. He would *not* make love to Clara Davencourt.

He looked at her again as the heat drained from his body and a shred of sense took hold. He had not given much thought to her reactions, being so wrapped up in his own. Now, scanning her face, he made a stunning discovery that sent his thoughts into turmoil again.

"That was your first kiss," he said slowly. He felt a little regretful. While he had been swamped with lust and thoughts of ravishment, she was experiencing something quite different. Something new. Something shocking. He should have guessed. He should have realized how important the moment had been for her. He shut his mind to the thought of how important it had been to *him*.

"Yes it was," she said.

Fleet was at a loss. He had taken greedily from her with no thought for her feelings. While he floundered, Clara had evidently regained full possession of her senses.

"Don't you dare say you are sorry," she said wrathfully.

Fleet smiled. "No. I'm not sorry." Her expression eased slightly. "It was nice," he added.

"Nice? *Nice!*" Clara took a deep breath.

He could see the hurt in her eyes. Nice was so bland a word for what had happened between them. Devil take it, how could he be making such a hash of this? He was supposed to be a man of the world. The trouble was that he was accustomed to dealing with women of the world, not inexperienced young ladies. He felt woefully out of his depth.

"Then I wish you a *nice* Christmas, your grace," she said, spun on her heel and walked briskly away.

SHE HAD BEEN KISSED for the first time. Thoroughly, expertly, ruthlessly kissed by a man who was a thorough, ruthless expert. She knew she should feel shocked or offended or both. The trouble was, it had been wonderful.

Clara curled up on her bedroom window seat and watched the snow falling. The clouds were breaking now, shreds of moonlight showing in the blackness, glittering on the white branches of the trees as the tiny flakes fell softly then finally ceased. It was very late and the city was quiet. Clara leaned her head against the cold pane and thought of Sebastian Fleet.

She supposed she had been in love with him from the start. That realization did not excuse her behavior but it certainly explained it. She should have slapped his face. Instead she had pulled him closer with a hunger that had startled her as much as it had no doubt astounded him. The experience had been like feast after famine, joy after long nights of loneliness.

She sighed, wrapping her arms about her knees and curling up tighter still. When he let her go she had realized what had been an earth-shattering experience for her was for him no more than a pleasant encounter with a pretty girl. The vast gap between the two of them—the experienced rake and the never-been-kissed debutante—had never seemed starker.

Now was the moment to accept the truth and relinquish her fantasy.

Sebastian Fleet would never love her as she loved him.

As she wanted to be loved.

As she *deserved* to be loved.

She pressed her fingertips to the cold glass. Outside the night was beautiful but frozen. The trees were still as statues. Above the trees swung a little star, glittering in the deep dark of the night, sometimes obscured by the scurrying cloud, sometimes shining bright, growing in strength.

Have hope.

Have faith.

Clara shook her head slightly. She slid off the seat and let the curtain fall back into place. The room was warm and quiet. She felt lonely.

"Perch," the Duke of Fleet said, taking the pristine, pressed newspaper from the tray his butler offered, "would you be aware of those shops that sell Christmas gifts for infants?"

Perch's eyebrows shot up into his hair. "Gifts for infants, your grace?"

Fleet gave him a hard stare. "Nothing wrong with your hearing this morning is there, Perch?"

"No, your grace."

"Do you know the answer to the question?"

"No, your grace."

"But you could find out."

"Of course, your grace." Perch bowed. "Would you wish me to purchase something appropriate, your grace?"

"No," Fleet said absentmindedly, scanning the

headlines, "I will do the purchasing myself. I merely need the direction."

"Of course, your grace," Perch said, "I shall see to it at once."

Fleet nodded, tucked the paper under his arm and headed toward the library. He wondered what Miss Clara Davencourt was doing this morning. He would not call in Collett Square to find out. After the fiasco of the previous night it was best to leave matters to cool. Looking back, in the frozen light of day, he wondered what on earth had possessed him. Before he had gone to the ball he had made a perfectly reasonable resolution to avoid Clara's company, which he had broken as soon as he had seen her. It was incomprehensible. He must have been drunk. He must have been bewitched. He must have been both bewitched *and* drunk at the same time. It must not happen again.

Even so, he knew that his behavior had been shabby. He should send her some flowers to apologize. Except that she would probably cut off the tops and return the stems to him. He smiled a little at the thought.

Two portraits flanked the entrance to the library. They were of the previous Duke of Fleet and his Duchess. Sebastian rarely noticed them, for they were as much part of the fixtures and fittings of the house as a chair or a lamp. Now, however, he stopped and regarded the painted faces. His father looked noble, wrapped in scarlet and ermine and adorned with the ducal strawberry leaves. His mother had a gentler face beneath her coronet. Wise and kind, she had put the warmth into his childhood.

The huge ruby betrothal ring of the Fleets gleamed on her finger, alongside the simple wedding band. They were both in the vaults of his bank and there they would stay; it felt symbolic, somehow.

His mother had never really recovered from the loss of her youngest, Oliver. It was all wrong to bury one's child. Whenever he thought of the burden he had laid on his parents, he felt the same crushing cold. If he had saved Oliver it might all have been different, but he had failed.

He hurried into the library and sat down beside the fire. Perhaps it was time to rearrange the portraits in the house. A couple of landscapes might look attractive in the hall. At least there were no pictures of Oliver to haunt his waking nightmares.

There was a tap at the library door. Perch entered.

"Hamley's Emporium is the best shop to purchase children's gifts, your grace," he said.

"Hamley's," Fleet said. "Excellent. I shall go there at once."

He felt a profound relief to be occupied.

IT WAS LATE when the knock came at the door of the house in Collett Square. Clara had been reading alone in the library in the big armchair in front of the fire. Martin and Juliana were attending a dinner party and Mrs. Boyce had gone to bed. Clara had fully intended to follow, but had become caught up in Miss Austen's *Sense and Sensibility* and stayed before the dying fire as the clock ticked past midnight.

She heard the knock and looked up, surprised anyone would possibly be calling at this time of night. She heard Segsbury's footfall across the floor, followed by the creak of the hinges and a low-voiced exchange.

"I regret, your grace, that there must have been some mistake. Mr. Davencourt and Lady Juliana are not at home...."

Your grace?

Clara sat bolt upright, her book sliding off her lap with a thud. Could this be Sebastian Fleet come to call at this hour? Impossible, unless he had arranged to take a glass of brandy with Martin and discuss the latest legislation going through the Houses of Parliament...

"It is no matter, Segsbury. My mistake, I believe." Fleet sounded distinctly ill at ease now. "If you would be so good as to give this to Mr. Davencourt. It is a Christmas gift for the twins."

There was a rustling sound. Clara's curiosity gave

her the excuse she needed. She opened the library door and went out into the hall.

"Miss…" Segsbury was as taken aback as a butler of his experience could be. "I apologize. I thought that you had retired."

"It is no matter, Segsbury," Clara said, with a smile. "Good evening, your grace."

"Miss Davencourt." Fleet sketched a bow. He did not smile at her. In the barely lit hall Clara could not read his expression, although she fancied his mouth was set in grim lines.

Her heart was tripping with quick, light beats. She had wanted to see Fleet again despite everything. She had been compelled in some way to force this meeting when she could have stayed quietly in the library and allowed him to go on his way. Now she wished she had not given in to that impulse. This hard-faced stranger was not the man she had wanted to see. Already he had distanced himself from her. Already the events of the previous night seemed like a fevered dream.

"If you will excuse me," Fleet said, "I was merely delivering this parcel." He gestured to the package now in Segsbury's hand. "It is a Christmas gift for your young nephew and niece. I hope I have chosen appropriately. It is a little difficult when one is not accustomed to shopping for children."

Clara felt a jolt of surprise. "You chose it *yourself?*"

A rueful grin touched Fleet's mouth. "I did."

"And you delivered it yourself, too. How singular!"

She saw his smile deepen and felt a jolt of pleasure inside. "Perhaps you could put the parcel somewhere safe, Segsbury," she said, "while I show the Duke of Fleet out."

Segsbury gave her a hard stare. He had been butler to Lady Juliana before her marriage and so was no stranger to unconventionality, but he had a very definite way of showing his disapproval of such inappropriate behavior. He looked at Clara for a long moment and she looked back steadily, then he bowed slightly.

"Very well, miss."

Neither Clara nor Fleet moved as Segsbury walked away with stately displeasure. The hall was quiet as his footsteps died away.

"I wanted to see you," Clara said.

"So it seems. It was not, perhaps, your wisest decision." Fleet's entire body was taut with what Clara assumed was anger.

"Last night—"

"Miss Davencourt, we really must *not* discuss this."

"Not discuss it?" Clara felt something snap within her. "What do you want to do instead, your grace? Sweep it under the carpet because it is difficult for us to face up to so inconvenient an attraction?"

"No," Fleet ground out. "What I want is to have you."

Clara felt a sudden, treacherous excitement. It caught like a flare, blazing into shocking and sensual life. Fleet's eyes darkened with concentrated passion. He took one step forward, grabbed both her arms and his mouth captured hers, swift and sure.

Clara instinctively moved closer to him. All conscious thought fled her mind. Her arms went about him, fingers tangling in his hair. He tasted faintly of brandy and strongly of desire. The kiss grew frantic, then rough, almost brutal. The shock of it sent a blaze of feeling right to the center of Clara's body.

His impatient hands were already pushing aside silk and lace, and when he closed his hand over her breast, warm and hard against her bare skin, she gave a desperate moan as she felt her legs start to buckle. He half pulled, half carried her through the library door, slamming it shut behind them.

Then they were down on the rug before the fire and she was clutching at his shoulders. His tongue and teeth had replaced his fingers at her breast, and she squirmed and arched in quick delight to his touch.

She was shaking; so was he. Clara noticed it with astonishment, for surely this man was supposed to be an experienced rake. Yet he touched her with reverence as well as ferocious desire, as though he could not quite believe what was happening. The sense of power the thought gave her, the sheer unbelievable seduction of his hands on her body, roused a driving need.

His lips returned to hers with a passionate tenderness and urgency that inflamed her. He moved over her, throwing up her skirts, sliding a hand up her thigh, over the soft skin to find the hot, central core of her. Her body shivered like a plucked cord beneath his touch.

"Sebastian…"

She felt as though she were dissolving into some desperate pleasure, and when he moved down to meet her unspoken plea for release with the touch of his tongue against her most intimate place, the sensation was too hot and too sudden to resist. Her body was speared by so violent a delight that she rolled over, stifling a cry against his chest.

She could feel his arousal hard against her thigh but even as she reached blindly for him, intuitively knowing what was needed, he was withdrawing, wrapping his arms carefully about her. Although he held her close, she somehow knew he was putting distance between them. The pleasure and the astounding intimacy she felt turned cold and started to shrink.

"Clara… sweetheart…we must not…"

If Clara's thoughts had been clear, she would have

noticed the harsh undertone in his voice, realized he was still trembling as much as she. Instead, she only knew that while her body still echoed with unfamiliar passion, Sebastian was trying to retreat, leaving her feelings too raw to bear.

"*We must not?* Sebastian, we already have!" Her voice cracked, and she felt him hesitate then draw her closer against him. The warmth of his arms should have been reassuring but it was not, for it already felt wrong. She had opened herself body and soul to this man, had allowed him the most shocking and unimaginable liberties. Now, in return, she had received nothing but humiliation.

She stifled a little sob and hid her face in her hands.

"Clara. Do not…"

Sebastian gently helped her to her feet as she pulled her disheveled dress tight around her. When he would have drawn her down to sit with him on the sofa she resisted, deliberately choosing a chair that set her apart from him.

"I am sorry." This time she realized that he sounded wretched. "I should not have done it."

"*You* should not have done it?" Clara's fingers scored the arms of the chair. "Do not take responsibility for something that I wanted as much as you! Indeed, if you had not stopped me…" Her voice trailed away as she realized she would have given herself to him totally, without reservation. But even then he had not been so emotionally engaged as she. He had known what he was doing. And he had stopped it. She bit her lip to stifle her anguish.

"I should never have sent for you yesterday," she said tonelessly.

"No." His word was uncompromising. "And I should never have come to you."

"It took me such a long time…" Clara gulped. "I thought I no longer had such strong feelings for you."

He was shaking his head but said nothing. She felt desolate.

"What are we to do?" she said. She looked at him properly for the first time and her heart turned over at the misery and self-loathing in his eyes. "I know that you cannot offer me what I want, Sebastian."

He closed his eyes for a moment. The pain was etched deep on his face. "Clara, to make you a promise and then break it would be intolerable."

She knew what he meant. He did not wish to have the responsibility of loving her. He could not swear to be faithful to her for the rest of his life. She remembered what she had thought the previous night: he could not love her as she wished to be loved, as she deserved to be loved.

"So what do we do?" she said again.

He did not pretend to misunderstand her.

"About this perilous attraction between us?" He smiled faintly and Clara's heart clenched with a combination of misery and longing. "There is nothing we can do. You are not a woman I can have by any means other than marriage. I accept that." His voice was calm but there was an undertone of emotion that seared Clara. She knew he wanted her and wanted her desperately.

The words fell into the silence. Despite the warmth of the room, Clara shivered. A little while ago, a mere half hour perhaps, she would have believed she was truly a woman bound by convention. Now she had tasted passion and her body ached for it. It would be fulfilling, overwhelming, to make love with Sebastian Fleet. She had sampled desire and it made her hungry.

"Sebastian."

He read her tone and she saw the leap of fire in his eyes. He came to his knees by her chair, taking her cold hands in his. "Clara…"

For a long moment they stared at each other, but then Clara shook her head. "I cannot do it, Sebastian. If it were only for myself I…" She broke off, unable even now, after all that had happened between them, to confess to what felt such an unmaidenly desire. She looked up again and met his eyes. "But you would lose my brother's friendship and gain nothing but the censure of those who had been your friends."

"It would be worth it for you." The sincerity in his tone was beyond question. His hands tightened on hers. "It would be worth it and more, a hundred times over, to have you even for a little while…."

For a moment, Clara's world spun on the edge of a different existence. She was a woman of independent means. There was no one else she would rather marry. She could not imagine there ever would be, for she loved Sebastian Fleet with all the stubbornness in her character. Yet upbringing and principle ran so deep. To lose her good reputation, to lose her family and friends, all the things she had once taken for granted, and to gain what? Not Sebastian's love, for he had sworn himself incapable of that. What was he really offering her? A few months of bliss perhaps, but with everlasting darkness at the end.

He released her suddenly and stood up, turning away. "No, I know it would not serve. I could not ask it of you, Clara, even if you were willing. You are not the kind of woman who could be happy with such an arrangement."

He was right. They both knew it. Clara felt her spirits sink like a stone. So this really was the end.

"So what do we do?" she asked hopelessly, a third time.

"We do not see each other again. It is the only way."

Clara shook her head. "That will not suffice. We are

forever in the same company. We cannot avoid it. It will be unbearable."

The shadows made the planes of his face even more austere. "Then I will go away."

"No!" The cry was wrenched from Clara. That she could not bear. Not to see him again would be painful enough, but to think that he had exiled himself because of her…

"Perhaps," she said, after a moment, "it will become easier in time."

"I doubt it." There was a smile in Sebastian's voice now. "Not when I cannot even look at you without wishing to kiss you senseless and strip all your clothing from you and make love to you until you are exhausted in my arms."

Clara made a small sound of distress, squirming in her chair with a mixture of remembered desire and unfulfilled passion. "Do not!"

"I am sorry." She knew he was not only speaking of what had happened between them. He was speaking of his inability to give her what she desired.

The library door opened with shocking suddenness. Both Clara and Sebastian spun around like a couple of guilty schoolchildren. Engrossed in their own passions and anxieties, neither of them had heard the front door open or the sound of voices in the hall, or footsteps approaching.

Segsbury, Juliana and Martin were all poised in the doorway. Segsbury looked genuinely startled to see the Duke of Fleet in the house a full half hour after the man's supposed departure. Juliana looked shocked and Martin merely furious.

Clara felt a bubble of hysterical laughter rising inside her. She was seated; Sebastian was standing a good few feet away. There was nothing remotely compromising in their demeanor. And yet she wondered what on earth was showing on their faces.

"A curious time of the night to be making calls, Sebastian," Martin said, and although his voice was perfectly pleasant it held a distinct undertone of menace. "Segsbury implied that you had brought some gifts for the children."

"I did." Clara saw Sebastian pull himself together with an effort. "Excuse me. As you say, it is late. I should be leaving."

For a moment it looked to Clara, frozen in her seat, as though Martin were not inclined to let his friend go so easily. Then Juliana drifted forward. "Dear Sebastian," she said, putting one hand on Fleet's arm, "how thoughtful of you to bring presents." She steered him toward the door and after a moment, Martin stepped aside, though there was still an ugly look in his eyes. "Segsbury will show you out," Juliana continued, "and we shall see you soon, I am sure." She relinquished his arm and Segsbury stepped forward, perfectly on cue, just in case the Duke had once again forgotten his way to the front door.

"This way, your grace."

Clara waited. Sebastian half turned toward her and Martin made an unmistakably threatening movement.

"Good night, Miss Davencourt," Sebastian said. There was nothing but darkness in his eyes. He inclined his head. "Davencourt, Lady Juliana…"

The library door shut with an ominous thud and Martin took a purposeful step toward her. Clara shrank in her chair.

"Martin, darling," Juliana said clearly, "I wonder if you might check on the nursery? I would be relieved to know that all is well."

Clara saw the tiny shake of the head that Juliana gave her husband and, after a moment, to Clara's inexpressible relief, Martin went out. She was so thankful not to have to explain herself to her brother that she almost burst into tears.

"Oh, Ju!" She hurled herself into Juliana's arms and clung tight, careless of what her sister-in-law would think. And after a moment Juliana hugged her back fiercely, with no words until Clara had slackened her grip a little.

"I am sorry, Ju."

"Do not be." Juliana caught her hand and pulled

her down to sit beside her on the sofa. "What happened, Clara?"

"He is to go away," Clara said, in a rush. "We think it is the only way."

"Yes," Juliana said quietly, "I think that may be true."

They sat for a moment in silence. "Perhaps you could go away for a little, too," Juliana said thoughtfully. "When your sister Kitty and Edward return to Yorkshire after Christmas."

"Yes," Clara said rapidly. "A change of scene. Perhaps that might serve."

"Clara—" There was anxiety in Juliana's voice now. "Forgive me, but did you... I mean, surely you did not..."

At another time, Clara might have laughed at her notoriously outspoken sister-in-law being so timid at confronting her. She shook her head. "We did not." She knitted her fingers together. "I would have given myself gladly to Sebastian tonight," she said, "but he was not so careless as I."

"Thank God," Juliana said, and there was a wealth of relief in her voice.

"I suppose so." Clara stood up. Her heart felt as bleak as winter. "I must go to bed. I am so tired. Thank you, Juliana."

Juliana's expression was sad. "If you wish to talk to me tomorrow, Clara, you will, won't you?"

"Of course." Clara managed a smile. "I love having you for a big sister, Juliana."

Juliana's answering smile was vivid and bright. "Thank you, Clara. I will see you in the morning."

As she went slowly up the stairs, Clara worried she would not be able to sleep, but when she finally came to lie down she was so exhausted that she remembered nothing from the moment her head touched the pillow.

There were no stars that night.

to know what would happen in the event of his untimely death abroad. It had reassured Seb to see Anthony, even if his cousin's thoughts were taking a morbid turn. It was good to know that with his passing, the Fleet succession would still be in safe hands. For half of Seb wished passionately for precisely that untimely death to which Anthony had alluded.

He felt trapped, and he hoped that different climes and fresh scenes might help him regain his perspective. All he had been able to think about in the fourteen days following his last meeting with Clara Davencourt was the sheer torment of wanting one thing and yet feeling incapable of gaining it. It was not so simple or so selfish as wanting Clara physically and being denied. He needed Clara in some deep sense that frightened him to analyze, and to tear himself away from her was to wrench out part of his soul. Yet to have her love and her trust felt such a huge burden and one of which he was not worthy. He would let her down; he would desert her. He could never meet her expectations or be what she deserved. The responsibility was too great and the image of Oliver was before him always. He had let Oliver die. He had let his parents down and caused them such a grief that could never be assuaged and he would never, ever, do that to another person again.

Sebastian had been walking with no fixed intention, so deep in thought was he. Now he found he had come out into the street by one of the pleasure gardens, the Peerless Pool. In summer it was the haunt of bathers who came to swim in the fresh spring waters. Now, the frozen lake was full of skaters. They circled beneath the high blue sky and their excited cries mingled with the cutting sound of skates on ice. The frozen branches of the lime and cherry trees seemed to catch the sound and send its echoes tinkling back.

Sebastian paused. It was a pretty scene and in the center of it skated a girl in crimson. He recognized Clara at once. She was surrounded by her family and friends. These were the very people with whom he would once have felt so comfortable. He found himself automatically moving to the marble steps that led down to the pool, then stopped. He had barely seen or spoken to Clara in the past fortnight, and to force himself on her party now felt awkward and wrong. Besides, now he looked more closely he saw that Lords Tarver and Elton were both in attendance, like twin ugly sisters waiting for Cinderella to choose between them. It made Sebastian feel ridiculously angry. Yet he knew that Clara might well be married by the time he returned from the continent and that he should feel relieved at the prospect. It was unfortunate that he was not even noble enough to want for her the thing that would achieve her greatest happiness. He did not want Clara enough to risk everything for her—the thought petrified him—and yet he did not wish her to find her happiness with anyone else. The tug of it was like an agonizing seesaw inside him. Risk all to gain all…he was so very close to it. And yet he turned aside to leave instead.

He almost missed it, had almost turned back through the gates where the doorman was still demanding his entry fee, when out of the corner of his eye he saw Clara fall. She had skated away from the others to the edge of the pool, where the ice ran beneath the branches of the bare trees. She was weaving her way under the trees, a snow queen all in red against the frosted white of the trunks. Then there was a harsh, horrible cracking sound and Sebastian saw the dark water run between the cracks in the ice, saw Clara clutch and miss the branch overhead, and did not wait to see more. He ran. The park keeper was still shouting for his money, unaware of the accident. The other skaters were still spinning and drifting on the other side of the pond. Sebastian scrambled down the bank, careless of the snow and the branches that tore at his coat and his face, and came down onto the ice near where Clara lay.

Someone else had seen now, and was shouting for help, but Sebastian reached her first. She was lying half on the ice and half in the icy water. She did not move. The ice cracked and shifted beneath his feet, but he ignored it. He caught a fold of her skirts and pulled fiercely.

"Clara!"

She moved then and tried to pull herself up out of the ice but it broke beneath her hands. He grabbed one flailing wrist. There was a pain inside him so immense and a panic so smothering that he could not speak. Her wrist was wet and he could feel his grip slipping. She was sliding from his fingers and he was powerless to stop her. There was an immense crack as the ice gave beneath her and she tumbled from his grasp. Seb saw the water close over her head.

The dark images that he had thought buried forever flashed across his mind with vividness. Oliver struggling against the ice, slipping away from him, disappearing from sight, his face white, his mouth open in a soundless scream... For a moment he was still with the horror of it and then he was lunging forward to seize hold of Clara before it was too late. His grasp met nothing but ice and air. He reached for her again and this time, to his inexpressible relief, he touched the material of her gown; he grabbed it and pulled. There was resistance, a ripping sound, and then her skirts were free of the clutching water and he was drawing her to him fiercely. They both tumbled backwards onto the snowy bank, Clara held tight in his arms. He pressed his lips to her hair and tried to pull her closer still, until she made a muffled sound of protest.

The others were arriving now, full of questions and anxiety. Juliana and Kitty plucked Clara from his arms and fussed over her. Martin was shaking his hand and saying something, but Seb was not sure what it was. He felt sick and shaken and afraid. Martin carried Clara up the bank. Seb could hear her protesting that she was quite well and he felt breathless with relief. They were calling for a carriage to take her straight home. Clara turned to look at him and held out a hand in mute appeal, but he turned away. He was too dazed to speak to her, both by what had so nearly happened to Clara and by the tragic memories it had stirred for him. He did not want her thanks.

The fuss and bustle gave him the chance to escape. He went to a nearby coffee house and, although he could see them looking for him out in the street, he stayed in his own dark corner until the last of their carriages had rolled away.

The coffee warmed him and gradually soothed his shaken emotions. He was able to force the fearsome images of the past back into the dark recesses of his mind where they belonged. Nevertheless, he knew that this was not the end. It could not be, now. For in those moments when he'd held her, he had confessed to Clara that he loved her. Not in words, perhaps, but in the expression in his eyes and the touch of his hands as he clutched her so fiercely to him; he had known it and so had she. And he knew she would seek a confrontation now, stubborn girl that she was. He would have to be ready.

CLARA CAME TO HIM that evening, as he had known she would. He could have gone to his club and avoided the confrontation but he planned to leave first thing in the morning, as soon as it was light, and so he settled upon a final evening at home. Now he knew it would be a final reckoning, as well. When he left, it would be with the truth between them. He would tell Clara about Oliver and explain once and for all why he was not worthy of her. He sat in his study with a glass of brandy untouched on the table beside him and he stared into the fire and thought of Clara. Who had he been fooling when he pretended not to care for her? She had stripped away all but the last of his defenses now. He loved her. He loved her desperately and he had done so for a very long time.

"When Miss Davencourt arrives, please show her into the study," he told Perch, and he was on tenterhooks as the clock ticked on toward midnight. Perhaps she had been injured more than he had realized;

perhaps she had taken a chill. It might be better if they did not meet. He could slip away in the morning and ask Perch to arrange for a message and a bouquet of flowers to be sent, wishing her a speedy recovery….

"Miss Davencourt, your grace."

Perch was ushering Clara into the room. She looked a little pale but he was glad to see that she appeared otherwise unharmed. He was quick to set a chair for her.

"You should not have come out tonight," he said. "You sustained a shock. Were you injured? You might have caught a chill…." He realized that he was rambling like a nervous youth. There was a spark of amusement in Clara's eyes.

"I am very well," she said. "I came to thank you, Sebastian. You disappeared so quickly this afternoon."

Sebastian shrugged awkwardly. He was feeling very ill at ease. Before she had arrived, he had been confident he would direct their conversation. Now he was not so sure. The balance of power between them seemed to have changed and he did not know how to change it back.

"Does Martin know that you are here?" he asked. "After last night…"

A shadow touched her face. "No one knows. I slipped out when they thought I was asleep."

He felt a rush of amusement followed by a jolt of despair. That was his Clara, so stubborn, so determined to do what she felt was right. Yet she was not really *his* Clara at all. He was about to tell her so.

She sat forward in the chair, looking directly at him. "Do you still intend to leave for the continent tomorrow, Sebastian?"

He looked away. "I do."

Her face fell. The bright light had gone. "I was hoping that you might have changed your mind," she said. "We all wished to thank you properly."

He looked up and met her eyes so sharply that she flinched a little. "Was that why you came here, Clara?" he said harshly. "To thank me?"

"No." She dropped her gaze. A shade of color stole into her cheeks. "I came here to tell you that I love you."

Sebastian looked at her. Her eyes were clear and steady. She was the most beautiful thing he thought he had ever seen. He felt an immense admiration for her courage, followed by a choking wave of love and an even sharper pang of despair. How many women would have had the honesty to behave as she had done?

She was regarding him directly but he knew she was nervous. She moistened her lips with her tongue. A tiny frown touched her forehead at his silence.

"My dear." He cleared his throat. He sounded nervous. That was not good. He had to hide his feelings from her at all costs. "You know that I hold you in the greatest esteem."

She moved with a swift swirl of silk to kneel at his feet. She put one hand on his knee. "No you do not, Sebastian. You do not hold me 'in esteem.'" Disdain colored her voice. "You *love* me."

He moved to raise her to her feet. He could not bear this closeness.

"You and I will never be equal, Clara," he said, trying to make her understand. "You are too open and truthful—damn it, you are too *good* for me. I am jaded. My soul is old."

Clara smiled. It devastated him. "You are making excuses, Sebastian. Do you think I do not know? You are afraid to let yourself love me."

He knew she was right. He had been building barriers against her from the moment they met, instinctively knowing that her love could be his undoing. And now the thing he feared most had happened. He was undone. He had to make her leave him before he disintegrated completely. He could not explain to her about Oliver. That would bring her too close and he would never recover.

"You are in love with love, Clara," he said, struggling to keep his voice neutral. "For me there is nothing between liking and lust. Do not try to dress up my desire for you as something it is not."

There was a stubborn spark of anger in Clara's eyes now. "Why are you lying to me, Sebastian? What is it that you fear?"

He feared so much. He feared that he would offer her his love and she would then have the power to destroy him. But more than anything he feared taking responsibility for another life. He had failed once before when he had allowed Oliver to die. He could not risk that happening to Clara, his one and only love. He said nothing.

"I know you love me," Clara repeated. "I saw it in your face today at the pool. That is why I am here!" She spread her hands wide. "You have only to allow yourself to care for me and all will be well." Her tone was less forceful now, as his silence was starting to undermine her certainties.

"I do care for you," Sebastian said, "but I do not care for you enough." He hated himself for what he was doing. He could see the color draining from her face and the spirit leaching from her eyes, and knew how much he was hurting her. "I acknowledge that people can love each other with the sort of passion you describe," he said. He could barely hear his own false words over the desperate beating of his heart. "But I do not love you like that, Clara," he said starkly. "I do not love you nearly enough. It would not be fair to you to promise otherwise."

Clara scrambled to her feet. There was a blankness to her eyes. She stumbled a little, bumping clumsily into the small table on which stood his glass of brandy. He wanted to pull her into his arms then and never let her go, to comfort her and beg her forgiveness. He was too afraid to do it.

"Either you are lying or you do not know the truth," Clara said. She did not trouble to keep her voice from shaking and he loved her for it; he loved her for the strength of character that made artifice unimportant to her. "I was wrong when I called you coldhearted," she added. "Your heart is a desert, Sebastian, a dry, shriveled place where nothing can live, least of all love."

He could not look at her. He waited until he heard the soft patter of her footsteps receding and then he finally looked up. The face that looked back at him from the mirror was barely recognizable. He looked so haggard. He looked a broken man.

He had hurt Clara inexcusably. But he had succeeded in driving her away and protecting himself from the terrifying risk of loving and losing her. He knew that he should feel glad, but his heart felt like the desert that Clara had so accurately described.

"Miss Davencourt? Miss Davencourt!" Clara was heading for the front door, hampered by the fact that she was blinded by tears. She tripped over the edge of the Persian rug, grabbed a table for support and almost toppled the priceless vase that rested on it.

"Miss Davencourt!"

Her arm was caught in a reassuring grip and she found herself looking into the face of Perch, the butler. She noticed, irrelevantly, what kind eyes he had. Then she also noticed that the door to the servants' stair was open and a row of anxious faces was peering at her from the gloom. Her curiosity was sufficient to overcome her misery for a moment.

"What on earth is going on?"

Perch steered her discreetly into the dining room, and the other servants trooped in silently. In the gothic shadowy darkness they lined up in front of her, candlesticks in hand, their expressions a mixture of hope and concern. Clara looked to the butler for enlightenment.

"Begging your pardon, Miss Davencourt," Perch said, "but we were thinking that you might have persuaded his grace…" He studied her face for a moment, shook his head and sighed. "No matter. Shall I procure you a cab to take you home, miss?"

The other servants gave a murmur of protest. It was clear they did not wish to let her go so easily without telling her their concerns.

"We thought you were to be the new Duchess of Fleet, ma'am," one of the housemaids, a girl with a round red face, said. "That's what Mr. Perch is trying to say. His grace has been sweet on you for as long as I've worked here."

Clara felt a rush of misery. She looked at their anxious faces and managed to raise a rueful smile. "Thank you, but I'm afraid I shall not be the next duchess."

"His grace must be mad," the hall boy whispered, rolling his eyes expressively. Perch shot him a warning look.

"We are very sorry to hear that, ma'am," he said. "We should have liked it very much."

Clara's desolate heart thawed a little. She looked at them all properly for the first time, from the brawny under-gardener to the smallest scullery maid and realized how extraordinary it was that they had all pinned their hopes on her. "I had forgotten," she said. "The duke is to leave on the morrow, is he not? Are you—" she hesitated "—will he be closing the house?"

A row of doleful nods was her answer.

"We are looking for new positions, ma'am. All except Mr. Dawson, his grace's valet. He travels abroad with his grace."

So, most all of them would be out of work as soon as Fleet left for the continent, Clara thought. It was another consequence of his departure and one she had not even considered. She felt horribly guilty.

"I am sorry," she said.

"Not your fault, ma'am," one of the footmen said stalwartly. "His grace is a fine man but in this case his wits have gone a-begging, if you will excuse my saying so."

"His grace has a picture of you in his traveling case, ma'am," another of the maids put in, blushing. "I saw him pack it when he thought no one was watching."

There was a hopeful pause.

"I do not suppose, madam," Perch said weightily, "that you would be prepared to give his grace another chance?"

Clara looked at them all. "I have already given him several chances," she said.

Perch nodded. "We are aware, ma'am. What lady could be expected to do more?"

There was another rustle of disapproval from among the assembled ranks. Clearly they believed their esteemed employer had run mad.

"Unless you could think of a winning scheme," Clara said, "it is pointless. And even then I am not sure that his grace deserves it."

The housekeeper and several of the maids shook their heads. "Men!" One of the girls said. "Hopeless!"

"Get him at a moment of weakness," one of the footmen suggested. "He'll admit to his feelings when he's in his cups."

The valet nodded. "That's true, ma'am. If we could get him drunk."

Clara stifled a laugh. "I am not certain I would want a man who has to be drunk to admit his love for me."

The housekeeper shook her head. "Begging your pardon, ma'am, we're thinking it was the business with Master Oliver that made him this way. Those of us who have been with the family for years saw it happen. The master changed. Terrible shock, it was. After that he turned cold."

One of the older housemaids nodded sadly. "Aye, such an affectionate little boy he was, but he blamed himself from that day forward."

Clara raised her brows. "Who was Master Oliver?"

The servants shuffled uncomfortably. "Master Oliver was his grace's brother," Perch said. "There was an accident."

"Drowned," one of the footmen put in. "Terrible business."

Clara was so surprised that she was silent for a moment. She had never heard of Oliver Fleet, still less that the duke had ever had a brother. He had never, ever mentioned it to her and, she was sure, not to Martin, either. But then, he was good at keeping secrets.

"I had no notion," she said. "How dreadful. I am so sorry."

The servants nodded sadly.

"His grace blamed himself. He has been as cold as ice ever since," Perch explained. There was a long silence before he continued.

"We know that you are too good for his grace, ma'am, being a true lady and generous to a fault, but if you could see your way to giving his grace—and the rest of us—another chance…"

The eagerness of their expressions was heartbreaking. Clara thought of the stories behind the faces, the families that depended on their wages, the fear of being without a job or a roof over their heads, the uncertainty of a servant's life. And yet it was not only that that had prompted them to throw themselves on her mercy. They had seen her come and go through Sebastian Fleet's life for two years and the sincerity of their regard warmed her.

"If you have a plan," she said, "I am prepared to listen to it."

Perch checked the clock on the mantel. "In approximately two minutes his grace will decide to go out to drown his sorrows, ma'am. We shall give him a few hours to become cast adrift, and then we will escort you to fetch him home." He looked around at his fellow servants. "We believe he will admit his feelings for you very soon, ma'am. His grace has almost reached the point where they cannot be denied."

There was a crash out in the hall. Everyone jumped at the sound of the library door banging open and Seb Fleet's voice shouting irascibly for his butler. He sounded absolutely furious.

"Perch? Where the devil are you, man? I want to go out!"

"Perfectly on cue," one of the footmen said.

Perch smoothed his coat and trod slowly towards the door, opening it and closing it behind him with his usual grave deliberation.

"You called, your grace?" Clara heard him say.

"I am going out," Fleet repeated. She thought he sounded murderous.

"Might one inquire where, your grace?"

"No, one might not, damn you! Fetch my coat!"

"May I then remind your grace that you are to travel at first light?"

Fleet said something so rude that one of the housemaids gasped and clapped her hands over her ears.

"Sorry you had to hear that, ma'am," the housekeeper whispered. "His grace is in a proper mood and no mistake."

Clara bit her lip to stop a smile.

The front door slammed. There was a long pause while they all seemed to be holding their breath, then Perch appeared once more in the doorway of the dining room.

"I've sent Jackman to follow his grace," he said. "We shall soon know where he has gone. Miss Davencourt—" there was a smile in his eyes as he turned to Clara "—may we offer you some refreshment while we wait?"

Chapter Five

SEB FLEET did not choose to drown his sorrows at Whites, but instead went to the Moon and Goldfinch, a considerably less salubrious place on the Goldhawk Road where he could drink himself to hell and back without anyone caring. Indeed, once the landlord had seen that his money was good he kept him so well-supplied with alcohol that Sebastian found himself by turns maudlin, then merry, then maudlin again in the shortest possible time. By three in the morning he had made several dubious new friends, turned down eager kisses from the landlord's daughter, and was comfortably asleep on the bar when he was shaken roughly awake. The door of the inn was open and a fresh burst of snow was swirling inside, pulling him from his welcome stupor.

"Sebastian! Wake up at once!" It was Clara's voice. Fleet groaned.

"This the missus, is it?" the landlord enquired affably.

"Not yet," Clara snapped.

Fleet shook the hair out of his eyes and tried to sit up. The room swam about him. His mouth felt like a cockpit. His eyes were gritty and his face was wet where he appeared to have fallen asleep in a pool of beer.

"You smell like a sewer," Clara grumbled. "Perch, Dawson, can you manage him?"

"Hello, my sweet love," Sebastian said with a slight slur, as his butler and valet struggled to lift him with all the finesse of a collier hefting a sack. He smiled at Clara as her cross-looking face swam before his eyes. He felt inordinately pleased to see her. He could not quite remember why, but he knew that earlier in the evening he thought he would never, ever see her again. Evidently he had been quite wrong. He struggled to remember the circumstances, failed completely, and lurched heavily against Dawson's side.

"How splendid that you are here, my darling," he called, as Perch and Dawson tried to maneuver him to the door. "I did not expect to see you." He staggered dangerously and almost knocked over the butler.

"Sorry, Perch. Don't know why you don't just leave me to sleep here."

"Yes, your grace." Perch sounded as though that was precisely what he would have done had he been permitted to have his way. "Miss Davencourt was concerned for you, your grace."

"Very wifely," Fleet observed. His head felt too heavy to think clearly. Here was Clara, turning his heart inside out again and making him feel as raw as an untried youth. He loved her so much that there was a lump in his throat at the thought of it. It was dreadful that she should see him this way. He must look terrible. He smelled. He was a disgrace. And yet she was still here, despite everything, and he really did not have the will to resist any more.

"I am not certain it is the proper thing for you to be here, Miss Davencourt."

Clara smiled. "I am here to discover if you love me, Sebastian."

"Love you?" Fleet asked. The question seemed so absurd that he started to laugh. "Of course I love you! I love you so much it breaks my heart."

"Excellent," Clara said. "You are drunk, of course, so that may make a difference. Will you still love me when you are sober?"

"Of course I will." Fleet squinted, his head lolling against Dawson's shoulder. "'Course I will! I love you to perdition, you little fool! Why do you think I keep trying to make you go away?"

"Hmm. It lacks something for a declaration, I think," Clara said. "I shall not propose to you again, however. A lady has her pride."

"Marry me," Fleet said. He tried to get down on his knees but Perch and Dawson held him up. It was probably best they did; he had a feeling that once he was down there he would never stand again.

"We shall talk about it in the morning," Clara said. "Now please be quiet, Sebastian, and get into the coach."

Fleet stumbled to the door, encouraged on his way by the profuse thanks of the landlord. The cold air sobered him somewhat and the falling snow on his face restored him to an unwelcome sense of reality. Clara was waiting patiently while Perch and Dawson hauled him into the carriage. She accepted Perch's hand up with perfect composure and settled herself opposite him, wrinkling her nose delicately at the combined scent of beer and tobacco.

"Clara," he said again, as the door shut on them. "This is no escapade for a lady. You really should not be here."

"If you were not here then neither should I be," Clara said calmly, wrapping the rug about them both. "I was worried about you, Sebastian."

Fleet pressed a hand to his aching brow. "I do not want you to worry about me!" The words came out almost as a shout and Clara put her gloved hands over her ears. "How many times do I have to explain this? This is exactly what I was trying to avoid!"

"It seems to me," Clara said, ignoring him, "that you have not permitted anyone to care for you in a very long time, Sebastian."

Fleet's head pounded. "Devil take it! Clara, have you not understood? I want you to leave me alone!"

His head was swimming, but in the dim light of the carriage lamps he saw that she was looking at him and there was a slight, satisfied smile on her lips. Fleet leaned his head against the seat cushions and closed his eyes in despair. He realized through the clearing fog of his inebriation that he'd declared his love to her. "Dash it, Clara, I am too befuddled to argue." He leant forward, suddenly urgent. "Yes, I love you to distraction but I wish to the devil that I did not! I would go to the ends of the earth for you but I can hardly bear it! The responsibility of it terrifies me."

"It is perfectly simple," Clara said briskly. "I care for you and in return you care for me." She put one small hand against his chest and pushed gently. "Go to sleep, now."

He wanted to argue but he did not have the strength. To sleep seemed easier. So he did.

HE WAS AWOKEN by the white light of a snowy morning illuminating his bedroom. For a brief, blissful moment he could not remember anything, then he flung one arm across his eyes and let out a long groan.

"I have prepared a nice posset for you," Clara's voice said. "I thought perhaps you might need something restorative for your head."

Sebastian opened his eyes. He might have known Clara would still be here. No doubt she sat up all night at his bedside to make sure he was quite safe. He felt exasperated and deeply grateful at the same time. She looked as fresh as though she were stepping out to a ball. Her dress was uncreased and her eyes bright. He looked at her and felt a hopeless feeling swamp him.

"Your concern is most touching," he said, sitting up in bed to take the steaming cup of sweet liquid. "I have sunk more drink than last night, however. I shall survive."

"You told me that you loved me last night," Clara said. "Do you remember?"

He looked at her. It was too late now for denials and lies. Much too late.

"I remember," he said. "Oh, Clara, darling, of course I remember."

She took his hand. "There is no need to look so

terrified, Sebastian. Love is not an illness. It will not kill you."

But to him it felt exactly as though he had contracted an unfamiliar and frightening disease. He had not tested love's boundaries yet. He did not know how far he could trust himself with it. Nevertheless, the need to tell Clara everything now was so acute he could not resist.

"When you fell through the ice yesterday I was so frightened," he said. His voice shook a little. "I thought that I was losing you, there in front of my eyes. It reminded me of when Oliver died." It had actually been worse than losing Oliver. Ten, twenty times more dreadful.

"Oliver was your brother," Clara said.

"Yes. He was four years younger than I was. I always protected him. Until the day I failed him."

The words came out in a torrent. He could not stop now if he tried.

"It was this time of year right before Christmas. We were supposed to be at our lessons but our tutor fell asleep and we crept out. It was too fine a day to stay indoors. We took our skates and went down to the old mill race." He swallowed painfully. "I can still see Oliver now. He skated out into the middle—the ice was hard, we did not realize the danger—and he was spinning around, his arms outstretched... And then he was simply not there." He stopped. Clara did not speak.

"I moved as fast as I could. The ice was cracking all around me. I shouted for help until I was hoarse but no one came. I could see him, under the ice, but I could not reach him. Every time I got close enough to grab him the ice would break beneath me and we would drift apart."

"What happened?" Clara whispered.

"Someone finally saw us. I do not know how long it took. The water was so cold. They brought ropes and ladders but I knew it was too late for Oliver. I was big and strong but he was only small. He was only eight years old! And I could not save him."

He half expected Clara to tell him that it had not been his fault. People had been saying that to him for years until they tired of reassuring him or thought that he was over the tragedy. But Clara did not say that. She held his hand and waited for him to continue.

"It was my fault," he said starkly. "I was the one who suggested we go skating that day. He always followed me. Then I could not help him when he needed me."

He gripped Clara's hand fast. "They rescued me first, you know. I was the heir." His mouth twisted bitterly. "The spare was sacrificed."

He was crying. He could not help it. He dashed the

tears away with his hand and found they fell all the quicker for it. He spoke in gasps.

"I have never told anyone this before. I thought I could lock it away but you have unmanned me. You made me feel again. You made me love you. Oh, Clara—"

Clara moved from her chair to the edge of his bed. She caught him and pulled him to her, drawing him down so that his cheek rested against hers. Her arms were tight about him and it felt protected and safe. For a second he hesitated, but it was out of nothing more than habit. Then he let go and felt himself fall, mind and body, to a warm safe place, where he was her strength and she was his.

He did not know how long they lay there, but when he opened his eyes, Clara's face was about an inch away from his, so he kissed her with love and gentleness. Her lashes lifted and she looked at him. He could see from her eyes that she was smiling.

"You need a shave," she said, running her fingers experimentally over the stubble that darkened his chin.

"And a wash. I fear I am most unwholesome."

"You are delightful." Clara rubbed her cheek against his rough one. "I love you, Sebastian."

He savored the words, tasted them. His entire body felt relaxed, released from a terrible torment. His eyes were heavy. He felt so tired. He did not want to resist and after a few moments, to his intense surprise, the sleep took him again.

CLARA DID NOT FALL ASLEEP. She lay looking at Sebastian with a small smile still on her lips. How ruffled and dishevelled he looked. If this was how he appeared when in a state of undress, how much more magnificent would he be when he was totally naked. And at least she might have a fighting chance of seeing that now. It had taken her a long time to realize that in permitting him to dictate her happiness she was helping neither of them.

She wriggled closer to the warmth of his body. He felt solid and strong. She ran a hand experimentally over his chest and he murmured something in his sleep and drew her deeper into the crook of his arm. He smelled faintly of leather and tobacco and lime cologne. Clara buried her nose in the curve of his neck and inhaled deeply. She felt almost light-headed with the warmth and the scent of him. It was a good job that he was asleep for she felt exceedingly wide-awake. Her body tingled. She remembered the way Sebastian had kissed her, the way he had used his tongue and his teeth on her bare breast, and she was shot through with a pleasure that pooled deep within her and made her body tense and wanting.

Then he opened his eyes.

For a long moment she stared into that deep, slumberous blue and saw his gaze darken with desire as he rolled over to pin her beneath his weight.

There was a very sharp rap on the front door followed by the sound of raised voices in the hall.

For a moment Sebastian was still, his body poised above hers, then he sighed and eased himself off the bed.

"What sort of hour is this for visitors to call?"

Clara squinted at the clock on the mantelpiece. "It is past one, Sebastian. You have slept the clock around."

Sebastian stretched. Clara stared. She could not help it. He was still in his breeches and shirt and she was riveted by the deliciously tight fit of the buckskins over his thighs.

"You could avert your eyes," Sebastian said mildly.

"I could," Clara agreed, "but I am not going to."

He smiled. "Hussy."

"I know. But I have waited a long time—"

His eyes darkened again. "No more waiting, I promise you." He bent over and touched his lips to hers and Clara's senses leapt in response to the light caress. She grabbed his shirt and pulled him down to her, kissing him fervently.

The sound of voices was coming nearer. Through the pounding of the blood in her ears, Clara could hear Perch's tones, soothing and respectful, and in response a voice she recognized all too well—Martin, sounding dangerously angry, along with Lady Juliana, high and anxious.

"We know she is here, Perch. She left a note."

Sebastian eased his lips from Clara's. *"You left a note?"*

Clara hung her head, blushing a little. "I thought it was the right thing to do. I did not want anyone to worry about me."

"Whereas now that they know you have been all night at my bedside they will be delighted," Sebastian said dryly. "Your brother is about to call me to account for being a scoundrel and for the first time in my life I am entirely innocent of all wrongdoing."

The door flew open and Martin Davencourt erupted into the room, Juliana at his heels. Clara's heart sank as she saw in their wake her sister Kitty, Kitty's husband Edward, Juliana's brother Joss, his wife Amy, Edward's brother Adam and Adam's wife Annis all jostling behind them on the landing.

"Why is everybody here?" she wailed.

A cacophony of noise broke over them and Clara put her hands over her ears.

"He is half-undressed!"

"She is fully dressed!"

"She is in his bed!"

"The place smells like a taproom!"

"Oh, Clara!" said Kitty, sounding both awed and disapproving.

"Scoundrel! Rogue!" Martin was not mincing his words. "To think I ever called you friend! To seduce my sister—" Before Clara could jump up, Martin had lunged at Sebastian and grabbed him by the remnants of his neck cloth, pulling tight. There was mindless fury in her brother's eyes. Clara heard Seb's breathing catch and saw his eyes start to bulge as, caught off balance, he tripped over backward onto the bed.

"I did no such thing, I swear!" he choked out, breaking off painfully as Martin pulled viciously on the cravat and brought tears to his eyes.

"Martin!" Clara leapt to her feet and hung on to Martin's arm. "Let him go! Nothing happened. I am the one to blame!"

Martin cast her one dark, angry look. "Oh, you need not think that I hold you blameless, Clara. I will settle with you when I have settled with him!"

Seb gave a despairing croak as the tourniquet tightened about his throat. Clara felt genuine alarm now. "Juliana!" She spun round to address her sister-in-law. "Do something! I promise nothing happened between us. Sebastian was too drunk—"

She realized this was not the most helpful defense, when Martin's breath hissed between his teeth with fury and he hauled Fleet to his feet, only to lay him flat out with one well-placed blow.

There was a silence.

"That was very unfair!" Clara said indignantly, scrambling to prop him up. "You have given Sebastian no opportunity to explain himself."

"It was the least I deserved," Sebastian said, fingering his jaw. "Would have done the same thing myself if I had a sister." He looked up at his angry friend and said, "Davencourt, my apologies. I have behaved abominably, even though it is true that your sister is quite unscathed."

"Because you were too drunk to seduce her," Martin said through shut teeth.

"Absolutely. And because I respect her and wish to make her my wife at the earliest possible opportunity."

There was a concerted gasp from the assembled company. Clara thought she saw a slight smile of satisfaction cross Perch's otherwise impassive expression.

"May I be the first to offer my congratulations, your grace," he said.

"Congratulations?" Martin's expression was like boiling milk. "Congratulations? I will *not* permit my sister to marry such a rogue."

"Martin, darling," Juliana said, putting a gentle hand on her husband's arm, "I completely under-

stand your misgivings but I do think we should consider the matter calmly."

"Calmly!" Martin spun around. "I am not calm!"

"I think we all realize that, dearest," Juliana said.
"Now, Clara, you will accompany us home. Sebastian,
you will join us for dinner tonight, if you please.
Great-Aunt Eleanor is staying and if you pass muster with her then I doubt anyone else will object to
your suit."

She took Clara's arm and propelled her forcibly toward the door.

"Ladies and gentlemen," Sebastian said, raising his
voice. "Might I beg one moment in private with my
affianced wife?" He caught Clara's hand as Juliana escorted her past.

Martin, who had started to look vaguely placated,
started frowning again. "Affianced? You try my patience too far, Fleet. You assume too much."

"One minute," Sebastian said. "Please." He kept
tight hold of Clara's hand.

Everyone backed from the room with good-
humored grumbling and Juliana dragged Martin out.

"One minute only," she warned.

As soon as the door closed behind them Sebastian
pulled Clara into his arms.

"I asked you last night but you did not answer," he
said. "Will you marry me?"

"Yes!" Clara said. "I am so glad that you asked. I had quite decided against putting my fate to the touch for a second time. A lady does not wish to appear too desperate."

Seb caressed her hair. "And the special license? Do you wish me to procure one?"

"Yes, please." Clara snuggled against his stroking hand. The latent sensuality of her behavior was doing terrible things to both his self-control and his clarity of thought.

"I am still a bit worried about your brother," he began, knowing there was another matter to be settled.

"We will persuade him," Clara said. She tilted her chin up. "Kiss me, please."

They were still engrossed when the door opened and Perch came back in.

"Mr. Davencourt requests his sister's presence at once," he said, straight-faced, "or he will go to fetch his duelling pistols."

SEB FLEET STOOD in the snow outside the house in Collett Square. It was late; the sky was black and cold, and the stars very bright. In all material terms the evening had been a vast success. Lady Eleanor Tallant, matriarch of the extended family, had given her seal of approval to the match between himself and Clara, and had dismissed Martin's objections in a few pungent words.

"Fleet is solvent, young enough to have his own hair and not require a corset, and influential enough to help your political career," she had said sharply. "You must have windmills in your head to object to such an offer." Then her face had softened. "He also dotes upon your sister, should that have more influence with you."

Martin had then reluctantly offered his hand, and Seb seized it gratefully.

"I do love her, you know, Davencourt," he said. "I would not wish to live without her."

He had seen the effort Martin had made to set aside the doubts and fears Seb knew were only for Clara's happiness. Things were *almost* back to normal.

Now he was supposed to go home and see his betrothed formally and respectably the next day, when arrangements would be made for him to join the family at Davencourt for Christmas, and for he and Clara to be married on Twelfth Night.

But there was one thing he had not done, one thing that required privacy rather than the benevolent observation of the family, one thing he wanted to give to Clara when they were alone.

He watched the lights go out in the house one by one and felt his feet freeze in the hard-packed snow.

Clara's room was at the back of the house and he let himself in through the small iron gate that led into the gardens. His footprints in the snow would give him away to anyone who spotted them, but this was too important not to take the risk. He suspected that for all their newfound harmony, Martin would allow him very little time alone with Clara until they were wed. Which was as it should be, of course. But he wanted her all to himself for a little.

He set his foot to the base of the ivy that climbed up the back of the house. It shivered under his weight but its branches were sturdy. At least the snow would break his fall if he misjudged the venture.

The ivy shook and trembled, sending showers of powdery snow to the ground, but he clung on as his fingers froze to the branches and he hauled himself up painfully to the first floor. The sharp twigs pricked at his hands and ankles.

He gained the ledge that ran around the first floor, then edged sideways past two windows until he came to Clara's chamber, at the end of the house. There was a faint light from behind the drapes. He hoped her maid was not still with her. He hoped she had not fallen asleep. He hoped he had not miscalculated and was outside Lady Eleanor Tallant's chamber instead.

He was wet and cold and scratched. The price of love. He smiled faintly and knocked at the windowpane.

Nothing happened. He knocked again, slightly more loudly. The vine creaked beneath his feet.

Clara's face appeared at the window, wide-eyed and astonished. In another moment she had thrown up the sash and was leaning out.

"Sebastian!" The whisper carried on the cold clear air. "What are you doing? You will fall!"

She grabbed his hand and pulled with all her might. Various parts of him caught on the latch or were squeezed in the aperture. Eventually he made a mammoth effort and half stumbled, half fell into the room and into Clara's arms.

"I came to tell you that I love you," he said, burying his face in her hair and holding her warm body against the coldness of his.

She eased back from him a little. The smile in her blue eyes was delicious. "You have told me that already today, Sebastian."

"I could not wait until tomorrow to tell you again. Besides," Sebastian said, gesturing towards the ivy, which would probably never recover from his onslaught, "I wanted to prove that I would do anything for you, even risk life and limb, flora and fauna, hauling my weight up to your balcony."

He released her and stood regarding her intently. In her flimsy peignoir and similarly transparent nightdress she looked luscious.

She gave a little giggle. "Dearest Sebastian, you have no need to prove anything to me. I know how much you love me."

He felt humbled by her generosity. "Clara, you do not understand. I will always think of you as too good for me." He slid his hand into his pocket. "I brought you this. It is a betrothal gift. I wanted to give it to you in private. I hope that you understand."

Earlier that evening, in full, approving view of the family, he had given her the Fleet betrothal ruby ring, which he had retrieved from the bank that very day. Now she was looking puzzled.

"A gift? But I thought—"

He held the box out to her. "Take it. Please."

Clara took it slowly, ran her fingers over the smooth, leather case, then opened the box.

"Oh!"

The huge ruby star pendant was nestling in the palm of Clara's hand now, its surface striking sparks from the candlelight. She looked up and her eyes were misty with tears.

"It is the most beautiful thing…"

She laid it reverentially in its box on the window seat, then came and took his hand and drew him down to sit on the bed beside her. She rested her head against his shoulder. "You know that there are things I need from you, Sebastian." She nestled closer. "You always claim that I am too good for you, but you are strong and courageous and loyal, and I admire those things."

Her nightgown slipped a little, the virginal white linen sliding from one rounded shoulder. Beneath it Sebastian knew that she would be soft and smooth, curved in all the most perfect places, warmly inviting.

He averted his eyes.

Her hair brushed his cheek—soft, confiding, innocent. She was tilting up her lips so that he could kiss her. His throat closed with nervousness. He gave her a tiny peck on the lips and withdrew hastily. Clara sat back, looking at his with a suddenly arrested expression.

"You do not intend to stay with me tonight?"

Sebastian stared at her in consternation. "Stay? Of course I will not stay." He knew that he sounded like a dowager. "That would be most inappropriate."

"So says the greatest scoundrel in London," Clara said.

"Clara, you are to be my *wife*. We must do these things properly." Seb wiped his brow. It was an excuse, of course. He wanted nothing more than to take her in the most improper ways imaginable, but he knew he could not do it.

Clara's lower lip quivered. "I am not certain I wish to marry you if you have become stuffy and proper all of a sudden. I do not want a reformed rake as a husband. I want a rake who will devote his attentions to me!"

Sebastian spread his hands helplessly. "You know I am yours, body and soul."

"And it is the physical side of you that intrigues me at present, I confess." She peeped at him. "No doubt I am shameless, but since you are to be my husband…"

She was tracing one finger down the line of his sleeve and when she touched the back of his hand, light as a breath of wind, he flinched as though scalded.

"No."

He could sense the uncertainty in her. She wanted him; she had courage, but in the face of his blank refusal she was too inexperienced to push for what she wanted. His heart twisted. He was hurting her again with a different sort of rejection now. He knew he had to explain to her. It was only fair. The difficulty was finding the words.

Clara covered her face with her hands. "Oh, dear! I was relying on you, Sebastian! I thought that one of us at least would know what to do."

"I do know the theory," Sebastian said. "Clara, I love you! I have never felt like this about anybody before—" He stopped.

Clara's eyes widened. She stared at him for a long moment. "Sebastian, you are afraid!"

He gave her a lopsided grin. "I confess it."

"When you said that I had unmanned you I did not think you meant..." Clara said, beginning to comprehend.

Sebastian looked down. He remained obstinately limp. He sighed.

"I am sorry."

"But what will happen on our wedding night?" Clara wailed.

Sebastian imagined that the longer their betrothal lasted, the more nervous he would become. Sebastian Fleet, the greatest rake in London, reduced to a quivering wreck by a slip of a girl.

Clara was looking at him, her blue eyes wide with apprehension. He felt a wave of hopelessness swamp him. Hell and damnation! The fact that he felt like ravishing her, the fact that he wanted to tear her clothes off and make mad, passionate love to her and yet he was somehow incapable of doing so was the last word in frustration. Theirs had been the most provocative courtship.

Then he saw a spark of amusement in Clara's eyes. The corner of her mouth lifted in a tiny smile. She traced a pattern on the edge of the sheet with her fingers and did not look at him as she spoke.

"Would you be prepared at least to try?" she asked demurely. "My governess always said that when one did not wish to do something it was better to grit one's teeth and take courage than to put off the moment."

Grit his teeth and summon all his courage. Seb drove his hands into his pockets in a gesture of contained fury. That was not how making love to Clara Davencourt should be.

"It is not that I do not *want* to, Clara," he said. "I want to kiss you and take you to bed and make love to you until dawn, but—" He broke off as he saw the rosy color suffuse her face.

"Do you really?" she said.

"Yes!" Seb almost shouted.

Clara looked around hastily. "Quiet! I do not wish Martin to find you here and have to explain that once again nothing has happened between us."

Seb gave an infuriated groan and sank down onto the bed. "This is humiliating."

He felt her wriggle across to sit beside him. Her breast pressed softly against his arm. She was warm and smelled faintly of jasmine and clean linen.

"Dear Sebastian." She was holding his hand in hers now and he let it rest there because it felt so comforting. "You must not worry about it. I shall not press you for my marital rights."

He looked up. She was so close that he could see the individual black eyelashes and the sweep of the shadow they cast on her cheek in the candlelight. Her cheek was round and smooth and he put up a hand to caress it. He smiled reluctantly.

"I suppose it is a little bit amusing...."

"Yes." She was nibbling at his fingers now, that full lower lip lush against the pad of his thumb. He felt a sudden fierce urge to kiss her that made him freeze on the spot. She withdrew slightly.

"I promise," she said solemnly, "to ask nothing of you that you are not prepared to give."

"Thank you." He started to relax. She gave him a little push and he lay back on the pillows, closing his eyes. When she lay down beside him he did not stir. Convention dictated that he should leave, but for once he was feeling completely at peace.

"Please hold me," Clara said, and he realized that in his selfish fears he had drawn so much on her strength and not given enough of himself back to her. He put his arms about her and drew her close so that her head rested beneath his chin and their hearts beat together.

After a moment he eased away a little and scattered little kisses across the soft skin of her face, paying special attention to those stubborn freckles that had always tempted him. He was trying not to think about what he was doing, trusting to instinct rather than past skill.

She turned her head slightly and her lips met his, then he felt the tip of her tongue touch the corner of his mouth. It set the blood hammering through his body and he opened his lips to hers, hesitantly at first, unprepared for the flash of desire that almost consumed him as their tongues touched, tangled.

Beneath the desire lay acute anxiety. He recognized it with incredulity. It almost paralyzed him. Clara was pressing closer, gently running her hands over his arms and shoulders, sliding the damp jacket from him so that he could feel the warmth of her touch through the linen of his shirt. She was resting her cheek against his chest now and he knew she would be able to hear the racing of his heart.

"I am sorry," he said, kissing her hair. "I do not wish to hurt you."

There was laughter in her voice. "I am no saint on a pedestal. You need not treat me like glass, Sebastian. I shall not break."

"No, but I am very afraid that I might."

She wriggled up until she was looking him in the eyes. "Then we shall break and mend together."

She saw the way his eyes darkened with sudden heat and felt a rush of the same excitement through her body with an undertow of fear. Now, at last, she sensed she was close to overcoming that last barrier that lay between them.

With one forceful movement he rolled her beneath him, his mouth crashing down on hers, scattering her own doubts and anxieties. Her senses reeled beneath the onslaught, her body arching, pleading for the fulfilment of pleasure. If he should hesitate now…

She felt his fingers rough on the fastenings of her chemise. He was trembling. She refused to give him time to think. She cast the chemise aside, caught his hand and placed it over her breast.

He groaned, but she knew with a flash of pure feminine triumph that she had won. His mouth was at her breast, hot and wet, and she ripped the shirt from his back so that she could touch his nakedness, skin to skin.

When he tore off his breeches and she felt the whole hard length of him against her for the first time, the shock splintered her. It was so strange but so exquisitely pleasurable. She arched again into his hands, and then his mouth was on hers as he came down over her, caressing her, parting her thighs to find that aching softness at the center of her.

He drew back a little.

"I will hurt you now…."

She sensed his reluctance and once again she was ruthless, straining for his touch.

"Then do so. Please…" Her voice broke on a ragged gasp. "Sebastian…"

The pause seemed agonizingly long, but then he was moving with one sure, hard thrust to claim her, and the pleasure and the pain raked her with fire and she gasped, but his mouth on hers silenced her cries. She clutched him to her, feeling her world shatter and reform as he took her with such thorough tenderness that her body melted into bliss. All she could be certain of was that she had his love and would never lose it.

"I LOVE YOU." Sebastian's face was turned into the damp curve of her shoulder. His breath tickled her skin. She could hear the profound relaxation and happiness in his voice and to her surprise it made the tears well up in her throat. Such a painful journey for a man who had rejected his feelings for so many years. She gave him a brief, fierce hug.

"I love you, too, Sebastian."

"I may not always be as good at showing my feelings as you are, my love. It was your sweetness and honesty that shamed me into such admiration for you. If I falter it will not be because I do not care for you."

She understood what he was trying to say. It would take time for him to unlock all the bitterness and unhappiness from the past. That did not matter for she would be there with him.

"As long as you can promise to love and be faithful to me alone," she said solemnly, "then there is nothing to fear."

She felt him smile against her skin. "I can promise that without a shadow of a doubt."

"Good." Clara turned to look at him. "This business between us, then—" she gave a little voluptuous wiggle "—this rather pleasant business of making love... Is it all settled now?"

His lips quirked into a smile. "I think it may well be."

She caressed his chest, feeling his muscles tense in

sudden response to her touch. "Do you think that we should do it again, to make certain?" she whispered.

In reply he pulled her down on top of him, tangling a hand in her hair, bringing her mouth down to his.

"Yes," he whispered against her lips. "Yes, I do."

CLARA KNELT on the window seat, the ruby star in its box beside her. In the faint light before dawn it seemed to have a radiance of its own. She looked from her own particular star to the one she had seen that night a few weeks ago as it paled in the dawn sky over the roofs of London.

Have hope.

Have faith.

She smiled a little.

Sebastian stirred and she went across to the bed, slipping into the space beside him.

"How strange," she said, as she cuddled close to his warmth. "I never thought this would be the season in which I found a suitor."

He smiled, drawing her closer into his arms. "I never thought it would be the season in which I found a *wife*. Clara Davencourt, my love, my life."

Enjoy a classic tale of romance that will
warm hearts this holiday season,
by **#1** *New York Times* bestselling author

NORA ROBERTS

GABRIEL'S *Angel*

Pregnant, alone and on the run to protect her unborn child, Laura Malone
finds herself stranded on a snowy Colorado road and at the mercy of
Gabriel Bradley. Fortunately he wants only to provide her shelter. As they
weather the storm together, a bond is formed and a promise made—one that
will keep Laura safe and one that will give Gabe a new reason for being....

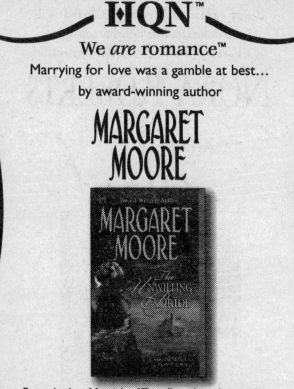

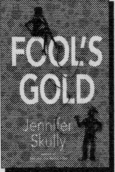

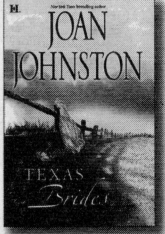